# Love and Terror in
## in
# HAVANA

## "REMEMBER THE MAINE"

*A Historical Romance Novel*
*by*

# MARK BARIE

Best wishes —

Barringer Publishing, Naples, Florida
www.barringerpublishing.com
Cover, graphics, layout design by Linda S. Duider

ISBN: 978-1-954396-44-9

Library of Congress Cataloging-in-Publication Data
*Love and Terror in Havana / Mark Barie*
Printed in U.S.A.

This is a work of fiction. All characters, organizations, and events portrayed in this novel are either products of the author's imagination or are used fictitiously.

# The Trilogy

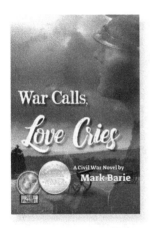 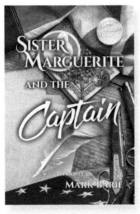 

Award-Winning author, Mark Barie, has created three heart-wrenching Historical Romance novels that will keep you spellbound until the very last page. The historical facts are accurate, his characters are compelling, and the stories are riveting.

Will true love triumph over the death and destruction of war?

Travel back in time, and discover for yourself the answer to this ageless question!

## Available at Amazon

## Other books by the author

Barie has also authored or co-authored several local (upstate New York) history books, all available at Amazon.com. They include:

### "Crossing the Line"

### "The President of Plattsburg"

### "The Boat People of Champlain"

**The author can be reached at:
authormarkbarie@gmail.com.**

# ÐEDICATION

*For the veterans of the Spanish American War.*

*May they rest in peace.*

A HISTORICAL ROMANCE NOVEL BY MARK BARIE

# ᑕABLE OF ᑕONTENTS

# ACKNOWLEDGMENTS

My heartfelt thanks and endless love to the one person without whom this book would never have been written. Her patience was endless, her sacrifices too many to count, and her guidance so very helpful. Thank you, Christine. You are and always will be the woman I love.

# ꓸIISTORICAL ꓢOTES

1. At the time of its destruction, there were two mascots on board the *USS Maine*. Pug, a dog, belonged to Captain Sigsbee. Tom, a cat, belonged to a sailor recently transferred from the *USS Minnesota*. Both animals survived the explosion. There were also plenty of rats on the ship. One of the rats was domesticated by a sailor, who trained it to eat from his hand and taught it tricks. The sailor named the rodent, Christopher. Although Tom the cat and Christopher the rat were never friends, they could be together in the same room without incident.
2. Isabella Hermoza is a fictional character. Her uncle, the Butcher, is a prominent figure in the history of Spain and is accurately depicted.
3. Substantive statements made by persons of historical note are accurately quoted.
4. Although the U.S. Navy knew that certain types of coal would, on rare occasions, spontaneously combust, they knew very little about coal-generated methane gas. The coal bins on board the *USS Maine* were poorly ventilated, if ventilated at all. Only after the ship was constructed did the navy make air vents in coal bins mandatory.
5. A coal fire would have to burn, unnoticed, for hours before it heated a bulkhead wall to a temperature sufficient to

explode gunpowder or live shells, stored in a nearby bunker.

6. Not a single piece of physical evidence was ever discovered, proving that a fire occurred in one of the onboard coal bins. Other coal-fired ships, which experienced these types of conflagrations, recorded heavy smoke, high temperatures, heat damage to bulkhead walls, and charred pieces of coal.

7. By today's standards, the wiring system on the USS *Maine* was crude and antiquated, as evidenced by the electric thermostats installed in the coal bins. The alarms continually sounded even though a coal fire never occurred on the USS *Maine*. The probability of a spark, caused by an exposed or damaged wire, was very high.

8. Dozens of ear witnesses have testified that two explosions occurred on the night of February 15, 1898. The first explosion, described as a small but clearly discernible report, cannot be attributed to the spontaneous combustion of coal. In the author's opinion, these witnesses heard the explosion of a methane-filled coal bunker.

9. Most modern-day experts have dismissed the idea that the USS *Maine* was destroyed by an underwater mine or torpedo. The evidence against this possibility includes the absence of a water geyser and the absence of dead fish on the water's surface. In addition, the constant movement of the ship, while tethered to a buoy, made the accurate positioning of a mine impossible. Moreover, the ship's 24-7 security detail, combined with the heavy boat traffic in Havana Bay made the secret installation of a mine or the unseen launch of a torpedo virtually impossible.

10. There are recorded instances where EMPTY coal bunkers exploded because they were filled with methane gas.

# Chapter One

## The Explosion

A thunderous blast rocked the tiny cabin.

Navy Captain Charles D. Sigsbee jerked to his feet. The deafening crash of metal against metal pierced the air. The deck beneath him trembled and lurched. The entire room tilted and listed to the port side. Personal items crashed to the floor. The lights went out. He gripped a desk he could not see. The explosions continued.

His mind raced with memories of warnings and precautions. When he left the Florida Keys just weeks ago for Cuba, Sigsbee received unsmiling advice from a friendly naval officer.

"Look out those fellows over there don't blow you up."

"Don't worry," said Sigsbee, "I've taken precautions against that."

Sigsbee took every precaution he could. After the *USS Maine* anchored safely in Havana Harbor, he issued a series of orders. The crew would be confined to the ship. He upgraded the standard anchor watch to a quarter watch, meaning that at any given time, one quarter of the crew would be immediately available. Night crews would man on-deck rapid-fire guns. All watertight doors would remain closed. He ordered steam in the two forward boilers, sufficient to operate the ship's 10-inch gun turrets and, if necessary, effect a quick get-away. He instructed the crew to stack live ammunition on deck, for the one- and six-pounder guns. All visitors to the ship would be closely supervised. He decided against dragging the harbor for underwater mines. Heavy boat traffic in the bay made it unnecessary. The political optics of such a move also contributed to his decision. Just the same, no boat, large or small, would be allowed to approach the battleship.

Sigsbee pivoted and took his first tentative steps toward the exit. Outstretched arms found nothing but air. As the captain groped his way through the darkness, an acrid smoke invaded his nostrils. He struggled to breathe. When he reached the exit, he paused and looked both ways. His eyes could not penetrate the inky darkness. When Sigsbee reached for the far wall, a panicked sailor slammed into him. Both men struggled to keep their balance. The captain barked.

"Who goes there?"

"It's Anthony, sir. Sorry, sir."

Private William Anthony served as the captain's orderly.

"The ship is blown up. We're sinking."

"I'll follow you," said Sigsbee.

After minutes of stumbling, a sliver of light brought them to the quarterdeck.

"What time is it, Anthony?"

"The explosion took place at 9:40, sir."

Another explosion, in the middle of the ship, bathed the two men in a blinding light. The rapidly rising water forced the captain and his aide to the highest elevation on the ship. While climbing the ladder to the *Maine's* poop deck, the captain muttered:

"The Spaniards have blown us up."

Sigsbee, greeted by all but one of his staff, turned to his Executive Officer, Lieutenant Commander Richard Wainwright.

"Flood the forward magazines, immediately."

The captain did not want the forward bunkers, filled with live shells, ammo, and gun powder, to explode. Wainwright flinched.

"Sir, the entire forward portion of the ship is already underwater."

"Then get the men to their hoses and post the sentries."

Wainwright disappeared into the flickering shadows. He returned, moments later.

"Sir, the water ducts have been destroyed. The hoses are useless, even if we had enough men to handle them. And there are no sentries to post."

The captain bit his lower lip and looked away. He could not return the Exec's unblinking stare. For the first time since the explosion, Sigsbee considered the devastation which surrounded him. His ship was sinking and hundreds of men were missing.

When the explosion of bursting shells temporarily subsided, the captain and his executive staff could hear the desperate screams of wounded and dying sailors.

"Help us. Please help us."

A series of lifeless, white objects bobbed up and down in the dirty water. Those sailors could no longer cry for help. Lifeboats, all but two of them from nearby vessels, scurried from one

5

floating cadaver to another. Occasionally, they discovered a badly burned sailor, screaming in pain. When a fallen smoke-stack, floating in the water, appeared at the captain's feet, Wainwright spoke up.

"Sir. We must abandon ship."

"I won't leave until everybody is off," said Sigsbee.

Wainwright leaned forward and whispered in the captain's ear. The raging fire now approached the ten-inch magazine. The detonation of such large shells would cause a huge explosion. Sigsbee bowed his head in surrender.

"Get into the boats, gentlemen."

The officers boarded a small rowboat. When Pug, the skipper's dog, miraculously appeared, an officer scooped him up and placed the ship's mascot on the gig. Sigsbee noted several strange rowboats, circling the wreckage. The tiny boats came from the *Alphonso XII*, a Spanish vessel, and an American steamship, the *City of Washington*. Their combined efforts retrieved only a handful of seriously wounded and badly burned victims. Sigsbee, fearing more and larger explosions, ordered them to leave the vicinity. He made one last desperate appeal for survivors.

"If there is anyone alive and onboard this ship, for God's sake, say so."

The captain and his officers strained to hear voices above the roar of explosions.

They heard more explosions. Nothing else.

No one spoke a word as the captain's gig slid through the water. The *City of Washington* would receive Sigsbee along with several dozen survivors. Numbed by the tragedy, the captain's thoughts drifted back in time. President McKinley ordered the *USS Maine* to Havana. The stated purpose of the trip, a "friendly peacekeeping mission," did not hide the real reason for the U.S. Navy's presence: To protect American life and property.

The Spanish government did not welcome the American government's clumsy attempt at a "peace mission." They viewed the *USS Maine* as a visible threat to Spain's precarious grip on the openly rebellious Cuban people. The native Cubans, struggling to achieve victory in their long-standing insurgency, greeted the U.S. battleship with a mixture of fear and joy. The rebels saw an ally. Older Cubans anticipated a long vicious war. Captain Sigsbee, skipper for less than a year, sailed into a political firestorm, made worse by the American newspapers. They accused Spain of atrocities against the Cuban people. The veracity of such stories could not be proven. It did not seem to matter. Freedom for the Cuban people, even if it meant war with Spain, became a battle cry. The destruction of an American battleship, while at anchor in a Spanish port, would likely lead to a declaration of war.

Once onboard the American steamer, Sigsbee insisted on visiting with the survivors. The ship's saloon served as a temporary hospital. Sigsbee, looking old and tired, walked among several dozen mattresses hastily positioned on the saloon floor. Several of the injured wore no clothes. Burns covered most of their bodies. A horribly disfigured sailor caught the captain's eye.

"What's your name, son?"

The man refused to give a name.

"My parents would be very upset, sir."

Sigsbee offered words of encouragement and sincere praise to every sailor in the room, conscious or not.

After his tour of the wounded, Sigsbee would take up quarters in the captain's cabin. The spacious chamber belonged to the skipper of the American steamer. Sigsbee lingered at the ship's railing and studied the wreckage that used to be his battleship. The *USS Maine* now rested, like a beached whale, on the bottom of Havana's shallow harbor. Portions of the vessel remained above water. Despite a slight rain, the remnants continued to burn, fueled by explosions deep in the belly of the beast.

When he reached his temporary quarters, Sigsbee composed a telegram to the Secretary of the Navy. He informed the secretary of the disaster and added a cautionary note:

> **Public opinion should be suspended until further report.**

Sigsbee could only guess who or what might have caused the explosion: an underwater mine or torpedo, one of the eight onboard boilers, the spontaneous combustion of coal, sabotage, or an accident. The possibilities crowded into the captain's mind along with the faces of dead, dying, and wounded sailors. He drifted into a restless sleep and woke early in the morning. A messenger brought the first of many reports delivered to the captain that day.

> **More than 250 dead or missing. Dozens more injured, many critical and unlikely to survive.**

February 15, 1898 would be seared into the memories of Americans everywhere.

# Chapter Two

## THREE YEARS EARLIER, CHRISTMAS 1895

"Merry Christmas, Walter."

Walter McDermott refused to acknowledge the holiday greeting from his work mate. He assumed that the man's words were spoken in jest, or, worse, a prelude to some sort of trick. Since his assignment on the *USS Maine*, currently anchored in Tompkinsville, New York, Walter suffered through a countless number of cruel jokes, personal insults, and underhanded tricks. Today would be no different.

Luther Burns cupped his oversized hands and yelled into his man-made megaphone.

"I said Merry Christmas, Walter."

Walter heard him the first time, despite the noise of the boiler and the nearby engine room. He rolled his eyes and nodded in silence.

"I brought you a present," said Burns.

Walter paused, an empty coal bucket in his hands.

"You brought me a present?"

"For Christmas," said Burns. "And a peace offering," he added, a reference to their last confrontation.

Walter reached for the gift. He waited a moment and examined the box. His darting eyes studied Burns' face for signs of treachery. Burns offer seemed sincere.

"Open it," said Burns.

Walter shook the box. Its contents made only a slight noise. Burns grinned. Walter took a deep breath and flashed a slight smile. He yanked at the ribbon. His trembling hands fumbled with the box. A giddy feeling churned in his stomach. He did not notice the faces which appeared around and behind Burns. Walter pulled at the bathroom tissue that hid his present from view. Now obsessed with his gift, he threw the tissue into the air. There it was. A single chunk of dirty coal. Nothing else. When his grin disappeared, Burns and his invited colleagues erupted in laughter. Walter's eyes moistened. He bit his lower lip. Burns rubbed salt in the wound.

"Merry Christmas, Walter."

Walter threw the box and the chunk of coal into the burner. He slammed the hatch shut and stormed his way through the scrum. With his jaw clenched and face set in stone, Walter marched through the gauntlet of jeers and raucous laughter. He did not stop walking until reaching his hammock in the bowels of the battleship.

Walter lay in his bunk and cursed himself.

Why do you fall for those stupid jokes, again and again, he asked. He blamed himself. He also blamed his late mother. "There is always hope," she would say. She drummed that mantra into the child's head. Walter's life offered no reason for hope. Hope was a useless exercise. It did not prevent his drunken father from beating his wife and child whenever he drank. Which was often.

Walter enlisted in the Navy when he turned 17. He wanted to sign up a year earlier but his mother took ill. He dared not leave her alone with his father. When she died, Walter received his final beating. His father's last words, "You'll never amount to anything," rang in his ears, still. Now 23 years old, he knew nothing but the Navy. His lack of height, five feet one, plus a round baby face, receding hairline, and long pointed nose, made the coal-passer look old and weak. He constantly suffered teasing and bullying at the hands of his shipmates. Complaints to a commanding officer usually made matters worse.

Walter would console himself with fantasies. Spectacular fantasies. Dark fantasies. In one daydream, he would save the ship's crew with a daring act of courage. In another, he would strike fear in the hearts of his crewmates, by maiming or even killing Luther Burns. He did it with a coal shovel to the side of the bully's head. Walter relished his fantasies. He used them to encourage a peaceful sleep when sleep would otherwise elude him.

Thus far, his dreams of violent revenge remained just that. Dreams.

"I have decided. You will not accompany me to Cuba."

General Valeriano Weyler stood erect and wore a steely look on his face. His niece, Isabella, almost a foot taller than her uncle, frowned. Isabella, an adopted member of Weyler's household since childhood, remained confident in her ability to charm and manipulate the man, at will.

"Uncle, must you always be so obstinate? I am a 19-year-old woman. You are the most feared general in all of Spain. Are you not capable of protecting me while I am in Cuba?"

The general furrowed his overgrown eyebrows, and rigorously smoothed the long bushy sideburns that framed his mustache.

"Isabella. Do not be disrespectful. I have raised you and supported you from childhood. And I know what is best for you."

Isabella rushed forward. She pressed his head to her bosom and squeezed.

"Oh, my precious uncle. I meant no disrespect. You have been like a father to me since the day my parents left this world. I love you with all my heart. But I must leave this place or I shall go mad. Please let me join you. Please."

She clasped his head in both hands, carefully caressing his perfectly coiffed hair. She gently kissed him on both cheeks and stared into his cold black eyes.

"Please?"

The general spoke in a loud voice.

"You must promise to obey my every command."

"I will be your most loyal soldier, your Excellency."

Weyler surrendered with a sheepish smile. Isabella beamed with joy.

"Thank you, my uncle. Thank you, thank you, thank you."

General Weyler waited until his stunningly beautiful niece left the office.

He retrieved the communication from Madrid and read it once more. Martinez Campos, the current captain-general in Cuba, would be summarily dismissed. Weyler would take his place. Spain's tiny island colony of Cuba had reached a tipping point. The rebels, their struggle for independence now years long, would no longer be tolerated. Weyler's mission, to end the rebellion as soon as possible, would include the capture or execution of their leaders, General Antonio Maceo and General Maximo Gomez. Weyler welcomed the assignment. As the former governor of the Canaries and the Philippines, the captain-general earned his well-deserved reputation for decisive action and widespread brutality. This assignment, he concluded, would be easily accomplished.

Weyler came from a military family. At the age of 15, he entered the Spanish military academy. After graduating as a second lieutenant in 1856, he served an additional seven years at the Staff Officers School. In 1863, the young soldier volunteered for an unpopular assignment in Cuba. It would become the most eventful year of Weyler's life. First, he won the national lottery. The enormous prize allowed him to purchase a large mansion on the island of Mallorca, his birthplace. He would be a wealthy man for the rest of his life. Shortly thereafter, he contracted yellow fever and nearly died from it. His survival led to a lifelong immunity from the deadly disease. And finally, he got what every young soldier wanted. A war.

While in Cuba, he took an assignment in the Dominican Republic. His role in quelling a rebellion earned him the Army's top honor, the Cross of San Fernando. Now a Lieutenant Colonel, Weyler transferred back to Cuba and fought in the 10-year war between Cuban rebels and Spanish loyalists. Again, he received a promotion, this time to General. A reporter posed a question to Weyler, as he basked in the victory.

"Is it true, my general, that your men returned from battle holding the severed heads of their enemies by their hair?"

General Weyler responded without hesitation.

"What do you think war is? In war, men have only one job. To kill."

From that day forward, Weyler became known as "The Butcher."

"Look, my uncle. The Cuban people welcome their beloved son."

Isabella waived her arm in a long flowing arc. All of Cuba, it seemed, came out to greet the new captain-general as the *Alfonso XII* steamed into Havana Harbor. Spanish and German war ships fired their artillery in salute. The ancient fortress, Morro Castle, with its huge guns defending the bay, also fired volley after volley in a noisy tribute to General Weyler.

As the boat slid into the harbor, its guest of honor stood in the bow of the ship, surrounded by dozens of officers. He basked in the glow of his many admirers. In the bay, war ships and merchant boats covered with bunting lowered their flags. Cheering spectators stood, jam-packed on a countless number of steamboats, tugboats, docks, and wharves. They screamed an enthusiastic welcome for their newly appointed leader. Another VIP crowd of senior military officers, along with the entire police department, the fire department, chamber of commerce officials, and distinguished guests, waited in a roped-off section of the street for the general to disembark.

After an onboard welcome by the city council, the captain-general came ashore. The surrounding streets, packed with people, cheered their new leader. Isabella shouted in the general's ear and pointed.

"Look, my general. For you."

She pointed to the balconies and the streets in the vicinity of the captain-general's palace. As far as the eye could see, ladies in colorful dresses and hats waved their adulation. They interrupted his arrival with constant presentations of floral arrangements, many of them shaped as crowns. It looked truly spectacular. Weyler happily paused and accepted their tributes.

The roar of the enthusiastic crowds continued until Weyler entered the two-story palace. It would be his home while in Cuba. When he approached the official who would swear him into office, an eerie, almost reverential silence descended on the large throng. Weyler swore the oath of office under a large crucifix, with his left hand on the bible and his right hand in the air.

Isabella rushed forward, just seconds before the huge swarm of people pushed closer.

"*¡Te quiero!*" (I love you!)

"But mama, I go in search of food."

"Your father went in search of food and now he is dead. You will not find food. You will find death," she said.

Roberto Alvarez insisted on leaving. The residents of Guatao, a small village southwest of Havana, suffered greatly as a result of the insurrection. Both sides stole from the poor, taking livestock, foodstuffs, and personal possessions. Both sides persecuted, tortured, and murdered the locals with impunity. Death by starvation became commonplace.

Roberto, now eighteen years of age and man of the house, felt duty-bound to feed his family. He turned to the door. His mother collapsed onto a kitchen chair, smothering her sobs with a worn and faded apron. Roberto's younger sister used her green eyes like daggers. The fiercely independent 13-year-old, soon to blossom into a beautiful woman, wore an emaciated look.

"Why do you make mama cry?" she asked.

Roberto said nothing. Ironically, Elena motivated him the most, in his desperate search for sustenance. The girl would not live much longer without food. The boy looked to his grandmother for support. She sat where she always sat, in their one-room shack, in a chair near her dying husband's bedside. Grandfather suffered from erysipelas, also known as Saint Anthony's rash. The illness caused an intense burning sensation. A few doses of penicillin would cure him. The lack of such medicines in Cuba would kill him. Roberto surveyed his family, one last time.

"I'm sorry," he said.

Grandmother reached for her rosary hanging on the bed post. *She looked so sad*, thought Roberto. The old lady made the sign of the cross and bowed her head. Roberto shut the door behind him.

He walked on the dusty road, in a southwest direction, but only for a short distance. Spanish soldiers would almost certainly be on patrol. His alternative, the dense forest and prickly underbrush, would be considerably more difficult but much safer. He used the nearby road as his compass and a machete to cut his way through the brush. Roberto searched his surroundings for something to eat. A banana tree, the pointed leaves of a yam plant, or even a slow-moving hutia, would suffice. The rodent, twelve to eighteen inches in length if you excluded its long tail, made a tasty meal.

Roberto's mouth watered at the thought of meat for dinner. The sound of voices disrupted his pleasant daydream. He scampered into a thicket of bushes and waited. In moments, he spied several dozen men with wide-brim floppy hats and baggy white uniforms. They wore ammunition belts, hung diagonally over their chest and back. Cuban rebels. Roberto resisted the urge to join them. His skills with a rifle, well known in the village of Gautao and beyond, would make him a welcome recruit. But a rebel cannot fight on an empty stomach.

The soldiers passed. He waited a bit more, unsure as to why. He heard new voices in the distance. He thought it odd that the rebels traveled in two separate groups. When the second entourage came into view, Roberto crouched lower and stopped breathing. They wore blue-gray uniforms and beige hats. They carried Mausers, unlike the Springfields, Remingtons, and Winchesters used by the rebels. The Spanish soldiers, numbering well over a hundred, followed the rebels. There would be a confrontation.

Worse, they traveled in the direction of Guatao.

Roberto shadowed the Spanish soldiers as they marched down the dirt road.

The rebels eluded the Spanish Army. A plethora of paths, streams, and back roads allowed the outnumbered insurgents an easy escape. Minutes later, shots rang out. Roberto stiffened. The Spanish soldiers reached the village of Guatao. Frustrated with their lack of success, they fired at random. The villagers screamed in terror, running in every direction. People Roberto knew as friends and neighbors fled their homes in a mad dash for a nearby sugarcane field. They fell to the ground in a hail of bullets. The soldiers banged on closed doors and murdered whoever answered. As they neared Roberto's home, he screamed. His warning could not be heard above the sounds of gunfire and the loud cries of the dying. In his heart and mind, he rescued his family. In fact, he stood in place, unable to move.

His eyes grew wide when mama opened the door. She clasped her hands in prayer and begged for mercy. The soldier used the butt of his rifle to bash her head in. The Spanish uniform entered the boy's home. Three shots and a cloud of smoke told Roberto that only one member of his family survived the onslaught. He envisioned his mama lying on the floor, his grandmother in her chair, and his grandfather, still in bed.

He prayed that Elena hid or escaped from the soldiers. A scream told him otherwise. The soldiers dragged her into the street. She yelled and kicked, biting them when she could. One soldier attacked the girl, ripping her flimsy dress and exposing the girl's adolescent breasts. Another soldier persuaded the predator to wait.

"There'll be plenty of time for that, later on."

They herded the females into a group. The soldiers tied the prisoners' hands. For good measure, they also tied the captives to each other. The men escorted their victims down the road, in the direction of Havana. Roberto turned and stumbled his way deep into the forest.

The thick brush and palm trees smothered his sobs.

Isabella remained just outside the door of her uncle's elaborately furnished office.

Weyler threw a stack of reports at a waiting aide. Papers flew everywhere. The terror-stricken officer scurried in circles to collect the clutter. Weyler glared at the wall and raised his voice.

"I have inherited an extremely grave situation. Worse than I imagined."

He dictated a series of pronouncements. Among other things, he called upon the rebels to surrender. He boldly announced that the war would end in 30 days. Civilians, foolish enough to aid the rebels, would be executed. All travel within Cuba would henceforth be restricted. Her uncle also announced a plan to herd Cuban peasants, now living in the countryside, into urban reconcentration camps. Isabella rolled her eyes, yawned, and walked away. Most of the time, her uncle could be a rather boring man.

She left the palace grounds and walked the streets of Havana, unmolested. The cold season in Cuba, all but over by the end of February, would be followed by a much more temperate climate, void of the rain that came during summer months. For Isabella, this would be a time of exploration, adventure, and shopping. Lots of shopping. Money never posed a challenge for Isabella. She received whatever she wanted and purchased what little she did not already own. In Spain, she attracted many friends. She regularly enjoyed being the center of everyone's attention. Cuba would be no different. Or so she believed.

A street leading away from the plaza, no larger than an alleyway, prompted her to investigate. Several of the vendors sold large, floppy straw hats, festooned with colorful ribbons.

One elderly lady loaned Isabella a small mirror to confirm the girl's selection.

"You are most beautiful, *Señorita*."

"I'll take it."

A last glance in the mirror triggered furrowed eyebrows and a frown. Several booths away, stood the large man she saw earlier, at the entrance to the palace. She saw him again, in the plaza. He wore a military-style floppy hat and a bushy, black mustache, overgrown and uneven. The rest of the man's clothes and army-style boots matched the color of his deeply tanned face and arms. She caught his stare. He immediately pulled the hat low over his face and turned in the opposite direction. A cold shiver triggered goosebumps on the nape of her neck. Isabella paid the old lady who made the hat, refused the change, and walked further into the alleyway.

Isabella Hermoza was the orphan child of Diego and Carmen.

Her father, killed in battle, served under the command of then Captain Valeriano Weyler. She remembered only that her father died somewhere in Santo Domingo. She recalled with clarity that day when her mother disappeared. The woman and "Uncle" Carlos, a frequent visitor to their home even before the war ended, abandoned the child to relatives. When they too grew weary of the effort and expense of a young girl, they dumped the child on the doorstep of her wealthy uncle.

Except for her name, the neglected waif-turned-pampered princess received nothing from her parents. Everything came from her wealthy uncle. He treated Isabella like his own. She quickly learned to take advantage of the man's generosity. Isabella's striking beauty, which included green eyes and long, flowing red hair, attracted attention wherever she went. Isabella's followers often remarked that the general's niece, with a burlap sack over her head, would attract no less a crowd. Her cunning charm, beguiling ways, and tempestuous tantrums allowed the young woman to obtain whatever she wanted. Always.

When Frank Lamb escaped from Isabella's view, he mingled with the large crowd at a nearby open-air market.

Hundreds of farmers and artisans hawked a large variety of fruits, vegetables, and handmade goods. Their intended customers, mostly well-to-do government employees, rarely agreed to the asking price. He watched as peasants sold their products for a fraction of what they originally requested. Frank offered the asking price for the items he purchased. In return, he received valuable information. The red-haired lady with the green eyes was none other than Weyler's beloved niece. The mercenary's instincts immediately kicked in. He sensed a hidden opportunity. Blackmail, ransom, access to Spanish military secrets. Whatever. The young lady could prove useful, if not lucrative.

Despite his potentially profitable discovery, Lamb wrestled with growing frustration. He arrived in Cuba almost a year ago. His mission, to aid the efforts of Cuban rebels, thus far produced no significant results. His backers in Key West would soon lose their patience. And he would soon lose the source of his funds.

Frank's previous experience in the military, a seven-year stint in the American Army, gave him the required appearance and demeanor. The 32-year-old former Lieutenant prided himself on being in excellent physical condition. He also claimed to be an expert in hand-to-hand combat. The regiment he served with, the 10th U.S. Calvary, consisted entirely of enlisted black men. Frank barely tolerated black people, even when they wore army uniforms. But for an altercation with an uppity Negro, Frank might still be with the regiment. The court martial found him guilty of assaulting an enlisted man. They ordered a dishonorable discharge. All for hitting a lazy blackie's backside with a shovel. Frank fumed every time he recalled the incident.

For now, the former soldier's bitter memories, and his plans for Isabella, would take second priority. He learned, just yesterday, that Antonio Maceo scored a victory against General Weyler's forces. The rumor mill reported of a possible meeting between Maceo and fellow general, Maximo Gomez. Together, they represented the insurrection's top leadership. If Frank could obtain an audience with them, his dream of becoming a dominant and well-known leader of the insurrection and over-throwing their colonial oppressors would be realized.

The adventure would also be good for his ego and his pocketbook.

Walter made a new friend.

"Your dish is empty, Christopher. You must have been very hungry," he whispered.

Christopher, one of many rats on board the *USS Maine*, took a liking to Walter—or at least the steady supply of food that Walter offered. Walter could not be certain of the rodent's sex. He named it Christopher, anyway. Walter's boyhood friend was named Christopher. The two boys did everything together. Until the old man, soaked in a drunken rage, chased Walter's best friend away. Walter reached into his pocket and retrieved a handful of scraps saved from lunch. The bottom of an old tin can, shorn to a half an inch in height, served as the animal's dinner plate. Walter carefully placed the food behind his large canvas duffel bag. The position of his low-hanging hammock, the duffel bag, and the walled corners of the room, made Christopher's dining area, invisible to all but searching eyes.

After several minutes, the furry little creature appeared, scurrying from the opposite side of the room. Walter watched with glee as the rat fearlessly attacked his meal. The pair first met several weeks ago. Although initially skittish, Christopher grew comfortable with his human benefactor. He would eat out of Walter's hand and learned to stand upright on his hind legs. Man and rodent became good friends.

"The captain wants the crews from one and two in the portside engine room in 15 minutes."

Christopher, fearful of the strange voice, abandoned his meal and ran for cover. Walter jumped to his feet. His job, as a coal passer for boiler number one, made attendance at the meeting mandatory. He also recognized the voice of Bill Horn, a fireman first class. Although Walter worked the third shift, Bill worked the second shift and they often saw each other in passing. Horn did not hang around to chat. Too bad, thought Walter. He liked the upstate New York native as one of the few sailors below deck who treated Walter with respect.

Walter waited, shoulder to shoulder, with his fellow coal passers, firemen, and boiler operators. He positioned himself in a far corner of the hot and humid chamber so as not to attract attention. A sudden hush and a flurry of salutes told him that Captain Crowninshield entered the room. Walter could see only a sea of heads and shoulders.

"As you were," said Crowninshield.

Walter remembered the tall, gaunt figure from their previous encounters. The ship's commanding officer wore no glasses, sported an overgrown mustache, and rarely smiled.

"I'm here to talk about coal," said the captain.

Crowninshield announced that, days earlier, a fire occurred on board the *USS Cincinnati*, a sister ship. Authorities blamed the conflagration on the spontaneous combustion of coal. Like the *Maine*, the *Cincinnati* carried several hundred tons of the soft, brown substance, for use as fuel.

"And gentlemen, on this ship, just like the *Cincinnati*, our coal bunkers are separated from our gunpowder and ammo bunkers by a thin bulkhead," said the captain.

Crowninshield went on to explain the specific measures that would henceforth be implemented. The new protocols, designed to avoid such fires, would be strictly enforced.

"I expect every man to do his duty," the captain concluded.

Walter waited until the room emptied and shuffled his way back to the enlisted men's quarters. He noted that Christopher had returned because the rat's dish lay empty. Walter studied the ceiling, thinking he might catch a few hours of sleep before the shift began. He performed a mental checklist of the fantasies that brought him pleasure and a restful sleep. Today, his creative brain spawned a new fantasy. One that would make him a popular hero. He would save the *USS Maine* from certain disaster by detecting and dousing a fire in one of the coal bunkers.

Walter fell asleep just as the captain pinned a large medal on the sailor's chest.

Roberto spent a sleepless night in the forest, fending off insects and tears.

At daybreak, he sliced a path through the vegetation and pointed himself in the direction of Guatao. The smell of death greeted the boy as he walked through a gauntlet of staring eyes, some of them lifeless. A woman, with two small children at her side, rolled a man's body into a freshly dug grave. The youngsters cried from hunger or grief or both.

Villagers who had attempted to escape the marauding soldiers by running into the sugarcane fields lay dead just short of their intended haven. Their bodies now fed the vultures and vermin of Cuba. Those that managed to escape and return to the village found their homes ransacked and destroyed.

Roberto took a deep breath and pushed open the door to the shack where he once lived. Grandfather, still in bed, wore a large crimson bib around his chest. Flies buzzed in and out of the man's open mouth. Grandmother slumped forward in her chair but remained seated. She appeared to be sleeping. The gaping hole in her forehead told the boy otherwise. Roberto shuddered when he first laid eyes on his mother. Her face, covered with blood, suggested that she initially survived the attack. Her eyes, wide open, seemed to follow him as he searched the rest of the room.

Elena's modest belongings lay undisturbed. Although five years separated them, the siblings were inseparable. He taught her to read and write. When food became scarce, he would give his portion to the girl. Roberto retrieved the torn and ragged shawl Elena wore when the temperatures dipped. He pressed his face into the material and inhaled. The suffering she would endure at the hands of her captors made him shudder.

The soldiers left nothing of value in their wake. The boy pulled on three sets of arms until each of his loved ones lay in the field behind the shack. After several hours of digging, the sweat-soaked boy-man stood next to three shallow graves. He rolled their remains in place like large bags of tobacco in a warehouse. Roberto covered his mother's head with her apron, unable to shovel dirt and stones onto her lifeless face.

He searched for, but could not find, the materials required for graveside markers. The stones which circled each grave would have to suffice. He started to pray. An angry look crossed his face. His grief slowly transformed into anger. A sweltering rage rose in his chest. He looked to the scattered clouds which dotted an otherwise unblemished sky. Roberto growled at the God that he had prayed to every day since childhood.

"You have brought nothing but death and destruction to me, my family, and my country. Why?" he asked. "How did we sin in your eyes? Was our sin so great that you would make us suffer and die as your punishment?"

Roberto glared at the stones which commemorated his family's slaughter.

"I too can rain death and destruction on those who have sinned. And I swear to you, on the graves of my loved ones, their deaths will be avenged."

# *Chapter Three*

## ⒯HE ⒭EBELS

Roberto's desperate search for Elena pushed him in the direction of Havana.

After one hour in the thick brush, his machete swinging constantly, the exhausted boy stopped to rest. Despite his fatigue, the rage in his heart continued to simmer. His shame, for being unable to aid his family, continued unabated. He did not know where the men took his younger sister. He knew only that the attackers walked in the direction of Havana. The dungeons at Morro Castle and *La Cabana* came to mind. His stomach churned as he imagined the horrors she faced. In the end, his torturous thoughts gave way to common sense. Havana would be overrun with Spanish soldiers. He could not go there.

He recalled some of the older men in the village discussing Matanzas. The port city lay north and east of Havana. They described the city as a hotbed of rebel activity. As a lone rebel, he could not possibly make a difference. But hundreds of rebels could attack and defeat the Spanish soldiers. Perhaps even locate his sister. He would join the rebel army.

The 65-mile journey would be impossible without food and a horse. Stealing a ride on a railcar, with a load of sugarcane, would solve his dilemma. He planned to keep the main road to his right and do his best to stay hidden. By traveling east and north he would soon reach the rail line that connected Havana to Matanzas.

Since the revolution began, sugarcane production fell precipitously. Both sides in the rebellion decided to destroy most of the sugar mills. They did not want their enemy to benefit from the revenue. The result, near-empty freight trains and fewer troops guarding those trains, would make Roberto's journey less difficult.

The sugar cane trains consisted of no more than a series of flatbeds. The stalks, many of them 8- to 10-feet in length, lay stacked on the railcar. Wooden uprights, positioned every 2 feet around the perimeter of the car, held the cane in place. A horizontal frame, also of wood, held the uprights in place. The box-like structure made boarding the flatbed car an easy task. The challenge would be to remain hidden during the journey to Matanzas.

The hissing steam from a stopped train told the boy that his illicit ride to Matanzas lay just ahead. The train, although parked in the middle of a sugarcane field, did not surprise the would-be rebel. Years ago, the owners of those fields clamored for railroad tracks nearer to the sugarcane. This would reduce the cost of transporting their cash crop. Roberto watched as mules and men filled the cars with large bundles of sugar cane. As he expected, the last car did not contain a full load of stalks, its cargo being only five feet in depth. That would be his home for the next couple of hours.

Roberto pushed and sliced his way through the forest. He needed to get ahead of the train before it departed. To avoid discovery, he would hop onto the last car, hundreds of yards east of where the men and mules loaded the cane. Minutes later, the fully loaded locomotive, struggling to pick up speed, announced its presence. Large puffs of smoke from its woodfired boilers and the deafening sound of steel on steel filled the boy's ears. Roberto waited until the last car came into view. He ran alongside, chose an upright in the middle of the flat bed, and leapt into the air. His muscular arms reached for the elevated portion of the wooden frame. He easily swung his body onto the bed of sugarcane stalks. The soft landing made him smile. Roberto scurried to the front of the car and selected a likely spot for his hideaway. He created a man-sized foxhole by pushing and throwing stalks in every direction. Roberto jumped in the hole and pulled a few stalks close, in the event he needed to disappear.

"Very nice work."

The man's voice, coming from the rear of the flatbed, triggered Roberto's defensive reflexes. In one smooth motion, he jumped to his feet and reached for his machete. The razor-sharp weapon, now raised above the boy's head, glistened in the hot sun. The man on the opposite end of the rail car, carried a sidearm. He ignored the weapon and raised both hands.

"Easy, boy. I surrender."

Roberto's eyes flashed. The stranger jerked his eyebrows into an arch and flashed a quick smile. The boy took a deep breath. His heart continued to pound. He slowly lowered his machete.

"The name is Frank. Frank Lamb. I jumped on just before you did."

"Why do you go to Matanzas?" asked Roberto.

The stranger lowered his hands. The machete rose, once again.

"That depends. Who am I talking to?"

"My name is Roberto Alvarez. You are an American," said the boy.

"Guilty."

Roberto pointed his machete in Lamb's direction.

"I am not going to ask you again. Why do you travel to Matanzas.?"

"I came to kill a few Spanish soldiers."

Roberto's eyes grew wide. The boy stood at alert. His grip on the machete tightened. He took notice of the two large ammo belts which crisscrossed Lamb's torso. When the American reached into his hiding place, Roberto yelled.

"Keep your hands where I can see them."

Lamb stood up with a burlap bag in his hand. The fabric bulged in every direction. He tossed the sack, tied at the end, in Roberto's direction. Roberto did not flinch.

"Since my arrival, I have yet to meet a Cuban who isn't hungry," said Lamb.

Roberto stared at the man and slowly untied the leather strap. His eyes darted between the bag and the stranger. A large grin covered the boy's face.

"There's more where that came from," said Lamb. "Eat up."

Roberto reached for the bag. He could see and smell several kinds of fruit, dried meat, plus two small loaves of bread. The boy shoved a hand into the bag of edibles. He held the machete in his other hand. As he wolfed down the food, Lamb tossed a leather covered canteen.

"Water. And you better slow down, kid, or you're going to lose your lunch."

When Roberto finished gorging himself, he asked a series of rapid-fire questions. Lamb revealed that he served previously with the U.S. Calvary and traveled to Cuba more than a year ago.

"Why do you wish to fight with the rebels?" asked Roberto.

"Our government supports the rebels," said Frank, referencing his country's public opinion and the likelihood of a congressional resolution.

Roberto thrust a finger at the man who fed him.

"But why do *you* fight?"

"Some people call me a mercenary. But I support freedom fighters everywhere," said Lamb.

"The rebel army has no money," Roberto announced.

"The rebel army has been ineffective and poorly managed. They need people like me, whether they can afford me or not," said Lamb. "Besides, I get my money from the states."

"What's in Matanzas?"

"I hope to meet some of the rebel leaders when we get there."

"I wish to join the rebel army."

"Why?"

"They killed my family and kidnapped my younger sister. I search for Elena and I search for revenge."

"Your sister, if she is not dead already, will not survive her captivity."

Roberto hugged his stomach and groaned in pain.

"Drink some more water. Slowly, this time," advised the mercenary.

Frank told the boy about Generals Gomez and Maceo. Roberto recognized the names. They would gather in a place called El Galeon, just northwest of Matanzas.

"I should like to accompany you," said Roberto.

"And so you shall, my friend."

Frank used two fingers on his left hand to smooth his moustache. He stared at the boy, all the while.

"You are very well-spoken for a young Cuban."

"My grandmother was my teacher. When I was a child, she taught me English, history, the arts, math, and science. I would spend hours at her side, each day. I read constantly. When she got sick, the lessons ended. We had only a handful of books, but she taught me well."

"Keep reading, boy. As much as you can. It's important."

"I no longer require books. I require bullets. And a gun."

"Do you know how to shoot?" asked Frank.

"The older men in the village would tell you that I am an excellent marksman," said Roberto. "But they too have been killed or imprisoned."

"I will get you a rifle."

The boy's fluttering eyelids permitted a weak smile.

"Get some rest, Roberto. I'll keep watch."

Frank did not have to repeat his directive. The boy disappeared into his foxhole.

Roberto 's eyes remained closed until the city of Matanzas appeared on the horizon.

"Walter, where are you? Come out, come out, wherever you are."

Walter groaned when he recognized the voice of his nemesis, Luther Burns. He hurried to finish dressing for the night shift. Burns and his followers worked the afternoon shift. Troublemakers, every one of them. With his shoelaces still untied, Walter jogged down the narrow passageway, hoping to avoid his tormentors. The strategy failed.

"There you are, Walter," said one of the men.

Another voice, off to the side, chimed in.

"Going somewhere, Walter? You forgot to tie your shoes."

And from the back of the five-person mob, Burns' grating voice.

"Maybe he doesn't know how to tie his shoes. He's just a witto boy, said Burns. "I think we should help him."

Several of the men stepped forward and hoisted Walter into the air. He turned his head so as not to collide with the low ceiling. Burns laughed.

"Let's tie his shoes so they never come off."

Several of the ruffians took hold of Walter's feet. Another man reached for the shoelaces.

"Gentlemen. Are you in need of assistance?"

The deep voice of Bill Horn jerked the men to a standstill.

Horn, one of the largest sailors on board the *Maine*, pretended to clear his throat. They lowered Walter's body to the ground. When Bill cleared his throat a second time, the bullies drifted off in different directions, unsmiling and clearly disappointed.

Walter's knight in shining armor could intimidate a man by his size alone. He stood six and a half feet tall. Horn said little, listened a lot, and enjoyed an almost universal respect from both subordinates and superiors. He hailed from Plattsburgh, New York, and sported a meticulously trimmed jet-black moustache. He wore a wedding ring. The fact that he regularly received scented letters from an address in Brooklyn triggered a lot of gossip. Bill shared nothing of his personal life with any of the crew. No one dared to make inquiries.

"Thank you, Bill," said Walter.

"Why do they pick on you so much?"

Walter scratched his head.

"I really don't know. I try like the dickens to avoid them."

"Do you have the night shift this evening?" asked Horn.

"Yes, sir."

"Me too. I'll check in on you."

Isabella threw her hands in the air.

"Why are you so angry? I walked to the plaza and did some shopping. Must I seek your permission each time I leave my room?"

Captain-General Weyler slammed his fist on the table.

"Yes. You must. The streets of Havana are not safe for a beautiful woman such as you. You could be kidnapped, attacked, or even killed."

Isabella pouted.

"I don't understand."

"I think you understand perfectly. You will henceforth be accompanied by two guards whenever you leave the palace. And you will not disappear for hours at a time without my knowledge aforehand."

Isabella wiped a few imaginary tears from her eyes.

"Please, uncle. You cannot do this to me. I am your loving niece. What am I to do in this dreadful place, all day long?"

"Do what you wish, little girl. But you will obey my orders or I will send you back to Spain."

Isabella's face grew red with rage. She scrunched her nose and drilled into the general's face with flashing eyes. With one arm, she swept the general's papers, rolled-up maps, and writing paraphernalia from his desk onto the carpeted floor. She leaned forward with clenched fists on the bare wood and thrust her face to within inches of her uncle's bushy moustache.

"I am *not* one of your soldiers. And you will *not* send me back to Spain."

Weyler rose from his chair. He stood on his toes to exaggerate his five-foot frame.

"Young lady, you have exhausted my patience. Leave this office at once."

Isabella stormed out of the general's chamber. She noted three guards, posted at the building's exit. Isabella scurried to a door on the opposite side of the cavernous lobby. That door opened to a long set of stairs leading to the second floor. She did not plan to return to her room. Nevertheless, she rushed up the stairs. When the girl reached her room, she opened the door and slammed it shut, remaining in the hallway. She then removed her shoes and ran the length of the hallway to the opposite side of the building. She peeked around the corner. Two of the guards, breathing heavily, stood on either side of the door. They protected an empty room.

Isabella flew down the back stairs and through a hallway. From the wafting aroma of food, she concluded the palace kitchen must be nearby. As she wound her way through the oversized kitchen, a series of surprised faces greeted her. No one dared to stop the captain-general's niece. She smiled at the guards posted at the rear of the mansion, quickly explaining that her uncle would soon join her for a stroll to the plaza. Both men, focused more on the woman's bust, offered no objection.

35

Her now leisurely pace brought her through the large Plaza De Armas and left, past the cathedral, to the nearby seminary. The naval storehouses, which lay ahead, held no interest for the adventurous young woman. She shaded her eyes and caught a glimpse of Morro Castle, just across the water. A small transport boat, tied to the dock and guarded by Spanish soldiers, took on a handful of passengers. Isabella rushed forward. One guard, an officer given the salutes he received, greeted her.

"You will identify yourself and state your business," said the soldier.

Isabella smiled sweetly.

"I'm new to Cuba and I wanted to explore the castles, over there."

Isabella pointed over the man's shoulders. He too seemed more concerned with the woman's plunging neckline.

"I am sorry, *Señorita*, that is not permitted."

She thought of dropping the name of her uncle but considered it unwise. Instead, she inquired about the building's history and current use. The soldier hesitated. Isabella feigned a dizzy spell. Her eyelids fluttered and she pretended to swoon.

"Oh my. I'm feeling a bit faint."

The officer ushered her to a cast-iron bench. He barked and several of the men hurried to a large trunk, positioned on the dock. They returned with a canteen. Isabella brought the container to her lips but did not drink. The water smelled foul.

"Thank you, officer. I'm feeling much better."

"What is it you wish to know about these structures?" he asked.

"Everything you can tell me. I am a student of history."

Isabella, rather bored, listened impatiently as the man recounted the year of their construction, their massive size, and their military importance.

"Are there soldiers stationed in the forts?"

"Only those required to guard the prisoners," said the officer.

Isabella snapped to attention.

"Prisoners?"

The guard's head slumped. His lips twisted into an angry frown.

"I am not at liberty to discuss such matters," said the officer, rising to his feet.

Isabella, her curiosity raging, threw caution to the wind. She stood and pulled the man closer with a wag of her index finger.

"I am the niece of Captain-General Valeriano Weyler. You will bring me to the Morro Castle. If you do not wish to cooperate, I will pursue the matter with my uncle."

The officer, initially stunned, recovered quickly.

"Yes. Of course. You were with the captain-general when he arrived. I stood guard at the palace. I remember you, miss . . ."

The man's voice trailed off, unable to recall the woman's name.

"Isabella Hermoza. Please, captain, I wish only to see the grounds."

She took several steps closer and whispered into the man's ear.

"Our visit and the prisoners you referenced will be our secret."

The captain wet his lips and gulped hard."

"As you wish, Miss Hermoza."

The officer escorted the young lady onto the transport. He ordered the other passengers to disembark and wait for the next boat. No one dared to object. The man's rank and the woman's beauty prohibited it.

Morro Castle, a superstructure on the island of Cuba, surprised and impressed the young lady. The officer took great pride as he recited the bastion's long list of armaments, its military importance, and its nearly impenetrable defenses. Isabella, her curiosity mostly satisfied, posed one more question.

"But where are the prisoners?"

"Please, Miss Hermoza. I am not permitted to discuss such matters."

A young soldier, message in hand and out of breath, appeared at the officer's side. The senior man blanched and ran off. He shouted over his shoulder as he left.

"Please remain at the dock, Miss Hermoza."

Isabella waited for her guide to return. She heard a door slam and walked to a far wall. A guard, not her guard, walked with his back to her, puffing furiously on a cigar, oblivious to the woman's presence. She glanced back to see if her officer friend returned. Not yet. The small door, from which the cigar smoking soldier exited, triggered her insatiable curiosity. She looked back once more. No sight of the captain. Isabella ran to the open door.

A short set of stairs greeted the woman. An awful stench invaded her nostrils. The light from a barred window, high above the stairwell, lit her way to another large door made of thick heavy wood. A small eye-level opening, protected by steel bars, offered no clue as to what lay on the other side. She turned away from the door, ready to leave. A large black ring, holding a single key, hung on the opposite wall. After several tries, the wooden door swung open.

She screamed when several large rats scampered across the stone floor. Isabella's scream alerted the prisoners. They rushed forward, dozens of them, jam-packed into cells on either side of the long aisleway. Desperate cries for food, money, and mercy filled her ears. She took a few halting steps forward, unwilling or unable to go back. A series of heads poked their dirty, emaciated faces through the bars. Outstretched hands reached for the beautiful woman but could not touch her. Isabella's stomach churned from the stench. She slipped and fell on the dirty wet floor. Her nose identified the cause of her accident. Human excrement. At the far end of the corridor, an inmate appeared to be sleeping on the floor. She looked closer. His emaciated body showed no sign of movement. A rat gnawed on the man's little finger. She blinked to clear the tears from her eyes. An old man, his skin covered with open sores, called out to her.

"Have you any food? Please? I have no family and I am dying," he cried.

She stepped forward, a hand in her purse. He grabbed at the beautiful dress. She panicked, turned, and ran. The skirt ripped.

She did not stop until she reached the large wooden door.

"Wake up, kid. This is where we get off."

Frank woke Roberto with a poke from a stalk of sugar cane. The boy jerked to attention and struggled to stand as he pushed the long stalks to one side.

"I was tired," said Roberto, a hand over his noisy yawn.

"Glad you got some rest," said Lamb. "We got some walking to do," he added.

"Where to?"

"A small village called El Galeon. If my sources are correct, we'll find both Maceo and Gomez there. With a good number of rebels."

Frank watched Roberto as the tall muscular teenager checked the machete strapped to his side. The kid shook remnants of sugarcane from his long black locks and brushed debris from his threadbare clothes. The pants barely fit the still-growing teenager. As Frank studied his young charge, he considered the possibilities. He could mold this impressionable young man into an effective soldier. Roberto, bitter and angry at the Spanish, would be the perfect candidate. The kid would complement Frank's evil repertoire of manipulation, blackmail, bribery, and mercenary ways. He would take the boy under his wing and change the kid into a younger version of himself. He would use the boy to secure a position of prominence in the Cuban revolution.

Frank and Roberto abandoned their coach of sugarcane, just outside of Matanzas. They would cross the Yumiri River and follow the northern coast of Cuba in the direction of the Sabana Archipelago. The 20-mile journey to El Galeon would not be on the main road. They hoped to avoid the Spanish patrols. Instead, they would travel through cane fields and jungle-like forests. Their arduous journey would require the rest of the day. As they approached what used to be a large cane field, outside Matanzas, Roberto and Frank came to a sudden halt.

"What happened here?" asked Frank.

"The Spanish soldiers burned the cane field. The Cuban rebels do the same."

"Why?"

"To deny the other side of food and money."

Both men had counted on the eight- to ten-feet high stalks to keep them hidden from view.

"We will be seen," said Frank.

Roberto jerked his head in the direction of a nearby area of small trees and thick bushes.

"This way."

The two men made a rush for the edge of the blackened cane field. Their fast-moving feet and the wind left small clouds of dust in their wake. Gunshots rang out. With a hundred yards to go, Frank stopped to rest. Roberto panicked.

"Mr. Lamb, we are not safe here. We have to—"

Roberto never finished his warning. Lamb spun to the ground, groaning and cursing as he clutched his upper arm.

"Goddammit. I've been hit."

Roberto, no stranger to bloody wounds, dropped to his knees. He ripped a sleeve from his tattered shirt, wrapped it around the bloody wound, and yanked on the knot.

"The bullet went clean through. You'll be fine."

Lamb shook his head.

"Of all the stupid luck."

The boy grabbed their things, yanked Frank to his feet, and pulled him forward.

"Come on. Let's go."

As they approached the lush field of green, more shots rang out.

"Faster," yelled Roberto.

The two men reached the cover of the forest in minutes. They ran until Frank could run no longer.

"I can't go on," he said, wheezing and doubled over.

Roberto crouched behind some tall bushes. His breathing was heavy but not labored.

"I'm too old for this shit," said Frank, secretly ashamed of his performance.

"We are safe now," Roberto announced.

When Frank caught his breath, he flashed a large grin.

"You're a natural soldier, Roberto."

Roberto scowled.

"A soldier kills the enemy does he not?"

"Yes. He does."

"I am not a soldier. Not yet," said Roberto.

He fell to a seated position, leaned his back against a tree, and closed his eyes.

Despite a busy work night of maintenance activities and hauling coal, Walter could not sleep.

He played with Christopher for hours. The fully-grown rodent, now accustomed to his human friend, did not object to being handled. He often demonstrated affection for the sailor. Walter taught it a few tricks, something he saw as a child when he attended a circus.

"Whatcha got there, Walter?"

Walter stopped breathing. The rat twitched his nose. Luther Burns stood in the doorway.

"Nothing," said Walter, allowing Christopher to climb into his cupped hands.

Burns leaned forward. His eyebrows shot up.

"It's a goddamn rat."

Walter slowly stroked the rodent . He gave Burns a suspicious look.

"His name is Christopher."

"Can I hold it?"

The rat crouched low in Walter's hands.

"No, I don't think so. He doesn't know you and he bites when he is frightened."

Burns ignored Walter's admonition. He reached for the animal. Christopher defended himself. Burns screamed in agony.

"The bastard bit me," said Burns, nursing a bleeding finger.

"I tried to tell you."

Christopher leapt from Walter's hands. He jumped off the cot and ran across the floor. Burns tried to crush the animal with an oversized boot. He missed his target by a wide margin. Walter smiled. Burns, his face now red with rage, yanked Walter from his cot. He punched Walter in the face. Walter fell back against the wall.

"I'm going to kill you *and* your stinking rat," said Burns, storming out of the room.

Walter wiped his bloody nose with a shirt sleeve. He focused on Burns' retreating silhouette.

"Not if I kill you first," he muttered.

The streets of El Galeon, clogged with hundreds of Cuban rebels, posed a challenge to Frank and his would-be acolyte.

"Now what?" asked Roberto, as the two men hid behind a small shack on the outskirts of the village.

"I say we just walk in," said Frank.

Roberto's eyes drilled into the side of Frank's head.

"Are you mad? We do not wear the rebel uniform."

"Nor do we wear the uniform of the Spanish Army."

"I say we wait until dark," said Roberto.

A chorus of metal clicks ended their argument. The sound of a half-dozen rifle hammers, pulled back in anticipation of firing, forced Frank's hands high into the air. Roberto did the same. An unseen voice announced what would happen next.

"First, you will meet the generals. And then, you will be shot."

Roberto twisted in place and protested loudly.

"We are here to join your ranks."

Frank tapped Roberto on the shoulder.

"Let me do the talking, boy."

Frank faced their captors.

"I am an American in support of Cuba libre. I wish to speak with General Gomez. I have weapons and ammunition for his army. Shoot me if you wish but you might want to consult your commanders first."

The senior rebel hesitated. Frank noticed the man's uncertainty.

"Well, boy? Are you going to pull that trigger or bring us to Gomez?"

The Cuban soldier barked his response

"Drop your weapons. Now!"

Frank nodded to Roberto. Another rebel scrambled to retrieve the hardware and ammo belt. They did not discover the hidden dagger strapped onto Frank's lower leg.

"Blindfold them," said the leader.

After ten minutes of walking, the soldiers pushed their prisoners into an enclosure. All conversations stopped when the two prisoners entered. A gentle voice spoke with authority.

"Remove their blindfolds."

Frank and Roberto twisted in every direction. The large, windowless shack housed piles of wood crates. Several of them lay opened. They contained rifles, ammunition belts, and machetes. Three closed cases, apart from the rest, were labeled "dynamite." A series of benches lined most of the four walls. Dozens of rebels occupied the benches or sat on the ground. Two men sat at a round table covered with rolled-up maps and papers. They occupied a pair of old chairs, their tapestry-like fabric neglected, torn, and dirty.

Frank recognized General Maceo from the many images in American newspapers. The rebel leader's wide mustache covered an unsmiling face. His dark skin and short, cropped hair gave the man a deadly serious appearance. Frank stepped forward with his arm outstretched. A dozen rifles rose into the air. Frank dropped his arm to one side and bowed low.

"General Maceo. You have returned to Cuba. The liberation of the Cuban people is now a certainty."

Maceo, visibly startled by the American's familiarity, rose from his chair.

"The American knows me but I do not know the American."

Frank explained. Although the two of them never met in person, Frank had followed the general's military career for years.

"Like most Americans, I support the Cuban cause."

Frank glanced in Roberto's direction.

"My friend and I would like to join your army."

Maceo turned to Gomez, his commander in chief. Gomez shook his head.

"I trust no one," he said.

Frank smiled at Gomez.

"Perhaps you'll trust me when I bring you weapons and ammunition."

"Perhaps I will," said Gomez, his frown turning into an almost imperceptible smile.

"And what shall we call our unexpected benefactor?"

"Lamb. Frank Lamb. And this is my associate, Roberto Alvarez."

Gomez reached for Frank's hand. A countless number of handshakes, exchanged in every direction, eliminated the tension. Frank and Roberto, invited to share a glass of rum, revealed the circumstance that brought them to El Galeon. When the discussion lagged, Frank requested mules and men to transport his expected shipment of arms and ammo. Gomez wore a suspicious look. The mercenary reassured the general.

"I expect the shipment will arrive next week at Boca Ciega beach. I can't haul it thirty miles without your help."

"You must be a man of great wealth."

"My backers, your backers, are in Key West."

Gomez jerked his head in the direction of an officer, nodding his approval. The man hurried from the room. The general rose from his chair, signaling the end of their meeting. Gomez spoke to Frank in hushed tones.

"Maceo goes to El Rubi in ten days. You must make the delivery before then."

Frank nodded.

"I have no funds with which to pay you, my friend."

"That's been taken care of," said Frank.

The general's eyebrows arched. He absent-mindedly rearranged several glasses on the table, all of them now empty. A wry smile crossed the general's lips.

"*Señor* Lamb has earned his rum."

Frank Lamb, emboldened by the words of the general, spoke in a loud voice.

"My weapons, please. Plus, clothes and a rifle for my colleague."

Roberto flashed a huge grin when one of the soldiers scurried to his side with a new rifle, several belts of ammunition, and a rebel uniform. Another rebel bowed his head when he returned Roberto's machete. Gomez cleared his throat and focused on Frank.

"Your men and mules are waiting. Good luck, Mr. Lamb."

Frank and Roberto walked out of the building. Gomez waited until they were out of earshot.

"Take two of your best men and have them followed."

An officer saluted and scurried from the building.

Isabella rushed through the side streets and back-alleyways of Havana.

Her panicked escape from Morro Castle placed the girl in an unknown location. She no longer saw any of the usual landmarks. The castle, Havana Bay, the bell towers of the Havana Cathedral, all vanished into the horizon. She was lost.

A train whistle gave direction to her frantic escape. She saw no one that appeared to be following her. Isabella rested on a bench at the railway station. The passenger train accepted a handful of customers. A warning whistle sounded, urging last-minute travelers to board. She considered boarding the train but did not know the locomotive's destination. Although she carried money, the girl did not possess the necessities of travel. The horrible memory of the underground prison at Morro Castle continued to haunt her.

Isabella's head jerked up when a man's loud voice interrupted her thinking. Several hundred yards away, on the walk and waiving his sword in her direction, stood an officer of the Spanish Army. He led three other soldiers, all of them now running toward Isabella. She jumped to her feet. The train was her only chance of evading her uncle's soldiers. The conductor's whistle blew its final warning. The engineer's assistant reached for the tiny wooden bench used by passengers to climb on board. Isabella yelled.

"Wait."

She scrambled onto the train. The soldiers shouted their objection.

"Halt. Do not let the train leave."

Their screams, lost in the loud shriek of the train as it gathered steam and moved forward, went unnoticed. Isabella chose a seat in the back of the first car.

A series of unwelcome looks from the other passengers confused her.

"The weapons and the ammo. They come from America?"

Roberto waited for an answer. A chill, unheard-of in the hot and humid climate of Cuba, raised the tiny hairs on the nape of his neck. He learned long ago to pay attention to such warnings.

"We will rest for a while," said Frank.

The soldiers took their respite in the shade of several large trees. Frank motioned to the boy.

"Let's take a walk."

They stopped when the soldiers could no longer be heard. Roberto watched Frank light a cigar and blow a series of smoke rings into the air. The older man smiled at the halo-like wisps of smoke, as they drifted and dissipated in the slight breeze. Frank spoke in a low voice.

"There is no shipment of arms or ammo."

Roberto's jaw dropped. Frank used his hand to muzzle the boy's mouth.

"Let's keep this to ourselves."

"But—"

Lamb placed an index finger to his lips and silenced the boy once again.

"We will do the next best thing," said Frank.

Roberto rolled his eyes and shook his head.

"And what is this next best thing? Because if the government troops don't kill us the rebel troops will."

Frank scowled.

"Just do as I tell you, boy, and we'll be fine."

"We are being followed. Or haven't you noticed?"

Frank looked over his shoulder.

"You will not see them. But they see you," said Roberto. "Gomez was truthful. He trusts no one."

Frank walked back to the rebel troops. He spoke to the captain in broken Spanish. Roberto overheard snatches of the conversation. They talked of a passenger train and wealthy travelers. The two leaders nodded in agreement. The captain announced their decision.

"We march to Matanzas."

Roberto fell in with the rebels, preferring their company to Frank's.

# Chapter Four

## THE TRAIN

Isabella did not understand the strange looks, urgent whispers, and smothered giggles of her fellow passengers.

She took note of her surroundings. A luxurious car, ostentatiously appointed with overstuffed chairs, velvet curtains in the windows and tables adorned with white linen. Such accoutrements represented the lifestyle to which she long ago became accustomed. When she noticed her reflected image in the window, Isabella understood the problem. Her fellow passengers did not take kindly to an invasion of their opulent lifestyle by peasants. And Isabella, her face covered in sweat, her shoes smelling of human excrement, and her dress ripped, looked like a peasant. She ignored their hostile reaction and moved to the far end of the rail car.

A Spanish soldier, stationed in the next car, stepped to the opening with a look of disapproval. He wagged his finger at Isabella and she followed him into the next car. A series of crude wooden benches, bolted to the floor, would be her uncomfortable perch for the balance of the journey. An older man, wearing a threadbare suit and sitting with a girl young enough to be his granddaughter, would be her only company. She needed to know her destination and waited until the soldier disappeared.

"Excuse me, sir. Where are you going?" she asked.

The old man's eyes glistened. The young girl, leaning on his arm, stared into space.

"I travel to bury my daughter."

He glanced at the girl.

"Her mother."

Isabella winced.

"I am so sorry," she whispered.

The old man cleared his throat.

"We travel to Matanzas."

Isabella vowed to give a few coins to the old man when they reached Matanzas.

Until then, she busied herself by studying the Spanish soldier's every move.

"I don't know how to play."

Walter declined the invitation to play poker with a half-dozen sailors.

They formed a circle around an overturned wooden crate. A familiar face sat among them.

"If you want to play, I can teach you," said Bill Horn.

He trusted Bill but hesitated. Luther Burns also played. As usual, the man's loud and obnoxious voice dominated the group.

"Oh, come on, Walter. I could use the money," said Burns.

The men laughed. Horn got Walter's attention.

"Play only if you want to. And don't bet money unless you're prepared to lose it," advised Horn.

Walter nodded his approval on the condition he could observe the proceedings for a few hands. Burns, anxious for the novice to join in, tried to shame Walter.

"You're worse than my grandmother, Walter. Let's see the color of your money," Burns yelled.

Walter glanced at his friend.

"You can take my place," said Horn.

Walter reached into his pocket and pulled out a wad of bills. Several of the men whistled. Burns wore an evil grin. The game, straight poker, seven cards with three 'in the hole', see-sawed back and forth, with no real winners or losers. Burns, using a combination of luck and outrageous bluffs, scored three winning hands in a row. Several players, forced to withdraw for lack of funds, left Walter, Burns, and two other players. Soon, it became a two-person duel involving Walter and the loudmouth. Burns recklessly raised the bets on each card. With one card to go, he claimed victory.

"My straight beats your stupid pair of sevens," said Burns.

"But how do I know that you have a straight? There are only four cards showing," Walter observed.

Burns shouted louder and shoved his money into the pile of currency which lay at the center of the scrum.

"Put your money in and I'll show you," said Burns.

The last card was dealt, face down, to each player. Walter frowned. Burns let go with a loud war hoop and tossed his remaining cards face-up on the make-shift table.

"Read 'em and weep," he shouted, pointing to his jack-high straight.

"A straight beats two of a kind. Is that correct?" asked Walter.

"That's right," said Bill.

"But what if I have two pairs?" asked the beginner.

Burns interrupted.

"That ain't good enough, sucker. The money's mine."

Burns reached for the stack of currency in their midst.

"I didn't know that," said Walter, clearly confused as he casually tossed his remaining cards on the crate.

The room went silent. Burns' trembling hands hovered over the winnings. Someone cursed in amazement.

"Son-of-a-bitch. Would you look at that. Four of a kind."

The room erupted into a deafening chorus of cheers, shouts of congratulations, and expressions of shock. Walter sat motionless, worried that he might have done something wrong. He turned to Bill.

"Are they laughing at me?" he asked.

"You won, Walter. The money's yours," said Horn.

Several of the men slapped Walter on the back. Burns, his face flushed pink, jumped to his feet and stormed out of the room. Someone scraped the pile of money in Walter's direction.

"If we get shore leave this weekend, you're buying the drinks, Walter," said one man.

Walter's unblinking eyes focused on the pile of currency and smiled.

"Well. This is a pleasant surprise."

Frank Lamb and his recruits decided to ambush the passenger train before it reached Matanzas.

Their thinking, to steal money and valuables, assumed that most of the passengers would disembark upon reaching Matanzas. From there, the train simply returned to Havana.

Felled trees, large rocks, and one abandoned ox cart, would stop the train. The soldiers, hidden in the thick brush, formed two groups, one on either side of the tracks. Smoke from the locomotive could be seen even before it rounded the bend. The soldiers waited for Frank's signal. Frank waited until the train slowed to a near stop. As agreed, two of the soldiers confronted the conductor and two had inserted themselves between the first car and second car. The balance of the troops, led by Lamb, infiltrated the luxury car, waiving their weapons and screaming instructions.

"You will surrender your money, your jewelry, and your valuables or you will die. Is that understood?" Lamb announced.

His perfect English and the sudden entrance of the robbers stunned the passengers into submission. One traveler, a middle-aged man, rose in protest. A rifle butt to the forehead sent the man crashing to the floor. The bloodied passenger emptied his pockets without further protest. Roberto walked to the second railcar and noticed one of the rebel soldiers harassing a young lady.

"The *señorita* will surrender her money and her valuables. Or you can come with me and we shall, how do you say, come to an understanding."

The woman jerked to her feet.

"How dare you address me in such a manner?"

When the soldier laughed, she slapped him across the face with her gloved hand. The man fell back a step, regained his balance, and shoved the lady back onto the bench. Roberto intervened.

"We are not here to molest the woman. Leave her be," he ordered.

The soldier placed his rifle on a nearby bench.

"I will now teach this peasant some manners," he growled.

The soldier jumped on top of Isabella, pushing her into a prone position. He tore at her blouse. Several buttons flew to the floor. The young woman's undergarment lay partially exposed. Roberto jumped forward.

"That's enough," he barked, using one muscular arm to yank the attacker off the woman. Roberto handed the man his rifle and shoved him to exit. The lady, trying desperately to catch her breath, focused on Roberto. The boy bowed low.

"Please accept my apologies, *Señorita*."

She studied the young man, stunned by his chivalry.

"Thank you, sir. You have defended my honor and I am grateful."

She removed a glove and extended her hand. Roberto blinked, reached out, and brought the lily-white skin to his lips. He stared into her green eyes all the while. When he released her hand, she almost forgot to withdraw the gesture.

"You are most welcome, *Señorita*," said Roberto.

"You wear the uniform of a rebel but you are clearly a gentleman."

"And you wear the clothes of a peasant but you are clearly a woman of standing."

"I would explain my appearance, but you appear to be in a rush."

"There is never enough time when one is with a beautiful woman."

"You are an educated man. Yes?"

Roberto leaned away from the woman. A slight frown crossed his face.

"And this surprises you. Why?"

Isabella smiled.

"A most pleasant surprise, I assure you."

Roberto's heart pounded in his chest. Isabella reached for her neck and flashed the jewelry on her hand.

"You have neglected to relieve me of my valuables, *Señor* rebel."

Roberto bowed low.

"The pleasure of your company is payment enough."

Frank interrupted their exchange.

"She can join us, but you'll have to share."

Roberto cringed. Isabella's eyes flashed with anger.

"I sincerely apologize for my comrade."

Frank lost his patience.

"Roberto, we have a war to fight. Get a move-on."

Frank exited the train. Roberto rushed to the exit. He turned and looked, one last time. She bowed slightly.

"I am in your debt, *Señor* Roberto."

Roberto blushed, stepped through the door, and jumped from the train.

Isabella rushed to the window, hoping for one more look. She saw Roberto as he slipped into the forest. The man in the hat turned, unexpectedly. She recognized him as the man in the plaza. The one who followed her. He caught her, staring in the window. She jumped back. Isabella whispered.

"*Señor* Roberto works for the American."

Frank Lamb and his small company of rebel soldiers reached General Maceo just a few miles west of El Rubi.

Unfortunately, the Spanish spies arrived first. When Frank approached the officer, the general's voice contained no anger. He wore a look of disappointment and sadness.

"The American is a liar."

Frank tossed a sack, half filled with gold coins, currency, and valuables. It landed at the general's feet. Maceo ignored the booty. He walked to a large rock and sat down. Frank retrieved the sack and dropped it at the general's feet, once more. Maceo shrugged.

"My men need rifles and bullets, not coins and jewelry."

"My American contacts don't believe you can win this war," said Frank.

Maceo, visibly angry, jumped to his feet with a snarl on his lips. The man's mulatto skin highlighted the general's white teeth, now displayed in a fit of rage. He shook an index finger at the American.

"Today, we will prove that your American friends are mistaken."

Frank sat apart from the rest of the men, cleaning his sidearm.

He looked up when a shadow blocked the hot sun.

"They call him the bronze titan for a reason," said Roberto.

Frank huffed and jammed his gun into its holster.

"Well, brown titan or not, my sources tell me we will be outnumbered and outgunned when we get to El Rubi," said Frank.

A sudden burst of activity in the camp ended their conversation.

Soldiers ran to the general, listened to his soft-spoken orders, and disappeared into the brush. Roberto approached, listening carefully. He reported back to Frank.

"The San Jacinto Sugar mill is just over that rise. There are three columns of Spanish soldiers. They've been there a while. A fourth column has just been discovered on the Lechuza Trail."

"I was correct. We are greatly outnumbered," said Frank, rising from his perch.

Maceo motioned for his horse and six mounted soldiers. Despite the dirty look from Maceo, Frank and Roberto followed on foot. The tiny rebel group made no noise as they approached the trail. When the fourth column came into view, Maceo gave the order to fire. After several rounds, Maceo turned onto a narrow trail, at a full gallop. Frank and Roberto ran hard to catch up with the general. After a sharp bend in the trail, Maceo and his men stopped at a tall, sturdy fence. Maceo's men begged him to go on, his mighty steed being the only horse that might possibly scale the fence. Maceo refused.

"Follow me," he ordered.

They galloped back in the direction of the Spanish Army, firing their weapons and screaming at the top of their lungs. Frank and Roberto followed but at a distance. Maceo shouted his next order.

"Draw your machetes."

The oft-told tales of machete-wielding rebels massacring hundreds of government soldiers, would soon be proven true. Or not. Clearly, Maceo assumed the government soldiers would run. They appeared stunned and confused.

The government troops remained in place, unafraid or paralyzed by fear. Maceo did not wait to discover which. He found yet another trail and returned to the rebel camp. When Frank arrived at the camp, exhausted and out of breath, he confronted Maceo.

"You were lucky, General Maceo. Very lucky," said Frank.

A nearby soldier, gripping his machete, stepped between the general and the American. Maceo waved him off.

"A number of my men speak the English language," he said. Frank bowed his head.

"I did not mean to offend you."

"We fight when we are able. We escape when we cannot fight," said Maceo.

"What do you hope to accomplish?" asked Frank.

"I have no other wish but for a free and sovereign homeland," said the general.

General Weyler slammed a fist on the desk and shouted.

"Escaped? How can that be? A handful of rebels escape the clutches of an entire army? You are worthless cowards. All of you."

The four officers, standing at attention, did not dare to look Weyler in the eyes. A door opened. The general's top commanders remained in place.

"I wish to speak with you, my uncle."

Isabella barged into her uncle's office, without knocking. General Weyler scowled at his recalcitrant niece. The officers breathed a collective sigh of relief. Weyler, flummoxed by the unexpected arrival of his uncooperative niece, barked his frustration.

"Find Maceo. Now."

The officers double-stepped to the exit. Each of them bowed hastily as they brushed past Isabella. She did not give her uncle a chance to speak.

"My dear Uncle, I have come to apologize to you and to beg for forgiveness."

Weyler rose and stepped to the front of his oversized desk. His eyes narrowed to slits. They drilled into Isabella's mournful expression.

"Am I to believe you? You are the woman who has repeatedly deceived me and disobeyed me."

Isabella, with an embroidered handkerchief already in hand, dabbed at the imaginary tears in her closed eyes. She spoke softly and slowly.

"I make no excuse for my outrageous behavior. I shall leave for Spain as soon as the arrangements are made. But I cannot leave without your forgiveness, my uncle."

Isabella rushed into his arms. The general, preoccupied with the menacing movements of General Maceo, saw no reason to waste time and energy on the silly antics of his young niece. He spoke into the girl's heaving chest.

"You mustn't cry, Isabella. You may remain in Cuba."

"I will go to my room," she said, sobbing loudly into both hands.

"And I will relieve the guards of their duties. But you must promise to seek my permission if you wish to leave the grounds."

"I promise. And I love you, my Uncle, I love you very much."

Isabella gave the general a peck on the scalp and turned away. The general smiled as she glided through the door.

Isabella, her back to the man, rolled her eyes and sneered.

General Maceo and his troops paraded through yet another small village in the eastern part of Cuba.

The rebel leader, greeted as a hero wherever he traveled, appeared unaffected by the people's adulation. They screamed their support even louder. Frank, with Roberto as his interpreter, listened to endless stories about the general and his exploits. He never smoked and would not allow it in his presence. Nor did he drink. Maceo allegedly suffered more than two dozen wounds since the beginning of the insurrection. And he regularly instructed his troops to count on no one's help, in the liberation of their homeland. Especially the Americans.

"It is better to rise or fall without help than to incur debts of gratitude with such a powerful neighbor," Maceo said.

Frank understood why Maceo so easily tolerated the mercenary's fake mission to secure arms and ammo. Maceo needed the shipment but he did not want to be obligated to the American. As they walked through one village, several ladies waved hats and handkerchiefs. One woman decorated her straw hat with a bunch of brightly colored ribbons. Frank came to an immediate halt.

"Is something wrong?" asked Roberto.

Frank flashed a big grin.

"No. Nothing is wrong. Nothing at all."

Frank's sudden epiphany made his head spin. The peasant girl on the train wore a disguise. The redheaded woman with the green eyes was none other than Isabella Hermoza, the Butcher's niece. After hearing Roberto's version of his encounter with the woman, Frank speculated that Roberto impressed the lady. And perhaps the lady impressed Roberto. If the relationship were to blossom, thought Frank, the possibilities could be endless. Frank remembered something else that Roberto said.

"Didn't you tell me that government soldiers kidnapped your sister?"

"Yes, sir. They did."

Frank thought for a moment.

"You have not searched for her?"

"Where would I look? She could be anywhere."

"The dungeons at Morro Castle are known to house female prisoners. You should go there first," advised Frank.

Frank knew a great deal about the dungeons at Morro Castle. A reporter friend of his once served time in the prison. He described it as a hellhole. They did not house women at Morro Castle but Roberto didn't know that. Roberto glared at the mercenary.

"Oh, I understand. Just walk in past the guards, wearing my rebel uniform, and conduct a search."

"We need a plan," said Frank.

"You have a plan?" asked Roberto.

"Yes. But we will need help from your friend at the palace."

"What friend?"

"The peasant girl you met on the train."

"She works at the castle?"

"Not hardly."

"Well then, what does she do?"

"Your friend's name is Isabella Hermoza. She is the Butcher's niece."

# *Chapter Five*

## UNEXPECTED VISITORS

"There will be no shore leave until further notice."

The announcement from Captain Crowninshield triggered a series of groans. An outbreak of smallpox on the mainland at Newport News, Virginia, made the prohibition necessary. The highly contagious disease, if brought back to the ship, could incapacitate the entire crew.

"Good news!"

Bill Horn woke Walter from a deep slumber. The coal passer, exhausted from a busy night of cleaning the boilers, rubbed the sleep from his eyes. Walter struggled to understand his friend's excitement.

"Unless someone threw Luther Burns overboard, I doubt very much that the news is good."

"The crew on the *Columbia* lost their shore leave, just like us."

Walter scratched his head.

"And that's your good news?"

"They're hosting a big party and we're invited," said Horn.

"Can I bring Christopher?" asked Walter, half in jest.

"Walter, your pet rat will not survive the party. Please leave him—wait a minute. You're making a joke."

"Yes, Bill."

Walter's feeble attempt at humor made both of them laugh.

On the night of the big shindig, approximately fifty sailors gathered on the deck of the *USS Maine*.

A series of rowboats would be used to ferry the men to the *Columbia*. Often described as an armored merchant ship, the *Columbia* featured four funnels, (smokestacks), and boasted a small complement of arms. No one would confuse it for a battleship.

Walter looked forward to the party, but not because he enjoyed the company of others. The *Columbia* featured the same double-ended marine boilers installed on the *Maine*. He wanted to speak with the men who worked in the *Columbia*'s boiler room. He anxiously waited for his turn to board one of the gigs.

"Walter, who's taking care of your rat?"

Walter recognized the irritating voice of Luther Burns. He stood with his back to the bully. Burns shoved his way through the throng of happy sailors. He towered over Walter and stood as close as possible. Walter ignored him. Burns leaned over and whispered in Walter's ear.

"I'm going to get my money back, Walter. It's just a matter of time."

Walter searched for Bill Horn, the only man on the ship taller than Burns. He caught a glimpse of Horn, just as he went over the side. Burns followed Walter to the side of the battleship and disclosed his plan.

"I'm going to wait until you're sound asleep. And then, I'm gonna break that rat's neck and take your money."

Walter shoved both hands into his pockets and pushed ahead.

He did not want Burns to see his trembling hands.

The party featured plenty of beer and lots of cigars.

Walter nursed a sarsaparilla and refused repeated offers to try a stogie. He did get to meet several boiler operators. They quickly abandoned the strange-looking man who wanted to talk shop at a raucous party. Well before the party ended, he caught the first gig back to the *USS Maine*. Back in his hammock, Walter welcomed his usual visitor. Always hungry, Christopher enjoyed the scraps of food Walter retrieved from the *Columbia*. He regaled his dark, gray friend with stories of the party, including the copious quantities of beer.

"I'm not sure what the big deal is," said Walter. "Beer doesn't even taste good," he observed.

Christopher rose on his two hind legs and turned away from his human benefactor. Walter cocked his head and frowned. The rat held his head high in the air and his nose twitched. Cigar smoke. Walter could smell it now. He recalled that rats enjoy a highly developed sense of smell. Christopher faced the exit. Walter could see a large shadow. The dark image belonged to Luther Burns. Walter didn't wait for Burns to enter the chamber.

"What do you want?" he asked.

Christopher squealed in pain. Walter, so rattled by Burns' visit, absentmindedly squeezed the rodent. When he loosened his grip, the rat scurried off.

"There's that goddamn rat," said Burns.

Christopher disappeared before Burns could take a step.

"Go away," said Walter, emboldened by his furry friend's escape.

"I brought you a cigar," said Burns.

"I don't smoke. And you're not supposed to be smoking in quarters."

"Now, is that anyway to show your gratitude? It's a gift, Walter. I left the party early, just so I can give it to you. Take it."

Burns stepped forward, a fresh cigar in his outstretched hand.

Walter took the cigar and tucked it in a shirt pocket, observing Burns the entire time.

"Aren't you going to smoke it?"

"I told you. I don't smoke."

Burns clenched his jaw.

"I'm here for my money."

"I won that money, fair and square."

"You cheated."

Walter sat up in his hammock, sliding away from Burns. With his back now against the bulkhead, the little man could go no further. Burns took another step forward.

"Give me the money or I'll make you eat that cigar."

Walter's mind raced. He rarely spent the money he had. And he had lots of money. Burns could easily kick the crap out of him. Maybe even hurt him. Walter swallowed the anger rising in his chest. Perhaps the money would make Burns go away.

"I'll make you a deal," said Walter.

"What kind of deal?"

"You can have the money, but you must promise to leave me alone."

"Give me the goddamn money."

"Deal?"

Burns hesitated. He pulled on his moustache and repeatedly blinked.

"Deal."

Walter made Burns turn his back. He retrieved the cash from its hiding spot.

"Here," said Walter.

Burns stood at Walter's side and counted the money. Twice.

"There was more money than this on the table."

"I'm giving you *your* money back. Not mine. You didn't win my money," said Walter.

Burns grunted his acknowledgment and stalked out the door.

Frank and Roberto, too busy marching to Maceo's next encounter with the Spanish army, could not plan for Roberto's visit to Morro Castle.

In late April, the *Competitor*, an American ship smuggling arms and men to the Cuban rebels, delivered thousands of rounds of ammunition and four dozen new recruits to Maceo. He led his expanded army to a mountain pass near Cicarajicara, in the Pinar del Río region of western Cuba.

Although exhausted from their long march, the troops, Roberto, and the American mercenary, dug trenches, erected fences, and installed barricades. The obstacles would be part of the reception they planned for the enemy's arrival. The rebels would confront six Spanish columns, totaling more than 1500 men, plus artillery. To reduce the enemy's effectiveness, the rebels planned to channel government soldiers through a narrow opening in a recently constructed wall.

When the battle commenced, Frank and Roberto contributed to the blistering rain of fire which decimated the Spanish troops. Lamb, forced to acknowledge the general's successful strategy, offered a half-hearted compliment.

"Maceo has very few troops and even less ammunition. But he makes good use of what he does have."

The cumulative effect of the barriers and bullets felled several hundred Spanish soldiers. The government troops responded by pushing their artillery pieces closer to rebel positions. When rebel losses approached twenty in number, Maceo called for an orderly retreat. Thanks to his earlier preparation, the rebel retreat escaped the enemy's notice.

"Let's get out of here," yelled Roberto.

When Maceo and his army reached safety, the solemn rebel leader allowed himself a smile.

"Gentlemen, the liberation of Cuba is at hand. I promise you."

The rebels cheered. Frank ushered his young friend to a secluded area of the camp.

"This isn't good."

"Why do you say that? We took out several hundred of them," yelled Roberto.

"How much ammo do you have left?" asked Frank.

Roberto searched the belts which crisscrossed his chest. He carried less than a dozen rounds. The young boy bit his lower lip.

"Look around, Roberto. We are all in the same boat. That little run-in with government troops took all the ammo that the *Competitor* brought to us and then some."

"What are you saying, Frank?"

"I'm saying we're not going to win this revolution by following General Maceo from town to town and praying for another load of ammo."

"What should we do?"

"I'm not sure yet. But we leave tonight,"

"I came here for revenge. That has yet to happen."

"You will get your revenge. But not here."

The rebels celebrated their victory and the rum flowed freely.

During the festivities, Frank and Roberto abandoned Maceo's army. During the hours-long journey back to Havana, Frank returned to the subject of Roberto's little sister. He didn't hesitate to give the boy a false hope.

"If she's in Morro Castle, she may still be alive."

"Why do you say that?"

"The locals are allowed to bring food. If they bribe the guards, the food gets to the prisoner," he said.

"Two of my cousins live near Guatao. They know of her capture. Perhaps they visit the dungeon," said Roberto.

Frank, pleased with the effectiveness of his ruse, encouraged the boy even further.

"I'm sure your cousins took good care of her. We should get to the castle as soon as possible, however."

The crew on the *USS Maine* received permission to reciprocate the *Columbia's* hospitality.

To pay for their party, each crewmember on the *Maine* donated a dollar. The ship's chaplain, trusted by everyone, accepted the job of coordinating the particulars. He and the crew took great pains to ensure that the party would be a huge success. The bugler trained a band and several of the men organized a minstrel show. A grand banquet, planned by the cooks and the stewards, would also take place. The meal would begin with oysters and end with ice cream.

Some of the more talented crew members, including Walter, worked on costumes and dresses, many with historical themes. They used braided rope to simulate longhaired wigs. The minstrel show, scheduled for midafternoon, would be followed by the banquet. At the end of the banquet, guests from the *Columbia* would return to their ship, don their costumes, and row back to the *Maine*. The evening went as planned and although several men, including Burns, got drunk, the dancing lasted until midnight. Everyone enjoyed themselves thoroughly.

And for that one evening, Luther Burns chose not to bully Walter.

Frank persuaded Roberto that Isabella would be key in his search for Elena.

Because of her uncle, she could access any prison on the island and perhaps even arrange for Elena's release.

"What if she says no?" asked Roberto.

"Bring her back to me. By force, if necessary."

"You make it sound so easy. Have you forgotten? She lives in a palace, surrounded by soldiers."

"The palace has a large kitchen. We will dress you like a peasant. You will gain access at the back of the building. Here, take these."

Frank gave the boy several coins.

"Use them to bribe the kitchen help or delivery boys."

"How will I find her?" asked the boy.

"She is most likely housed on the second floor. But it will not be easy. There are dozens of rooms. I suggest you follow the servants. Discreetly, of course."

Frank relieved the boy of his hat, rifle, and ammunition belts. He also suggested that Roberto arrive at the palace without his boots. Frank chose to remain at the edge of town. He urged Roberto to use the back streets and alleyways.

Roberto approached the large structure at the rear of the building. He hid behind a nearby stable. In minutes, he spied several peasants, laden with crates and sacks. They entered the building after being questioned by two guards. The soldiers, posted at the rear entrance, questioned the visitors, but only briefly. They seemed more interested in the contents of the crates and often sampled the fresh produce. Roberto grinned when one of the guards removed a dead chicken from the errand boy's sack. The soldier secreted the animal in the nearby bushes.

The young rebel nervously fingered the coins in his pocket. A servant, also barefoot and struggling with two overloaded crates, appeared at the far end of the alleyway. Roberto scanned the horizon and ran in the boy's direction. The kid appeared to be no more than fourteen or fifteen years of age. Roberto's offer of assistance triggered a suspicious stare. Roberto flashed a single coin. The servant swiped the money from Roberto's hand and immediately surrendered the heavier crate. They approached the sentries together.

As they did before, the guards inspected the crates and ignored the delivery boys. After each guard took what they wanted, Roberto and his new friend carried their crates down a long hallway. The young boy explained that the service entrance to the kitchen lay just ahead. A staircase, apparently used by the servants and waitstaff, offered Roberto the opportunity he hoped for. He surrendered his crate and offered the delivery boy a second coin.

"You must leave the building by another way."

Neither of them wanted to arouse the guards' suspicion.

Roberto climbed the stairs and peeked into the hallway. For a moment, he stood transfixed by his surroundings. The carpeted hallways, the walls adorned with artwork, the gold-plated lamps, and mahogany woodwork, polished to a bright luster, fascinated the boy who lived his entire life in a one-room shack.

Approaching voices forced him to the nearest door. It would not open. The second door, also locked, pushed the teenager into a panic. When the third door opened, he did not care if someone occupied the room or not. Although stuffed with old furniture and damaged artwork, the room was devoid of people. He waited until the voices passed and opened the door a sliver. A distant knock, a woman's voice, and a servant who bowed low, suggested that Isabella occupied a room at the far end of the hallway. It appeared to be on the corner of the building with a second-floor view of the street below. Roberto took a deep breath, left the safety of the storage room, and knocked on the last door in the hallway.

"I will not join the captain-general for dinner and I do not wish to be disturbed again. Do you understand?"

Isabella marched to the door a third time. Her jaw dropped when she flung the door open and saw Roberto. The boy's heart pounded in his chest. His head swiveled as he looked in every direction, to verify that he stood alone. Isabella used her hand to stifle a scream.

"Miss Hermoza. I mean you no harm. May I enter?"

Isabella opened her mouth, as if to speak. Her lips moved but the words did not come. Roberto, ready to run, desperately repeated his request.

"If I am seen, I will be executed. Please. I require only a moment of your time."

Roberto bowed his head and clasped his hands together, just as his grandmother did. Isabella stepped away from the door, using a nearby dresser to steady herself. Roberto entered the room and carefully closed the door. He wanted to lock it but feared the girl would panic.

"Thank you, Miss Hermoza, for sparing my life."

Isabella took several deep breaths and slowly regained her composure. She spoke in barely audible tones.

"The gentleman rescued me in my time of need. It is the least I can do," she said.

Roberto nodded. Isabella smiled. She turned her back to the boy and took a few steps toward a nightstand. Roberto did not see her open the drawer. When Isabella spun around, a six-inch stiletto flashed in her hand. She thrust the blade in the direction of her unexpected visitor.

"And now, my friend, you will leave me or I shall scream."

Roberto instinctively raised his hands and stepped back. With his back to the door, he reached blindly for the doorknob.

His eyes never left the girl. He thought of Frank's directive. Clearly, the woman would not go peaceably. She might even be willing to use the stiletto.

"I apologize for having frightened you. I will do as you request."

Roberto turned slowly to open the door. Isabella tossed the knife onto the bed.

"Wait."

Roberto's head twisted.

"How did you find me? What is it you want?" she asked.

"It is not difficult to locate the captain-general's niece."

Isabella persisted.

"Why did you come here?"

Roberto started breathing again. He faced the girl and spoke softly.

"I search for my little sister. She was taken from our home by the Spanish soldiers. I have reason to believe that she is being held at Morro Castle."

Isabella's eyes grew wide.

"Why did the soldiers take your sister?"

"They attacked my village. She is 13 years old and I fear she . . ."

Roberto's voice cracked. He stared at the girl through glassy eyes. Isabella pointed to a chair.

"Lock the door. You may be seated, over there.

Roberto swallowed his emotions, locked the door, and walked to the chair. Isabella sat on the edge of her bed.

"How old are you?" she asked.

"I will be 19 in December."

"And your family? Have they searched for your sister?"

Roberto related the horrific details of the massacre at Guatao. Isabella's face blanched white. A loud knock forced Isabella to her feet. She brushed past Roberto and yelled at the door.

"Why have you disturbed me yet again?"

"Isabella. This is your uncle. Why do you refuse to dine with me this evening?"

Roberto lunged for the blade and stood with his back to the window.

"Please, Uncle. I am not well. I must rest."

"Do you have the fever?" asked Weyler.

"No, my Uncle. I do not have the fever. Please Uncle, do not embarrass me."

The general mumbled his response.

"Oh. Uh. I do apologize. Perhaps breakfast. Good evening."

Isabella, her ear to the door, listened for the sound of retreating footsteps. She turned to face her visitor. Her eyes darted to the blade in Roberto's hand. He returned the stiletto to its hiding place in the nightstand.

Isabella's eyes softened.

"And now, we are both safe," she said.

"Can you help me?"

"Your sister is not in the dungeons at Morro Castle."

Isabella's bold statement startled Roberto.

"But Frank said she might—"

Isabella interrupted.

"Frank? The American you take orders from?"

"I take orders from no one," he muttered.

Isabella wagged a finger at the boy.

"Your American friend has not seen the dungeons. I have."

"What did you see?"

Isabella's eyes glazed over. She spoke softly, in a monotone, as if in a trance.

"Two cells, perhaps five- or six-paces wide, openings on either end. Doors made of steel bars. Dark. Rats everywhere, and a foul smell. And at least 100 men in each of the two cells."

Roberto caught the woman's eyes. She snapped out of her trance and spoke with a firmness in her voice.

"There are no women or girls in those dungeons," she announced.

Roberto slumped in his chair, struggling to hide his disappointment. Isabella jumped to her feet.

"I will ask my uncle to help us."

Roberto rushed to her side. He wanted to hold her hands.

"No. You mustn't. It could put us both in danger."

"You, perhaps, but not me," she said, turning to check her appearance in a large mirror on the wall.

Roberto spoke without thinking.

"No. I won't allow it."

Isabella spun around and scowled.

"Excuse me?"

The boy attempted a recovery.

"I meant no respect. Please forgive me."

"Do you wish to save your sister or not?"

"You trust this man they call the Butcher?

Isabella stepped forward. Her eyes burned into Roberto's face like hot embers. She spoke in an angry whisper that echoed in Roberto's ears.

"This man is not a butcher. He is my uncle. And yes, I trust him to do the right thing."

Roberto could no longer hide his frustration.

"And these people in the dungeons at Morro Castle. Did your uncle do the right thing by them?"

Isabella's initial shock morphed into white hot anger. Her open hand struck the boy's cheek. The loud smack reverberated in the oversized room. Roberto fell back a step and massaged the pink handprint on his face. He reconsidered Frank's order to take the woman prisoner.

"If you do not cooperate, I must take you with me."

Isabella rushed to the nightstand. Roberto reached the girl, one step too late. She shoved the blade under the boy's chin.

"Perhaps I shall take you as *my* prisoner."

Roberto's face blushed a deep pink.

"A gentleman does not strike a woman."

"You are not a gentleman and you will leave me, immediately. If I see you again, I will have you shot."

Roberto glared at the woman. He reached for her knife hand, held it in place, and used his remaining hand to retrieve the stiletto. He tossed the weapon onto the bed.

"The fruit does not fall far from the tree."

Roberto slammed the door behind him and jogged down the hallway. The second floor storeroom would be his escape route. Its windows faced a deserted alleyway. He jumped, slicing his foot on a sharp rock, and spraining his ankle in the process. The boy limped and skipped his way through several side streets, circling back in Frank's direction. Moments later, they stood together hidden behind a shack, on the edge of a charred and dusty cane field.

"What happened?" asked Frank.

Roberto took one hop toward Frank and swung hard with a closed fist. Frank fell to the ground, blood spurting from his nose. Roberto pointed an angry finger at the man.

"You lied to me, Frank Lamb. And if you ever do that again, I will kill you with my bare hands."

Frank scrambled to his feet while reaching for his sidearm.

Roberto lowered his head and charged the American like an angry bull. The two men rolled and grunted in the dirt. Frank threw a punch. It landed harmlessly on Roberto's shoulder. Roberto, on his knees, pulled Frank to a sitting position. His closed fist hit Frank squarely in the jaw. The older man fell back, his head hitting the dirt with a dull thud.

The man's eyes disappeared into the back of his head.

# Chapter Six

## ELENA

"Fire her up."

The order caught Walter by surprise. It came with less than an hour remaining on the night shift. The *USS Maine* would travel to Fort Monroe, a dozen miles from the docks at Newport News, Virginia. A full head of steam in the boilers would be required. Walter made quick work of his coal passer duties. He emptied bucket after bucket of the bituminous fuel into the fire pans of both boilers. He continually checked the pressure gauges and simultaneously adjusted the draft valves to ensure an adequate flow of oxygen. Too much pressure would lead to an explosion.

The ship would soon be underway. Walter waved a goodbye to the incoming crew and headed for the exit. A puff of steam in the vicinity of the manhole cover caught his attention. He came to an abrupt halt. The manhole covers included a large round gasket through which no steam should escape. Walter noticed a growing cloud of steam just above the manhole. The white puffy jets grew larger and increased in frequency. He turned to his coworkers and screamed.

"The manhole cover is leaking!" he yelled.

Before they could respond, the cover blew. The thick metal plate flew into the air, ricocheted off the metal bulkhead, and hit Walter square in the chest. The room filled with hot steam. Boiling water shot from the opening at the top of the boiler. Walter fell to the floor, clutching his chest. One of the crew members raced to the exit. A second man pulled at his clothes. His head and torso, drenched in boiling hot water, left him blind and helpless. Walter stumbled in the man's direction. He pushed and pulled the burn victim to the exit.

A half-dozen boiler operators, firemen, and coal passers arrived on the scene. The drafts were closed, depriving the fire of oxygen. The coal, soon reduced to hot embers, no longer heated the water. The men, now out of danger, began the clean-up.

Several sailors escorted their injured colleague to sick bay. Walter stayed behind and looked for a place to rest. He sat on a bench, absentmindedly reaching for his chest. His fingers found a sticky substance. He looked down and noticed a growing splotch of deep red. With trembling hands, he unbuttoned his shirt. The sight of oozing blood from the large gash on his chest made Walter swoon. His eyes fluttered and he listed to one side. Someone screamed.

"Get him to sick bay. Now!"

Walter strained to recognize the man's face just inches from his own.

The stranger used his thumb and index finger to keep the patient's eyes open. Walter resisted, brushing the man's probing hands to one side.

"Who are you?"

"Doctor Heneberger," said the man. "Do you know where you are?"

Walter, not entirely awake, struggled with the answer.

"The boiler room . . . I think."

"You're in sick bay on the *USS Maine*."

Walter stared into space, a frown on his face.

"I remember now. The manhole cover blew."

"Mr. McDermott, you have suffered a deep gash to your chest. It required dozens of stitches."

Walter reached for the large white bandage wrapped around his torso. The movement made him wince.

"Several of your ribs appear to be broken," said the doctor.

"I must get back to my hammock. Christopher is . . ."

Walter's voice trailed off. His eyes closed and his head tilted to one side.

"Make yourself comfortable, Mr. McDermott. You are going to be here for a while."

Walter surrendered to a deep sleep.

Isabella threw herself on the bed.

The voices in her head screamed at each other. Roberto falsely accused her uncle and insulted her in the process. The voice of the old man in the dungeon also clamored for attention. The young woman's confused thinking and conflicting emotions triggered a torrent of tears.

When the sobbing subsided, Isabella made herself presentable and proceeded to her uncle's office. She caught the captain-general in one of those rare moments when he sat alone at his desk.

"May I speak with you, Uncle?"

"Of course, you may, Isabella. Are you feeling better?"

"Why do the rebels refer to you as the Butcher?"

Weyler's face grew solemn. He rose to his feet. With hands clasped behind his back, he walked to the front of his desk. Isabella saw a man at peace with himself, strolling casually, as if on a walk through the gardens. She did not see a Butcher.

"Isabella, my dear. Do you recall why her Majesty's government sent me to Cuba?"

"To end the rebellion."

"Precisely. When we confront the rebels, they are always given a choice. They need only to put down their weapons."

Weyler continued.

"If they choose to use those weapons against us, do we not have the right to defend ourselves?"

"Yes, my uncle. Of course, you do."

"And for this, I am called the Butcher. Do I appear as a Butcher to you?"

Isabella rushed to his side, pulling the man's head to her bosom.

Weyler hid his smile in the woman's frilly blouse.

Roberto, a machete at his side and with a rifle pointed at the American, studied the mercenary as he regained consciousness.

"Welcome back, Mr. Lamb."

Frank rubbed his jaw and dabbed at his bloody lip with the sleeve of his shirt.

"I guess I had that coming."

Roberto, his jaw clenched, gave the man a menacing look.

"Yes. You did. I may be younger than you but I do not deserve to be lied to."

"The rifle's yours. I'll be out of your hair by nightfall," said Frank.

Roberto's head snapped up. He grabbed the American by the jacket and pulled him to his feet.

"What happened to fighting the Spanish government?"

"A soldier must be able to trust his fellow soldiers. You don't trust me anymore so I'm out of here."

Roberto stepped away, sat on his haunches, and drew circles in the dirt with his finger. He studied his artwork in silence. He cleared his throat.

"I still need your help finding my sister."

"What's in it for me? Besides a bloody lip."

"You help me. I'll help you."

"Fair enough. I have some information for you. Call it a peace offering."

"What information?"

"Information about your sister. But I want something in return."

"What?"

"Help me with Isabella Hermoza."

"She despises me."

"That's not what I saw on the train."

"I told her the truth about her uncle. She threatened to have me shot if she ever saw me again."

"If we can't get to her, we have to go after her uncle."

"Impossible."

"Difficult, perhaps, but not impossible."

"And my sister?"

"It's a long shot. But one of the American newspapers reported on the massacre at Guatao. The Spanish soldiers took prisoners, as you know. Mostly women. According to the article, the soldiers marched the prisoners to Marianao."

Roberto sprang to his feet. He jumped in Frank's direction.

"I know Marianao. It's 4 maybe 5 miles from Guatao."

"Roberto, she may not have survived. You mustn't get your hopes up."

Roberto gnawed on his lower lip.

"I must know for certain. We go to Marianao tonight."

Walter fidgeted, forced to remain in sick bay until approved for work.

The medical staff thought him anxious to return to his duties. Walter did not reveal the reason for his anxiety—Christopher the rat.

"You have visitors," said an orderly.

Walter's eyes turned into slits.

"Who would visit me?"

In walked a gaggle of sailors, Luther Burns leading the way. Walter's stomach churned. He lay back on the pillow and feigned sleep. Burns announced his arrival in a loud voice.

"We bought you a get well present, Walter."

Walter, with some pain, turned his back and drew his limbs into a fetal position.

"I'm tired, Burns. Please leave me alone."

Burns persisted.

"Look what we got you. It's your pet rat."

Walter felt a rush of adrenalin and twisted his body. He groaned in pain, his broken ribs not yet healed.

"We caught him in your bedding," said Burns. "He won't bother you anymore."

Walter struggled to a sitting position and reached for the cracker tin in Burns' outstretched hand. The patient held his breath and popped the lid off the container. The box contained a dead rat. Walter showed no emotion. Burns, upset that his present triggered no response, threw a temper tantrum. He knocked the tin from Walter's hand. The rat flew across the floor.

"That's the little bastard that bit me."

"Christopher bit you because you frightened him."

Walter pointed triumphantly at the dead rat.

"And that's not Christopher. Now go away."

The hike to Marianao did not require a great deal of time.

As often happened in Cuban towns and villages when Spanish troops arrived, they did great damage. They did not stay for long, however. When the food ran out or new orders arrived, the soldiers left. In their wake, a handful of men, ordered to maintain public order, stayed behind.

Roberto, inflamed with the thought of rescuing his sister, wanted to attack the local jail. Frank implored him to wait until dusk. The boy soldier reluctantly agreed. Four men guarded the jail. They sat on rickety wooden chairs, positioned on the side of the building in the shade. None of them appeared to be on high alert, taking their evening meal inside and returning to the chairs for a short siesta.

"We wait until dark. If they are expecting reinforcements, the additional men will arrive before then. If there are no reinforcements, we will have the element of surprise," said Frank.

When the sun disappeared, Roberto worked his way to the rear of the building. If possible, he and Frank would avoid gunplay. Frank approached from the front of the structure; his hands held high. He made as much noise as possible.

"Gentlemen. I come in peace," he yelled.

All four of the guards jumped to their feet. The senior man spoke broken English.

"You are Americano."

"I must speak to the officer in charge," said Frank.

Roberto used Frank's loud voice to smother the sound of his approach. Visions of Elena flashed in his head. His grandfather's blood-covered chest appeared. He swung his machete with a vengeance, nearly decapitating his first victim. The man fell to his knees. A dull thud could be heard when the body hit the dirt. The soldier nearest him turned to investigate. Roberto swung at the man's neck. A geyser of crimson liquid sprayed onto Roberto's dirty white uniform. The soldier stood for a moment, his eyes open and a pained expression on his face. He fell to the ground.

The remaining soldiers twisted in place. Frank pulled his knife across his first victim's throat. After a slight gurgle, the man fell, face forward, in the dirt. The fourth soldier, seeing Roberto's machete, blood dripping from the blade, panicked. He turned to run. Frank blocked his path. The soldier dropped his rifle and threw both hands into the air.

Roberto pushed him against the jailhouse wall. He interrogated the man with a series of rapid-fire questions. The soldier babbled, unable to provide the answers that Roberto wanted to hear. The boy raised his machete high above the soldier's head. The man began to beg and dropped to his knees. When he began to pray, Roberto planted the machete deep into the man's skull. Frank blanched and turned away.

Roberto ran to the front entrance. The locked door would not open. He swung wildly with his blade until the wood splintered. He took a few steps back and crashed into the door. He fell face forward, onto the floor. Several dozen inmates witnessed his forced entrance. He approached the cell doors asking the same question, repeatedly. An older woman, almost too weak to walk, raised her hand. Roberto urged her forward. The large cell afforded standing room only. Most of the prisoners, women and older men, looked emaciated and deathly ill. Roberto pulled on the iron bars, but to no avail. He screamed.

"We have to unlock these doors."

"Here," said Frank, holding a large ring with a single key.

"One of your friends out there didn't need it anymore."

Roberto, his jaw clenched and beads of sweat covering his brow, grabbed the key. He shoved it into the iron door and pulled the old woman forward. They walked to the door, his arm around her waist. He escorted her to the side of the building, opposite from the grisly scene of her massacred jailers. She walked a bit further and pointed to the open field which lay behind the jail. Roberto saw four mounds of dirt. A crude cross, made of tree branches, marked each gravesite. Roberto turned away, fell to his knees, and covered his face with both hands. The old woman placed a hand on his heaving shoulder. Frank joined them.

"I'm sorry, my friend."

Roberto's head twisted slowly in Frank's direction. He spoke in a whisper.

"I swear on my sister's grave. I will get my revenge, Frank. Do you understand me? I will get my revenge or I will die trying."

"I still haven't found Christopher."

Walter complained to Bill Horn when the fireman first class walked out of the engine room. The recovering patient would not be allowed to return to his workstation for another week.

"I'm sure he'll show up," said Horn, doing his best to comfort the man.

"But I have left food for him every day and it hasn't been touched."

"You were in sick bay for more than a week. Sooner or later, Christopher will discover the food."

"Did you know that Burns visited me in sick bay?"

"That's good, isn't it? Maybe he's come around now that you've returned the money, he lost."

"He brought me a dead rat. Thought it was Christopher."

"Oh. That's not good. Maybe I should talk to him."

Walter stepped forward, eyes wide and riveted on his friend.

"No. Don't do that. It will only make matters worse."

"Suit yourself."

"I'm thinking Burns should have an accident, just like I did," said Walter.

"What are you saying?"

Water studied the ceiling.

"Nothing."

"Walter?"

"I'm just saying that anything can happen onboard a battleship."

"You're playing with fire, Walter."

"Yes, Bill. That's my job on this ship."

Roberto, thinking of his grandmother, shared his food with the old woman.

They sat together on a crude bench in the village plaza. He discovered that she, too, lost her family in the war. Her town, unmolested by the Spanish soldiers, fell victim to rebels. The town's residents, falsely accused of aiding and abetting the Spanish Army, paid a high price. The rebels robbed the peasants and burned their homes to the ground. The old woman described how her daughter returned to their burning home, not once but twice. On her second trip, to retrieve a portion of their meager possessions, her hair caught on fire. Then her dress. She screamed and ran into the street. The soldiers laughed. The woman's clothing, now fully engulfed, brought the victim to her knees. The mother rushed forward. The soldiers stopped her. She watched, as her daughter burned to death. Roberto looked away, determined to keep his quivering lips out of view.

"What is your sister's name?" she asked.

"Elena."

"I will never forget her eyes. As black as my daughter's hair."

Roberto nodded glumly, shaken by the old woman's horrible story. It required a few moments before he realized the importance of what the woman said. He snapped to attention and twisted in place. Roberto grabbed the woman by her shoulders. He pulled her forward, his face just inches from hers.

"The dead girl's eyes. They were black? Are you certain? Are you absolutely certain?"

The old lady shook with fear.

"Yes. I am certain. Very beautiful eyes, too."

Roberto shook his head in disbelief. The woman's face twisted in sorrow. She began to sob.

"I am so sorry, my friend."

The boy jumped to his feet, pulling at his hair with his hands, and walking in circles. He returned to the old woman and kissed her on both cheeks. His wide grin morphed into a giddy laugh.

"I love you, old woman. I love you."

She smiled through her tears.

"I don't understand."

"Elena's eyes are green," he shouted, an exuberant look on his face. "A bright, beautiful green."

The old woman smiled.

"My sister is alive," Roberto screamed.

He shoved the last of his food into her hands and ran off in search of Frank.

Isabella, dressed like royalty, opened the door to her room and peeked in both directions.

Her uncle promised no guards at her door. Much to her surprise, he kept his promise. Nevertheless, when she arrived in the lobby, Isabella informed the Captain of the Guard of her decision to go for a walk. The officer motioned to two of his men and the threesome stepped into the bright sunlit day.

Isabella wandered aimlessly through the Plaza de Armas. She inspected the vendors' wares, sampled some of the food stuffs, and enjoyed the smiles and admiring looks of the people. Her last conversation with the captain-general put the woman at ease. He was not the Butcher that Roberto described. Her uncle sought only to end the rebellion. She rested on a bench, parasol still in hand, next to an old man. He put his newspaper down, and welcomed her arrival with a tip of his hat.

"Good afternoon, *Señorita*."

Isabella smiled and nodded. When her security detail drew close, one on either side of the bench, he stiffened. Without excusing himself, he hurried off, leaving his newspaper behind. Isabella shrugged, uncertain as to why the man would behave so strangely. She collapsed the parasol and retrieved the paper. The recent issue of the London Times, rarely seen in Cuba, would give the bilingual woman an opportunity to practice her English.

The paper, likely smuggled into the country, included an article which referenced her uncle in rather unkind terms. In fact, the author criticized the captain-general and praised the rebels.

> *With an army of 175,000 men, with materials of all kinds in unlimited quantities, beautiful weather, little or no sickness among the troops, in a word, with everything in his favor, General Weyler has been unable to defeat the insurrectionists.*

The correspondent went on to describe the leader of the Cuban rebellion, General Antonio Maceo, as able to evade the government troops at will. It described Maceo as clearly in control of the rebellion. Isabella threw the newspaper to the ground. For a minute, she sat on the bench, fuming. Surprising her security detail, Isabella jumped to her feet, grabbed her parasol, and scooped up the crumpled paper. The girl stormed back to the palace, her guards struggling to keep pace with their angry charge.

"This newspaperman writes that my uncle is incompetent."

Isabella slammed the paper on the captain-general's desk. Her uncle made no move to read the article. He turned to his attendants and waved them off. When the office door closed, Weyler turned to his angry niece.

"Isabella, my love. You should not trouble yourself with the propaganda of western journalists. They are fools. The lot of them," he said.

"Have you read it?"

"Yes, I have."

Isabella paced back and forth across the width of the office. She slammed herself into a chair. Seconds later she resumed her pacing. The sound of her hot breath, whistling in her nostrils, called attention to her hot pink face. She stopped in front of her uncle's huge desk.

"Well, Uncle, what are we going to do about it?"

The captain-general smiled.

"My dear Isabella. I am most appreciative of your concern. But these are matters over which I have no control. The newspapers will write what they wish and I will do what I must."

Isabella, on the verge of exploding, could not regain her composure.

"First you are the Butcher. Now you are incompetent. I hate these rebels. I hate this place. And I hate that you are here, alone, and surrounded by fools."

The general leaned forward.

"Do you wish to go home?"

Isabella took a deep breath. She fell into the chair. Her head slumped forward and she sobbed into her hands.

"Yes, my uncle. I think I do. I wish to go home."

Frank, deep in thought, puffed on a cigar.

He watched as large billows of smoke dissipated in a mild breeze. Frank calculated that the death of Roberto's sister would make the boy easier to deal with. He abandoned the idea of kidnapping the Butcher's niece. He would, instead, ignore the niece and go after Weyler.

"She's alive, Frank. Elena is alive."

Frank, sitting on the ground with his back to a large tree, could see the dark outline of Roberto's muscular frame, etched against the midday sun.

"Roberto, you must not get your hopes up."

"Elena has green eyes. The dead girl's eyes are black. The old woman swears it."

"We have to talk," said Frank.

"Yes. Of course. Where shall we search for her next?"

Frank stared at his young friend, a blank look on his face.

"Roberto, I do not know the answer to that question. We may never find her."

Roberto lunged for his friend, violently pulling Frank to his feet.

"Do not say those words to me, ever again. Do you understand me?"

Frank placed his hands on the boy's chest and pushed, but not forcefully.

"Easy, boy. I am not your enemy."

Roberto retreated. He turned his back to Frank and spoke softly to the clouds.

"I am happy that she lives but worried that she suffers."

"We will search for Elena. But we must also deal with the enemy."

Roberto turned and faced his would-be mentor.

"And how do you plan to do that?"

Frank focused on the rifle, strapped to the boy's side.

"You once told me that you were an excellent marksman."

"Yes, sir. I am."

"The captain-general is only 5 feet tall."

Roberto stared, unblinking, at his friend.

"The captain-general? You would assassinate the captain-general?"

"A snake, without its head, does not live for very long," said Frank.

Walter returned to the night shift, his chest and rib cage still sore and tender.

Without Christopher to keep him busy, the days dragged on. He grew despondent, depressed, and bitter. Walter slept for most of the day, a marked departure from his long-standing requirement of four to five hours of daily sleep. When the evening shift ended, he lingered, hoping to catch his friend Bill Horn.

"Walter. Isn't it past your bedtime?"

The voice belonged to Luther Burns. The man's face at the exit inflamed Walter like never before. He closed his eyes and shook his head in disgust. When he turned toward the doorway, Burns blocked Walter's path.

"You haven't found your rat yet, have you?"

Walter focused on the far wall and spoke through his clenched teeth.

"I am not in the mood, Luther. Please let me pass."

Burns addressed him like a schoolteacher would talk to her grade-school students.

"We should talk, Walter. I would like to help you. If we work as a team, we can find little Christopher."

Walter tightened his grip on the coal shovel he carried.

"And then we can kill the little bastard."

"I'm asking you for the last time. Please let me pass."

Burns spread his legs and raised his arms, blocking the entirety of Walter's exit. Walter exploded like the steamy hot water that almost killed him. The short man turned and held the shovel as a ball player would his bat. Burns did not see it coming. With both hands on the handle, Walter swung hard. The blade of the shovel hit Burns in the stomach. Burns lost his morning meal. His lungs emptied of oxygen. He fell to his knees.

Walter, drowning in his own adrenalin, reloaded his shovel. This time, Burns could see the blade coming. He raised his arm and swayed to one side. It didn't matter. The blow to his head sent the man crashing to the floor, unconscious.

Walter stepped over the motionless body and returned the shovel to its proper place. Surprised by the calm efficiency with which he dispatched Burns, Walter carefully unfolded his hammock. He checked the corner of the room, where Christopher usually appeared. Christopher's dish lay empty.

Walter grinned himself to sleep.

# Chapter Seven

## Yellow Fever

Isabella would return to Spain on the *Antonio Lopez*.

Although partially destroyed in an explosion, the refurbished ocean liner became a military transport ship. With a brisk speed of 14 knots, Isabella would enjoy a quick journey back to her homeland.

Packing for her return trip to Spain exhausted Isabella, despite the help of two lady servants. Isabella collapsed onto the bed, wiping the perspiration from her forehead. The older maid servant became concerned.

"Are you not feeling well, Miss Isabella?"

Isabella, her face flushed, did not respond. Her eyelids fluttered and closed. She slipped into unconsciousness. The older maid shouted to her junior counterpart. The younger woman ran out the door.

"I apologize, your Excellency. Miss Hermoza appears to have contracted the yellow fever."

The doctor, summoned by Weyler's staff, bowed low and left the woman's bedchamber. Weyler, who had contracted yellow fever years earlier, knew the often-times fatal results of the dreaded disease. He hoped and prayed that his niece would not succumb to the widespread malady. He scowled at the Cuban ladies who tended to his niece. The natives of Cuba rarely contracted the disease. He also recalled his decision to bring the girl to Cuba. He honestly thought the rebellion would be over in a matter of weeks. The insurrection he inherited proved much worse than what he imagined. He should never have allowed her to join him in Cuba.

Now, she might never leave.

"But where and when will I be given the opportunity to shoot the captain-general?" asked Roberto.

Although anxious to wreak his revenge on the Spanish Army, Roberto did not disguise his skepticism. Still preoccupied with his missing sister, the teenager cared less for the rebel cause and much more for the only surviving member of his immediate family. Frank sat against the tree, deep in thought.

"There's got to be a way," he muttered.

"It will require a miracle," said Roberto.

Frank looked at Roberto with wide open eyes. His face lit up. A slight smile crossed his face.

"That's it," he said.

Frank grinned and laughed out loud.

"That's it," he said again, shrugging his shoulders as if the solution had been obvious.

"You're a genius!" he yelled, holding his hands aloft in Roberto's direction.

Roberto closed his eyes and blew locks of hair from his face.

"It must be an American characteristic. The ability to speak without making any sense."

Frank ignored the insult and jumped to his feet.

"Come with me. And I will show you."

Frank found his oversized hat, pulled it low over his forehead, and verified that the hunting knife, strapped to his lower leg, remained in place. Roberto shook his head vigorously from side to side.

"You can't go into the city. It's too dangerous."

"We are not going into the city. Follow me."

Frank led Roberto to the edge of a cane field, one of the few not yet torched by the rebels. In moments, the City of Havana appeared on the horizon. Frank pointed.

"What do you see?"

Roberto, thoroughly confused, frowned his displeasure.

"Havana."

"Look closer."

"The bell towers of the cathedral."

The boy's head slowly turned in Frank's direction. Roberto's eyes narrowed to slits.

"Of course," said Roberto. "Of course."

The two men hurried back to their hiding spot. Frank explained his thinking.

"The captain-general and his niece attend the Catholic Mass, every Sunday, do they not?"

Roberto shook his head vigorously.

"Yes. During the week, he tortures and kills my countrymen but on Sundays, he is God's most faithful servant."

Frank acknowledged the irony with a quick nod.

"The seminary is very near the cathedral. Can you climb onto its roof?"

"I would want to inspect the building beforehand."

"Yes. That would be wise," said Frank.

"But how do I escape the entire Spanish army, once I have assassinated their leader?"

Isabella suffered for days with headaches, muscle aches, and a fever.

When the symptoms subsided, she declared victory.

"I am feeling so much better, Uncle. I wish to go for a walk."

The captain-general, still scolding himself for bringing the girl to Cuba, caressed her long red hair and placed a single hand on her cheek

"But you are not well, my princess. The disease remains. In two or three days, it will return with a vengeance."

Weyler described the toxic phase of yellow fever. The disease attacked the victim's organs. The patient would often become jaundiced. If the disease worsened, internal bleeding occurred. This produced a "black vomit." Patients would retch dark red blood.

Isabella's face twisted into a sob. She turned her head into the linens.

"I do not want to die. Please don't let me die, my beloved Uncle."

"You will not die," he said, reminding the girl that he contracted the disease and survived.

She reached for his hand and blinked back the tears.

"Pray for me, Uncle. You *must* pray for me."

Weyler looked away. His voice cracked.

"I will pray for you."

Before the girl could respond, the captain-general exited the room.

It required two full days before Luther Burns regained consciousness.

He scanned the room and noted several other beds, all of them empty.

"Hey. Where is everybody?"

He tried to sit up. His throbbing head made it impossible. A medical orderly appeared in the doorway.

"Oh, you're up."

Burns, in no mood to be pleasant, demonstrated his sarcastic ways.

"Well, you don't miss a thing, do you boy?"

The orderly's grin disappeared.

"I'll get the doc."

"I'm Doctor Heneberger, Mr. Burns. How are you feeling?"

"I've got a headache."

"You have a concussion. You will be here for at least one more night, so we can keep an eye on you."

"Wonderful," said Burns, staring at the ceiling.

"Can you tell me what happened?"

Burns struggled. The throbbing pain made it difficult to think clearly. He blinked repeatedly, as if a clearer vision meant a clearer head. A picture of Walter, coal shovel in hand, came into focus. Burns remembered. Walter wanted to leave. Burns blocked the little man's way.

"Well, doc. As near as I can recall . . ."

Burns lowered his voice and then stopped talking, altogether. The doctor leaned forward, peering into Burns' eyes.

"Are you feeling dizzy, Burns?"

Burns experienced no dizziness. It occurred to him that ratting on Walter might not be his best option. How and why did the smallest man on board the *Maine* manage to beat the crap out of one of the largest sailors on the ship? The story would not reflect well on Burns. He would be the laughingstock of the ship.

"No. I'm fine. Really," Burns snapped.

The doctor persisted.

"But what happened?"

"I was headed to the door of the engine room and remembered that I forgot my wrench. I ran into the open door and that's the last thing I remember."

The doctor did not challenge his patient's story. The bruises on the side of Burns' head could easily have resulted from an unexpected collision with an open door.

"Get some rest, Burns. If the headache is gone by tomorrow, you can report for duty."

As predicted, Isabella's condition worsened considerably.

A priest, brought in to administer the Last Rites, anointed the girl's eyes, ears, lips, nostrils, and hands. The Catholic ritual, given to Christians close to death, would erase the girl's sins and ensure her eternal salvation.

Despite the sacrament, her skin took on a dull shade of yellow. She continually vomited. Its pink color indicated a modest amount of internal bleeding.

"I have canceled your passage on the *Antonio Lopez*," said the captain-general.

Isabella, too weak to protest, could only nod her head.

"Is there anything you require? Anything I can do?" asked her uncle.

Isabella whispered her response.

"I am sorry. I am sorry to have caused you so much trouble."

Her eyes closed and the captain-general barked at the nurses.

"I want her moved into my quarters. Do it immediately."

Isabella's health improved after one week in General Weyler's living quarters.

The around-the-clock care and meticulous attention given her by palace staff did not guarantee her recovery. But, it made a difference. As her health improved and her strength increased, Isabella took the opportunity to explore her luxurious surroundings.

The ornate chamber, massive and opulent, fascinated the woman. A secret panel on the throne room wall opened the door to her uncle's bedroom. The big brass bed, canopied in silk, lay framed by several chairs of cane plus a large couch. Flowers, in full bloom, appeared on every surface. Dozens of books filled a bookcase. A crystal decanter, with six matching glasses, sat next to a hand-carved wine rack, filled with bottles of imported wines. A large bathroom, with walls of blue marble, included several dozen Turkish towels. Isabella squealed with delight.

Another secret panel opened onto an enclosed balcony. A spectacular view of the palace garden greeted the woman. On this sunny day, Isabella's nurses permitted her to occupy an adjoining sitting room, just off the bedroom. Its dainty lace curtains, when fully opened, exposed a panoramic view of the harbor.

"Do you like it?"

Her uncle's unexpected arrival prompted Isabella to rush forward. Two female nurses, hurried to her side, catching the woman before her wobbly legs gave out. She kissed her uncle on both cheeks.

"I love it. But, where are *you* staying. I have taken your bedroom. It is so unfair and yet, so generous."

Weyler placed a hand over his heart and bowed.

"When your health returns, I shall occupy my quarters once again."

Isabella, now in bed and surrounded by a bevy of staff, spoke between long yawns.

"Thank you, my Uncle. Thank you."

# Chapter Eight

## ASSASSINATION

Roberto traveled alone to the cathedral, carefully inspecting the nearby seminary.

Row after row of windows marked the cells which housed candidates for the priesthood. If he arrived just before dusk, Roberto calculated he could easily reach the roof. He would use the stone encasements, which surrounded each window, as footholds. From the roof, he would have a clear view of the wide-open plaza. The large square delivered church-goers to the cathedral's oversized, double doors.

Roberto fumed when he thought of Frank, unable, and perhaps unwilling, to risk daytime travel on the streets of Havana. While the American sat in the shade of a large acacia tree, the kid planned an assassination attempt. He could easily be captured and executed.

Roberto put his fears on hold and focused on the escape plan. He would enter a first or second floor window of the seminary and appropriate the robes of a seminarian. In this way, the intended assassin could escape among the crowd, unnoticed. When he returned to the hideaway, Roberto expressed his frustrations.

"I am assuming a great deal of risk. You, on the other hand, risk nothing."

Frank barked a response.

"My backers will make you a wealthy man."

"A dead man cannot spend his wealth."

Frank persisted.

"Your entire family was killed or captured. Now, you have a chance to avenge their death and bring peace to your homeland. And yet, you have doubts?"

Frank jumped to his feet and paced from the shade of the tree to the overturned oxcart.

"But Frank . . ."

Frank interrupted.

"If you are not willing to avenge the death of your own family, I am surely not going to waste any more of my time and money on this so-called revolution. People like you do not deserve to be free. Freedom is not given to you. You must earn it."

Frank walked toward the woods, conveniently leaving his pack behind. Roberto panicked.

"Are you leaving?"

Frank yelled over his shoulder.

"There is no reason for me to remain."

Roberto yelled.

"I am not afraid to die. For my family or for my country."

Frank kept walking. Roberto chased after him and spun the man around. The boy's glassy eyes flashed with anger and frustration.

"I am not afraid. I swear. I am not afraid."

Frank concluded that his devotee, only 18 years of age and easily manipulated, required both the carrot and the stick. He grabbed the boy's shoulders and pulled him close.

"You have become like a son to me, Roberto. And I know you won't disappoint me. But understand this. You have it within your grasp to end this revolution, avenge your family, and become a very wealthy man."

"I understand," said Roberto.

Frank released the boy and flashed a broad smile. Roberto hung his head and blushed.

"On Sunday, you go to the cathedral."

"Yes, sir."

Walter chuckled as he replenished Christopher's food dish.

The rat, munching on leftover bread, spotted Walter and stood on his two hind legs. Walter obliged his pet, lifting the rodent into the hammock. They carried on like best friends. While teaching Christopher yet another trick, Walter heard approaching footsteps. Christopher twitched his ears in protest. Walter pulled the blanket over the rat.

"Has he returned?"

The inquiry came from Bill Horn. Walter held Christopher aloft.

"Look."

"He looks healthy. How are *you* feeling?" asked Horn.

"I'm fine. Except for my scar, you would never know I got into an argument with a boiler," said Walter.

Horn leaned against the wall. His usual smile disappeared.

"Luther Burns got into an argument with a door," said Horn.

Walter cleared his throat and sat up in the hammock, his feet dangling off the side. Horn's unblinking gaze made the coal passer uneasy. Walter focused on the rat.

"I didn't know that," he lied, pretending to remove a piece of dirt from Christopher's rump.

"Burns is a very vindictive man, Walter."

"Yes, I know."

"Be careful, Walter. Be very careful."

Isabella surprised her uncle, appearing in the doorway of his office.

"Isabella, my love, you are feeling better," said Weyler.

The young woman floated into the room, spun in a circle, and bowed.

"Yes. I am feeling much better. But I will miss my luxurious accommodations," she giggled.

"A small price to pay for your good health."

The happy pair, interrupted by the arrival of two generals, responded simultaneously.

"I'm sorry."

"You are busy," she said. "I will go now."

"I will not be at table tonight," said Weyler.

Isabella, on her way out the door, stopped and turned.

"I understand, my dear Uncle. Will you be joining me at the cathedral on Sunday morning?"

"It would be my honor."

Roberto used the green fruit of a guava tree for target practice.

Frank whistled his admiration when Roberto hit each target with ease. They retired for the evening, the boy struggling to sleep. When Roberto prepared to leave, the light of dawn not yet visible, Frank rose to see him off.

"Take this with you," said Frank, handing the boy the leather sheath and knife he always carried. Roberto looked confused.

"But you do not use the machete. The knife should remain with you."

"I hear that seminarians can be very aggressive."

The mercenary's silly attempt at humor made them both grin.

The two rebels embraced and the teenager walked into the dark.

Roberto's journey to the seminary, longer than usual because he chose a circuitous route, calmed his nerves.

He encountered only one person, a local merchant, pulling a milk cart by hand. The man acknowledged Roberto with no more than a quick glance. It became the habit of Havana natives to avoid the stares of soldiers, street vendors, and visitors. Such encounters could lead to harsh interrogations, arrest, and even imprisonment. On this day, the widespread paranoia of Cuban nationals worked in Roberto's favor.

As he anticipated, climbing the rear wall of the seminary required stealth and strength. It posed no difficulty for Roberto, his catlike skills and physical strength well beyond most men of his age. When he reached the roof, Roberto hid behind the two-foot-high parapet which surrounded the seminary's rectangular roof. Using his hat as a pillow, he slid down to an almost prone position and watched the sun rise.

He stole occasional glances over the top of the small wall. Soon, the church bells announced that mass would begin shortly. Several dozen seminarians, in two long rows, processioned to the cathedral. The seminary would now be easier to access. Roberto's forced entry and hurried departure might go entirely unnoticed.

Roberto stiffened when the sound of boots on stone reached his ears. He grabbed the rifle, rolled onto his stomach, and peeked over the wall. Roberto drew a sharp breath. The captain-general arrived, surrounded by his entourage. Five soldiers led the way and five more walked behind him. Roberto focused on the beautiful woman who walked hand in hand with Weyler— Isabella Hermoza.

Despite the circumstances, he recalled her grateful kiss on the train. Roberto wondered if two such polar-opposite people could ever enjoy a loving relationship. He could see the flowing red hair from beneath her shoulder-length veil of white lace. He marveled that one woman could be so beautiful, so intelligent, and so strong. After today, his daydreams would come to an end.

When Roberto first aimed his weapon, Isabella, almost a foot taller than her uncle, blocked the boy's view of the target. Weyler and the girl reached the first of a half-dozen steps leading to the cathedral's oversized, double doors. A priest emerged to greet his VIP visitors, accompanied by two altar boys. Dozens of church-goers waited for the captain-general and his niece to enter. Isabella bounded up the stairs. Weyler fell behind, his stature a clear impediment. For a moment, the assassin enjoyed an unobstructed view of his intended victim. Roberto tightened his grip on the barrel. His trigger finger eased into place. The 1893 Mauser, given to him by General Gomez, would be deadly accurate.

He took a deep breath and exhaled. The last bit of oxygen left his lungs. He increased the pressure on his trigger finger. An unexpected movement distracted him. It was the girl. Isabella stopped, retreated one step, and reached behind her for the general. Once again, she stood between the man and the bullet that would kill him. When Isabella and her uncle reached the entrance, the cleric blessed them and ushered the couple into the church.

Roberto rolled onto his back.

"Now what?"

The service would not end for at least another hour. He did not relish the thought of waiting on a hot roof, for all that time. By then, his otherwise unoccupied escape route would be filled with returning seminarians. The streets and walkways would be clogged with pedestrians leaving the cathedral. Roberto concluded that his mission failed. *Perhap, next Sunday*, he thought.

Climbing off the roof proved difficult. He crawled to the far end of the roof with the rifle strapped to his back. As planned, Roberto utilized the window casings and ledges as footholds. After climbing over the edge, he heard voices below. He turned to investigate. Two government soldiers puffed on their cigars. Roberto spun in the other direction. His rifle swung with him and smashed into a window. Glass shattered and fell to the ground. A cleaning lady arrived at the window to investigate.

She screamed. Roberto leapt off the edge. He landed a few feet from the soldiers.

They reached for their rifles, which leaned against the seminary wall. The blade of Roberto's machete flashed in the sun. The soldier closest to Roberto fell first. The man's head oozed blood and brain matter. The grisly spatter covered Roberto's face. The boy needed a few seconds to clear his eyes. The second soldier aimed his rifle. Roberto rushed forward. A loud report, followed by a puff of smoke, slowed the boy's forward movement. Once again, the blood-covered blade of Roberto's machete found its target. Blood flowed from the man's chest wound. The soldier staggered. Roberto could not afford to wait for the man's certain death. He ran in the opposite direction.

The mid-morning sun rose high in the sky. Pedestrians, vendors with their oxcarts, and at least one Spanish soldier, spied the bloodied rebel, as he flew down the alleyways and back streets. The boy did not stop running until he reached the edge of the city. The safety of the cane field allowed Roberto to stop and catch his breath. No one followed. A sticky substance glued the front of his shirt to the boy's chest. He pulled on it and looked down.

A growing stain of dark, red liquid covered Roberto's chest.

The *USS Maine* received new orders on June 4, 1896.

The battleship would leave Hampton Roads, Virginia, and proceed to Key West, forthwith. The visit, scheduled for 52 days, would keep the boiler crew and Walter busy. Walter, free of any further harassment from Luther Burns, approached his duties with gusto.

One morning, shortly after his shift ended, Walter prepared for bed. When he climbed into his hammock, mostly undressed, the entire thing fell to the floor. Walter groaned in pain when his head hit the deck. He let loose with a series of curse words. The profanity surprised him. He rarely allowed himself such unchristian expletives.

After repairs to the oversized sling, Walter and Christopher enjoyed their usual early morning rendezvous. The sailor slept without incident and rose by mid-afternoon, intent on visiting the ship's mess. Both Walter and his rodent friend looked forward to their first big meal of the day. He slipped into his uniform, reached for his cap, and instantly noticed a large hole. The head covering, about 10 inches in diameter and with no visor, would ordinarily lay straight on a sailor's head. In this instance, Walter could feel his scalp protruding through the large hole. The two decorative ribbons, normally hanging at the backside of the headgear, also went missing. Walter fumed when he considered the likely expense of replacing the hat. His prime suspect, Luther Burns, triggered a reaction.

"I'm going to kill that bastard."

Isabella's uncle rescheduled the woman's return trip to Spain.

Although plagued with second thoughts, the girl said nothing. After mass at the cathedral, the bishop's words rang in her ears. Being thankful to the Lord for all of one's blessings was not enough. Good Christians showed their gratitude with good works. The prelate recited the corporal works of mercy. He implored those who listened, to "feed the hungry, give drink to the thirsty, cloth the naked, shelter the homeless, and visit the sick." Isabella, despite her wealth and luxurious conditions, did none of these. The bishop's admonitions triggered a twinge of painful guilt. She also thought of her miraculous recovery from the yellow fever. Why should she be spared, when so many others suffered and died from the disease?

Her time in Cuba, soon to be nothing more than a series of fond memories, contributed to Isabella's reluctance. She recalled the highlights of her trip: the enthusiastic crowds which greeted her and her uncle, the sunny days spent shopping in the plaza, and her extravagant accommodations. Roberto's handsome face also flashed in her mind. She would remember him, forever. Their meeting on the train, his lips on her hand, that giddy feeling in her stomach, and even the argument in her room. No one challenged Isabella. Everyone acceded to her wishes. Everyone except Roberto. Somehow, that too, appealed to her. She shared none of her misgivings with the captain-general.

Isabella's tearful goodbye at the palace exacerbated her anxiety.

"I will miss you, my beloved Uncle. Please return to Spain as soon as you are able."

After arriving at the docks, she dismissed her two-person security guard and sat on a nearby bench. Isabella noted that passengers boarding the *Antonio Lopez* did not do so without first undergoing a lengthy interrogation. Port authorities peppered each man with a series of questions, designed to confirm their good health. The pointed questions about fevers, body aches, and dark vomit, made her stomach turn.

A man, appearing deathly ill, attempted to board the ship. The authorities resisted. The captain insisted.

"He is my nephew. A member of the crew. I cannot leave him behind."

The official, with whom the captain argued, refused to budge.

"We have been instructed by her Majesty's government to allow no transport of any individual who shows signs of the yellow fever. You will comply, captain, or you will not leave this dock."

The sick man, now perched on a crate and shivering in the hot sun, clutched at a blanket wrapped around his shoulders. Isabella watched the man retch onto the dock. When several dockworkers arrived at her side, preparing to load the woman's luggage, she waved them off.

"Leave them. I will not be boarding the ship."

Her announcement surprised Isabella but she did not waiver. Overcome with pity, she hurried to the sick man. She pulled him to his feet and ushered him to her place on the bench. He spoke with difficulty, so violent were the chills.

"Th-th-thank you, *Señorita*."

Isabella affected a weak smile.

"I too, suffered from the fever. You can and will get better," she said.

Her statement, most likely a lie given the man's black vomit, triggered a wave of guilt. She ran to the ship and approached its captain. Isabella informed the man that her uncle, Captain-General Weyler, requested she remain in Havana. The captain did not question the beautiful young woman.

After several inquiries, Isabella learned that at least four military hospitals operated nearby. In addition, in Regla, a small city just 3 miles by land across the bay, she would discover more government-run hospitals. All of them, financed by the Spanish government, catered to victims of yellow fever. Although housed in large tents and abandoned warehouses, the facilities offered food, shelter, and medical care. Isabella solicited the assistance of a local merchant. His horse-drawn cart carried Isabella and her patient to the nearest treatment center.

It required three attempts before Isabella could locate a hospital willing and able to accept the sickly crew member. Only after her patient was given a bed, no more than a mattress on the floor, did Isabella realize that she too needed a place to spend the night. The hospital doctor, after witnessing the wealthy woman's compassion, stepped forward.

"Your dedication is obvious. Perhaps you would be willing to assist us on a regular basis, *Señorita*. What is your name?"

Isabella thought it best not to disclose her true identity. She recalled the name of the transport.

"Lopez. Isabella Lopez," she stammered, holding her hand aloft.

"It is my pleasure, *Señorita* Lopez."

"But I am not a nurse. My only experience is having suffered through the disease myself," she added.

"We will instruct you as necessary. I will show you to your quarters."

Roberto stumbled and staggered into the hideaway and collapsed to the ground.

Frank dragged the boy into the shade of their overturned ox cart.

"What happened?"

Roberto did not respond. Frank removed the boy's shirt, gathered it into a ball, and pressed it on the boy's upper chest. Although bleeding profusely, Frank calculated that the bullet, which entered the boy's upper right chest, near the clavicle, did no damage to any vital organs. He cleaned the wound with a splash of water from his canteen. He sliced several long strips of material from the sleeves of Roberto's shirt. The strips, used to tie the bandage securely to Roberto's shoulder, worked well.

The bleeding continued. Roberto needed to have the bullet removed. He would then require stitches and a thorough cleansing of the wound. Although he witnessed only one battle back in the states, Frank knew that without treatment, Roberto's wound would become infected. An out-of-control infection would lead to the boy's death.

Frank could hear the boy's labored breathing, as he sat with his back to the large tree. He contemplated the alternatives. None of them appealed to him. Abandon the mission *and* the boy. Deliver the kid to a government hospital which would put both at risk. Or locate a rebel camp in the countryside and seek their help. The journey alone would be dangerous, exhausting, and perhaps fatal to his patient.

In the end, the mercenary compromised. He would strip the boy of his clothing and deposit him at a nearby government hospital. The doctors would be forced to guess the boy's true allegiance. Frank stared at the overturned oxcart. One of its wheels lay on the ground, broken in two. How would he get the boy to a nearby hospital?

Frank tossed and turned for most of the night.

The American mercenary rose at dawn.

After checking on the boy, he trotted to a nearby shed. He used a stone to break the lock and opened the door just wide enough to allow entry. Frank slipped into the darkness and waited for his eyes to adjust. A tiny, barred window, its glass broken long ago, allowed enough of the sun to penetrate the darkness. Empty crates, a few farm tools, and several broken harnesses lay covered with dust. An old wheel, in relatively good shape, rested against a far wall. A pile of filthy and tattered clothes lay in the corner.

Frank returned to the hideout, his meager discoveries in tow. He pulled Roberto's weary frame to the shade of the tree and struggled to repair the broken-down ox cart. Several hours later, the ox cart featured a replacement wheel, fastened to the axle with no more than a piece of knotted leather. The contraption rolled forward when Frank pulled on it.

He fashioned a human harness with the remaining leather and donned some of the filthy clothes. He covered Roberto's now naked body, with the balance. After stashing his own clothes and weapons, Frank pulled a hat low over his head and began the backbreaking journey into Havana. He did not ask directions to the nearest government hospital for fear of being identified as an American. Instead, he waited patiently, studying the steady stream of oxcarts. After a few hours, he spotted a driver towing a cart, its cargo covered with a blood-stained blanket. A deathly white arm, waving from the rear of the wagon, told Frank its destination. A graveyard. The cart's origin, therefore, must be a hospital or a prison. After an hour of waiting, the cart returned. Frank followed. The driver made two stops. First at a small jailhouse and then at a large warehouse on the water's edge. The driver backed his cart to an oversized door. He disappeared inside the building. Moments later, he returned to the cart with an assistant. Each of them carried one end of a crude litter. They made several trips to and from the building, each time carrying a shrouded body.

Frank waited until sunset. He pulled his makeshift ambulance to the door. Roberto, in and out of consciousness and now running a fever, muttered aloud, He wanted a drink of water. When Frank pulled him, headfirst, from the cart, Roberto's feet slammed into the dirt. The boy groaned in pain. Frank propped the teenage rebel up against the door.

No one could leave or enter the building without noticing the wounded man.

# Chapter Nine

## THE NURSE

Isabella blushed each time a patient complimented the nurse-trainee on the dress she wore.

It seemed silly to wear such frilly clothes amid so much squalor and suffering. She owned nothing else. She made a mental note to sell at least a portion of her massive wardrobe. She would donate the funds to military hospitals. They suffered from shortages of linens, bandages, medicine, and a large variety of supplies.

A constant parade of soldiers greeted the woman every morning. Most of them exhibited signs of the fever. Some of them enjoyed a temporary respite from their symptoms, the result of a days-long remission. Others suffered through the final stages of the dreaded disease. They bled from the nose, their eyes, and mouth. They vomited repeatedly, spewing a dark hideous liquid of partially digested blood.

In less than a week, Isabella witnessed the death of several dozen men. Although totally exhausted and rarely taking time to eat, the young woman said "yes," when the doctor asked her to visit additional military hospitals in and near Havana. He trusted her to assist with patient care, cleaning, and the prompt disposal of bodies.

"We are most indebted to you, Isabella. You have been an angel, sent from God," said the doctor.

Isabella could not recall a time when the days left her more exhausted, more challenged, or more satisfied. Despite the squalor, the sickness, the death, and her inexperience, Isabella made a difference in the lives and deaths of her patients. And she did it without the accoutrements of power and wealth. She did it on her own. Her heart burst with pride.

She rode on the cart used by the hospital to transport the dead. After three stops, she instructed her driver to return to their home base.

"Forgive me, *Señorita*. We have just one more stop," said the driver.

Isabella, too tired to object, nodded her approval. This hospital, on the water's edge, operated to capacity. It smelled of dead bodies, human waste, and vomit. When the driver could locate no one to assist him, Isabella stepped forward. Two more bodies left the hospital, for the last time. On her last trip to the wagon, she noticed a patient. He sat on the floor in the corner of the oversized room. The man's skin hung on his bones, like rags on a clothesline. A bandage, bloodied and soiled to the point of being gray, hung loosely from the right side of his chest. It appeared to be an unhealed gunshot wound, red and dripping with puss. The young man appeared emaciated and feverish. His eyes fluttered open and closed again.

When he saw movement nearby, an outstretched arm rose in the air. He begged for water. She could feel the hairs on the back of her neck rise in protest. After she swung the last body into the back of the ox cart, Isabella instructed her driver to wait.

The young woman returned with her canteen. The noise of her approaching footsteps attracted the patient's attention. The young man's eyes opened wide. He studied the girl with a long, unblinking gaze. His parched lips trembled and his chest heaved. With great effort he spoke a single word.

"Isabella."

When the *USS Maine* docked at Key West, the captain announced there would be no shore leave.

The prohibition would remain in effect indefinitely. An onshore outbreak of yellow fever triggered the decision. The *Maine* would also be designated as a quarantine steamer. No vessel would be allowed near the Key West area until its passengers' health and vaccination status could be confirmed. Because the battleship required almost constant mobility, its boiler operators, firemen, and engine crew enjoyed little down-time. Walter finished his shift, exhausted.

When he reached his hammock, ready for a good night's sleep, Walter stopped and stared. His hammock no longer showed signs of yesterday's repairs. He ran down the hallway and found Luther Burns in the engine room.

"I know it was you, Burns."

Burns looked straight ahead.

"I don't know what you're talking about, Walter."

"You messed with my hammock and then you changed your mind and made everything right again."

"I think you've been spending too much time with that rat."

Burns brushed Walter's hand away and walked out. Walter raised his voice and pointed an accusing finger.

"His name is Christopher and if anything should happen to him, I'm coming after you, Burns. Did you hear me, Burns? I'm warning you."

Burns kept walking.

Frank traveled to the U.S. Consul's office.

His backers in Key West arranged access to the consul's telegraph office. Frank needed to communicate with Key West as soon as possible. From his perspective, the rebel cause in Cuba would soon fail. More arms and ammo, already in short supply, would assist the insurrection. But Frank wanted something bigger and better than another boatload of guns and ammunition. He wanted Weyler out of the way or the United States dragged into the fight. Either possibility would ensure the rebels' success. He also bragged about the attempt on Weyler's life, predicting that another attempt would soon be made.

Key West did not comment on Frank's analysis of the war effort or his claims about the assassination of Weyler. He received a cryptic note about the next shipment of arms and ammo, instead.

**"Three Friends," Boca Ciega Beach, early July**

Frank knew what that meant. A filibuster. (Smuggled goods.) The *Three Friends* would arrive at Boca Ciega beach near Havana with a shipment of arms and men in early July. Frank, with no viable alternatives at his disposal, began his search for General Maceo.

Roberto, jostled awake by the bumpy ride, stared into the wide-open eyes of a corpse.

Too weak to change positions, he surveyed his surroundings. The cart carried four dead bodies, stacked one on top of the other. Apparently, the driver thought Roberto too required burial. A bit premature, thought the teenager. With effort, Roberto raised an arm and groaned.

"We are almost at our destination. Be still," a woman's voice announced.

When Roberto recognized Isabella's voice, he closed his eyes and smiled at the clouds that floated by. He recalled the encounter on the train with Isabella. He remembered the look on her face when he appeared at her bedroom door. And he remembered her angry face when he stormed out of the room at the palace. Despite all of that, or perhaps because of that, she rescued him from certain death.

Roberto thanked God and His angel, Isabella, for watching over him.

Isabella watched as Roberto slept.

Her stomach growled with hunger. She could barely keep her eyes open. And she dared not look into a mirror. Her thoughts, confused and conflicted, made matters worse. She questioned the hasty decision that brought her to this place. She remained in Cuba without her uncle's knowledge or permission. And, as of today, she could now be justifiably accused of aiding and abetting the enemy. Friends and family, back in Spain, would not believe the circumstances of her current situation. Truthfully, she too did not fully understand why she did what she did. But here she sat, caring for the young man who dared to call her uncle a butcher.

"Isabella."

The boy's weak voice brought the woman to his side. She reached for a damp rag and pressed it against the boy's sweaty forehead. The would-be nurse, with no more than a few weeks of real-world experience, checked her patient's bandage. Pleased with her handiwork and even more pleased that he no longer bled from his surgery, she assumed an air of authority.

"You are in a Spanish hospital, reserved for government soldiers who suffer from the yellow fever."

Roberto nodded his understanding. The young woman wet her lips and took a deep breath.

"Roberto. You cannot remain here. Do you understand?"

The boy, straining to focus, whispered his response.

"Yes, Isabella, I understand. And I thank you for the kindness you have shown me."

She expected him to object. Protest. Perhaps even yell. He accepted her decision without complaint. She stepped away, bathed in guilt, but too frightened to openly welcome the sworn enemy of the Spanish government.

"I must go now. I will check on you when I can."

Roberto did not acknowledge her. He fell asleep.

Frank hiked the distance to Boca Ciega Beach.

His attempt to enter the enemy camp did not go well. Maceo's regiment in that area served under the command of José Maria Aguirre. Aguirre enjoyed a widespread reputation for blowing up bridges, railroads, telegraph lines, and buildings. He took credit for the near-miss which previously occurred at Weyler's palace. The man knew his dynamite.

After relieving him of his rifle and hunting knife, the rebels arranged for the Americano to meet Aguirre. A large tent served as the rebel commander's headquarters.

"General Maceo reports that you are not to be trusted," said Aguirre.

Frank called the rebel's bluff.

"You wish for me to leave?" asked Frank.

Aguirre twitched.

"Maceo also says you have access to arms, ammo, and money. Is that true?"

Frank scowled.

"You are expecting the *Three Friends* within a fortnight. That should hold you for a while."

Aguirre, trying to frown, surrendered to a smirk instead.

"You know about this shipment?"

"There's more where that came from," said Frank.

"We require a great deal more arms, ammunition, and men."

Frank shrugged.

"Additional shipments will not guarantee your victory. Weyler has to go."

"The Americano speaks of great things. But such talk costs you nothing."

Frank stepped closer.

"Weyler attends mass with his niece every Sunday."

"His niece has returned to Spain. Your information is old."

Lamb's eyes darted from one wall of the tent to the other. Aguirre smiled and winked.

"You Americans believe yourself to be so smart. I prefer the Butcher in Havana to the snakes in America."

Frank shook his head in disagreement.

"Those snakes in America will pay handsomely for Weyler's head. I can arrange for, shall we say, a retainer. But first we need a plan."

"We?" asked Aguirre.

"Bring me to Maceo. We will do this together."

"Very well, Mr. Frank. You are now one of us."

The rebel leader stepped forward, his unsmiling face just inches from Frank.

"For now, anyway."

"But I have no clothes," said Roberto.

With only a scar to show from his encounter with government soldiers, Roberto reached for the bed covers. He threatened to expose himself. Isabella stepped back, using two open hands to block her view of the boy.

"I will purchase the clothes myself. Please do not embarrass me."

Roberto surprised himself. That he would be so familiar with the beautiful woman had less to do with his courage and more to do with a full stomach and good nursing.

"I thank you, Isabella. You have been most gracious to this humble rebel."

Isabella put an index finger to her lips.

"Shhhhh. You must not speak like that in this hospital."

"I am indebted to you," said Roberto.

"Yes. And now, my debt to you is repaid," she said.

A reference, Roberto assumed, to the attack on her person while riding the train. He grew serious, caught her nervous eyes, and spoke in a whisper.

"Isabella, you and I are very much alike."

The woman frowned.

"How do you mean?"

Roberto focused on the far wall. A tiny window admitted a single ray of sunlight.

"We both seek justice in a land where there is no justice."

Isabella took a deep breath, releasing it from her lungs, slowly and silently.

"Yes. I want justice. For government soldiers and the Cuban people, alike. But the fighting will continue. Rebels like you, and soldiers like my uncle, will not give up. The bloodshed will go on forever."

Roberto noticed her glistening eyes. He sat up in bed and reached for her hand. She jumped back and scowled.

"Are you insane?"

An orderly interrupted their visit with a handful of clothing. Isabella grabbed the garments and tossed them on Roberto's lap.

"Please get dressed and leave us, at once."

"Your words tell me to leave but your eyes tell me to stay."

"Get dressed."

Roberto, with no gun and no machete, stood in the doorway.

He wore the clothes of a businessman, along with boots, two sizes too large and reaching almost to his knees. His dark brown hat, surrounded by a visor, looked like something an artisan would wear. Roberto could be described as neither a Cuban rebel nor a Spanish soldier. Isabella ushered him to the exit. She looked in every direction, anxious that no one could overhear their conversation.

"Your sister. Have you made any progress?"

"No. A woman in a jail just outside of the city said the soldiers buried a young girl. But it was not her."

"Where will you look next?"

Roberto's head drooped. He removed his hat.

"I do not know."

He managed a smile.

"*Señorita* Isabella Hermoza, I am most grateful to you and I will never forget your kindness."

Isabella spoke in a loud whisper.

"Lopez. You must call me *Señorita* Lopez."

Roberto rolled his eyes. He leaned forward and placed a hand on each of her shoulders.

"I will continue to search for Elena but I will always rejoice that I found you."

He leaned in and gently kissed the woman on both cheeks.

Isabella stood motionless, her unblinking eyes staring into Roberto's face.

He walked through the door and down the street.

# Chapter Ten

## SURPRISES

Frank watched as the large tug stopped just short of the Boca Ciega Beach.

The *Three Friends*, with its 350,000 rounds of ammo, arrived to the cheers of its friends on the island of Cuba.

Aguirre let go with a war whoop when 65 fully armed men disembarked from the boat. Aguirre's soldiers rushed to greet the new recruits and immediately began the work of unloading the ship's cargo. Aguirre needed every man he could get. In fact, he recently dispatched several of his officers to recruit additional volunteers. He intended to wait at the beach for at least an additional week. Frank grew impatient.

"When do we meet with General Maceo?" asked Frank.

Aguirre scowled.

"The American has not yet learned the ways of the Cuban Revolutionary Army."

"What's to learn? Consuming large quantities of rum and doing nothing?"

Aguirre pulled his sidearm from its holster and brought it to Frank's forehead.

"I will not tolerate insubordination."

The men that surrounded the Cuban officer stood in shocked silence. Frank decided to bluff his way out of the confrontation.

"Gomez and Maceo will be very upset if you pull that trigger. But do what you must."

Aguirre blinked. Frank grinned. Aguirre threw his head back and laughed.

The Cuban rebels laughed with him.

The *USS Maine*, ordered back to Norfolk, Virginia, required three days for the journey.

All eight boilers on board the ship would be in use. Walter checked the pressure on boiler number one. He checked it again and again. Despite the buckets of coal, he shoveled into the burner, the pressure did not rise. After two more buckets of the bituminous fuel, the pressure remained unchanged. With just minutes to go before the shift changed, he anticipated a nasty reception.

"Walter, what the hell are you doing?"

"Thank God, it's you."

Bill Horn, hearing the noise of a boiler at full steam, rushed to the pressure gauge. He cut off the air to the burner and remained in place until the boiling water inside the tank grew calm. Walter, his eyebrows in a bunch, did not understand Bill's reaction.

"Why did you do that, Bill?"

Bill, his face red with anger, pointed to the pressure gauges.

"Look at it, Walter. A couple more buckets of coal and she would've blown up."

"I think the gauges are broken."

"There's nothing wrong with the goddamn controls," said Horn, stepping closer to Walter and studying the little man's face.

"Is there something wrong with you, Walter?"

"I'm fine, Bill. Really. I'm fine."

Walter's eyes, glassy but fixed on Bill's face, said otherwise.

"I think you need some rest. I'll explain it to the chief. Now get out of here."

Walter shuffled off, scratching his head, and talking to himself.

"I swear the needle didn't budge," he grumbled.

When he reached his hammock, Walter checked the dish which held Christopher's food.

Christopher, too busy eating to acknowledge his human friend, did not dine alone. Much to Walter's surprise, Christopher brought a friend. When Walter tried to shoo the uninvited rodent away, it bit Walter on the finger. He winced and cursed the unwelcome rodent. Walter sucked on his wound and fell asleep.

When Walter woke up, late that afternoon, Christopher's dish lay empty. He shook an index finger at the empty dish.

"I'm not surprised. Your friend eats like a pig."

Walter checked his finger. The bite, completely healed after just a few hours, left no scar. Walter thought for a moment.

"He did bite me," said Walter. "Didn't he?"

Walter decided on a walk, topside. He strolled the deck, enjoying the fresh air and dockside view of the Norfolk shoreline.

He noticed a lone sailor walking down the gangway, headed to shore. Walter cocked his head, wondering how the man received shore leave when nobody else could.

When he looked again, the lonely figure lay on the dock, in a crumpled heap. Walter, unsure whether he imagined the incident, yelled to the officer of the deck. The two men scrambled to the collapsed sailor. They rushed him to sick bay and yelled for a doctor. The deck officer, forced to return to his workstation, left Walter with Doctor Heneberger and the stricken sailor. Walter watched as the young man's color changed to a ghastly gray. Heneberger could do nothing. He turned to Walter.

"I'm very sorry. Was he a friend of yours?"

Walter, unable to take his eyes off the corpse, shook his head and shuddered.

"No, sir. I didn't know him at all."

William Cosgrove, Walter learned later, received his discharge papers just weeks earlier. He died of a cerebral hemorrhage. Walter returned to his hammock, intent on a few more hours of sleep before the night shift commenced. He could not sleep. His body trembled. His clothes, soaked with sweat, made him shiver. He tossed and turned for several hours. At one point, he fell asleep and woke to the sound of a man's blood curdling scream.

The scream came from Walter.

Roberto, despite his new wardrobe, thought it best to use the backstreets as much as possible.

He traveled to the hideaway, where he and Frank planned the assassination attempt. He doubted that Frank still camped there. It would be Roberto's base of operations, until he figured out his next step. When the boy's empty stomach growled, Roberto thought of the fruit and vegetable markets which dotted the streets of Havana. With no money there would be no food. Out of habit, he reached deep into his pockets. Roberto discovered a single coin made of gold.

"Isabella Hermoza, you are an angel," he said to himself, flashing a wide grin.

He selected a vendor at the very end of a small marketplace. The old woman shook her head when he presented the gold coin. She pressed it into Roberto's palm.

"I have only a few pesos," she said.

"But I must pay you for the food."

"We will meet again. You will pay me at that time," she said, smiling at the handsome young man.

"I promise you, my friend. I shall return."

A half dozen mangoes later, Roberto stood at the end of the cane field. The overturned ox cart was gone but he immediately recognized the large tree. The hideaway, its grass and dirt still trampled, lay empty and bare. He sat in the shade of the tree and thought briefly about Elena.

Most of his thoughts focused on Isabella.

Frank considered a visit to the hospital where he abandoned Roberto.

He quickly dismissed the thought. The boy most likely succumbed to his wounds. In any event, such a visit would be too risky for the Americano. He decided on a visit to Key West. His backers operated from that Florida city. A steamship, the *Olivette*, regularly carried mail from Cuba to Key West. Perhaps, the captain would be willing to take on a passenger.

"I seek passage to Key West."

Frank spoke with the two crewmembers who stood top side on the *Olivette*. The two, armed men guarded the entrance to the 250-foot steamer. They directed Frank to the captain.

"Who are you?" asked the captain.

"Frank Lamb. I require a ride to Key West. I will pay you well."

The captain extended a hand.

"I'm the captain. My name is Randall. You look and sound like an American."

"Yes, sir, I am."

"You're welcome to come along. And you can keep your money."

The two Americans struck up a friendly conversation. Randall complained about Weyler's recent edict, stopping all tobacco shipments to the states. Frank complained about the progress, or lack thereof, of the so-called revolution.

"Well, it was nice for a while," said the captain. "I moved people and tobacco to Florida. Made lots of money. Not anymore. Now, all I do is run the mail between here and Key West."

A knock on the entrance way interrupted their conversation.

"We've got company, sir."

Frank noticed two Spanish soldiers on the deck. They brushed past several crewmembers and appeared in the cabin doorway.

"Your ship is detained until we have completed our inspection," said the older officer.

"What are you looking for?" asked the captain.

"That is none of your concern," said the uniformed man.

The captain laughed.

"Do you really think I'd be sitting here at the dock, in broad daylight, with a couple of tons of tobacco in my hold?"

Both soldiers pivoted and began their search. When they disappeared below deck, Frank spoke in a whisper.

"Are you still moving tobacco?"

"No, the supply has dried up."

"What *are* you carrying?"

"Mail, mostly. Not much profit in that."

"I may have a solution for you," said Frank.

"What's that?"

"A full load of cargo from Key West.

"What kind of cargo?"

Frank's eyes darted to the deck. The Spanish soldiers, now topside, approached the cabin.

"You are free to leave."

"Thank you," said Randall.

When they disembarked, Frank turned to the captain.

"We will talk on the way to Key West."

As the shores of Key West came into view, Frank and Randall reached an agreement.

Randall would move men, arms, and ammo from the Keys to the eastern shore of Cuba. The captain stipulated a single caveat. He wanted no dynamite on board his ship. Frank made a mental note to relabel the crates.

A boarding house, with a small eatery, greeted the American mercenary as he left the docks. A colored server offered him several choices. He chose the fresh fish. While waiting, he noticed a young girl who cleared and cleaned the tables. She wore long dark hair and a sad, desperate look in her bright green eyes. Frank muttered to himself.

"It can't be."

He jumped to his feet.

"Elena."

The girl's head jerked up. The dirty dishes on her tray rattled.

"Elena, is that you?" Frank asked, again.

She dropped the tray. Porcelain shards flew everywhere. A short, fat man, rushed over. He grabbed the girl by the hair and pulled her to the floor.

"Clean it up, you idiot. You are nothing but a worthless whore. I don't know why I let you stay here."

Frank took a few steps forward, his fists clenched at his side. The fat man took notice. He kicked the girl in the ribs while staring at Frank. She rolled into a fetal position. Several pieces of porcelain sliced into her arms.

"You got a problem, mister?"

Frank took a knee, pretending to re-tie the string on his boot. When he rose, the blade of his hunting knife glimmered in the brute's eye.

"Touch her again and I'll slice you like a Thanksgiving turkey."

"I own this place and she works for me. You can go to hell."

Frank ignored the owner and walked to the girl. He plunged the knife into the wooden table and pulled the girl to her feet. The fat man eyed the knife. Frank removed the porcelain from the girl's arms and clothing.

"Tell you what I'm gonna do," said Frank. "I'll let you have the knife."

Frank reached for the blade, flipped it in the air, and offered the knife to the owner, handle first. The fat man backed away. From a safe distance, he shouted his objections.

"You're crazy. The bitch is nothing but a useless whore. If you want her that bad, take her. But I paid good money for her. You owe me twenty bucks."

Frank studied the floor. Without looking up, he threw the knife. The blade missed the man's head by just inches. The weapon sunk deep into the wall. The metal made a loud twang when it pierced the wood.

"Pay the girl."

"I don't pay her. She works for food and a roof over her head."

Frank brushed by the owner and pulled his weapon from the wall. He pointed the blade at the man's throat.

"I said pay her. Now."

The man reached into his pocket and retrieved a few pesos. Frank's knife broke skin. A trickle of blood could be seen.

"More," said Frank.

The fat man removed all the paper money in his pocket and threw it on the floor. Elena scooped up the currency. Frank, with one foot behind the owner's legs, pushed with his free hand. The owner fell onto a table and rolled to the floor. The dirty plates and cups flew everywhere and shattered into pieces. The owner groaned.

"Say goodbye to your former boss, Elena."

The girl walked over and stood at the man's feet. She spit on him and spoke to him in Spanish. Frank grinned when he recognized the Spanish word, *"el cerdo."*

She called him a pig.

Isabella, with a rare moment to rest, sat on a nearby dock. Her bare feet dangled just above the dirty waters of Havana Bay.

She wrestled with a series of conflicting thoughts. Does her uncle know that she remained in Cuba? If she continued her work in the hospital, how would she replace her quickly depleting funds. She also thought of Roberto. Did he continue his search for Elena? Did her uncle's army pursue him? Capture him? Or kill him? Her eyes welled up with tears. An unexpected shadow blocked the heat of Cuba's midday sun.

She looked up and easily recognized the Captain of the Guard at her uncle's palace. Neither of them spoke. He removed his hat and sat beside her on the dock. The heels of his boots triggered a series of ripples in the water.

"The captain of the *Antonio Lopez* reports that you refused to board his ship," said the officer.

"He is correct."

He stated that you remained in Cuba at your uncle's request."

"I did."

"He also witnessed your care and concern for a sick and dying man."

"And still, you will follow my uncle's orders and return me to the palace. By force, if necessary."

"I will not use force. You are not my prisoner."

"I will not return to the palace, unless I am forced."

"Your decision is most disappointing."

"Because you are afraid of my uncle and do not wish to anger him?"

"No, Miss Hermoza. Because *you* are afraid of your uncle and do not wish to anger him."

Isabella's eyes drilled into the officer's face.

"How dare you?"

The officer did not flinch.

"I have known you for only a short while, Miss Hermoza. But from the day we first met, I saw in you an exceptionally strong and courageous woman—afraid of nothing and fiercely independent. There is much to see beyond your obvious charm and stunning beauty. Or so I thought."

Isabella looked away. She struggled to see the Havana skyline despite eyes brimming with tears. She hung her head and spoke just above a whisper.

"The Captain of the Guard is wise in the ways of women."

"I will leave you now, Miss Hermoza. What shall I say to your uncle?"

"I will tell him myself."

"You look like a peasant woman."

The greeting from her uncle surprised Isabella. She assumed he would be screaming and slamming his fist on the desk.

"A beautiful dress is of no use in a hospital filled with sick and dying men," she said.

Weyler used a thumb and index finger to smooth his moustache.

"You are the niece of her majesty's representative in Cuba. Why do you humble yourself? Where is the honor in being a nurse?"

"I am extremely proud, my dear Uncle. I am proud of my work. I am proud of the lives I have saved. And I am deeply honored to be with Her Majesty's soldiers when they leave this world and go on to their reward in heaven."

Weyler blinked. He rose to his feet and stood at the window, with his back to her.

"You have changed, Isabella."

"Yes, Uncle. I have dark circles under my eyes. My hair has not been brushed in weeks. I am covered with dirt and blood and I smell like vomit. I cannot remember the last time I had a decent night's sleep and, every night, I dream of the dozens of men that have died in my arms. But I will not apologize to you or anyone else, for my conduct. Never."

An unexpected silence enveloped the room. Weyler used both hands to smooth his unruly hair. The window reflected his image as he brushed at several pieces of imaginary lint on the sash of his uniform. He turned, walked to Isabella's side, and clasped both of her hands with his.

"Isabella, my princess, tell me. What is it that you want?"

Isabella's eyes filled with tears. She looked to the ceiling, blinking repeatedly, hoping they would subside. After a moment, she regained her composure.

"I want the suffering to stop, my beloved uncle. But, I know it won't. Until then, I will help the soldiers. I must help them. I will help them to live and I will help them to die."

Weyler pulled her hands to his lips. He kissed them both. Slowly. Softly. He wore a look of sadness, his eyes almost glassy.

"What happened to the spoiled little girl that used to be my niece?"

"She is not here anymore, my beloved Uncle. She finally grew up."

Isabella stepped forward and kissed the man on both cheeks. They hugged. He motioned to the guard at the door.

"See to it that my niece is transported to wherever she wishes to go. You will use a wagon. She will instruct you as to the supplies and food stuffs she requires. Do exactly what she says."

Isabella smiled through glassy eyes. Her uncle stepped forward. In his outstretched hand, he held a leather pouch. It jingled with the sound of coins when he pressed it into her hands.

"You will visit your uncle, from time to time, yes?"

"Yes, of course."

"May God be with you, my princess."

Frank left the café at a brisk pace.

Elena gripped the American's hand and repeatedly looked over her shoulders.

"You're safe now, Elena."

The girl replied in Spanish. Frank resorted to sign language, rubbing his stomach, and resting his head on clasped hands. She smiled, rubbed her own belly, and nodded in approval. In moments, the two of them sat at another eatery. Frank watched, wide-eyed, as the girl attacked several bowls of fresh fruit, three helpings of bread, and some cold chicken.

"You were hungry," he observed.

The girl took a deep breath.

"Food. Yes."

Frank, pleased that she knew a few words in English, waited for her reaction to his next word.

"Roberto."

The girl leapt to her feet and scrambled to his side. She used both hands to pull his head forward.

"Roberto. Please. Roberto."

"Yes. Roberto, yes. I will bring you to him."

He winced at the sound of his own words. For all he knew, the boy could be dead. He should just dump the girl at the first opportunity. He maneuvered her back to the chair.

"I'm going soft," thought Frank. "The last thing I need is an orphaned kid," he muttered.

The girl looked puzzled. Frank forced a smile. Maybe he could do both.

"Roberto. Yes. Now eat," he said, pointing to her plate.

When she finished her food, Frank searched for the *Olivette*. Captain Randall agreed to house the girl in a small storeroom until he returned. A few old blankets on the floor did the trick. Elena fell asleep in just a few minutes. Frank promised Randall he would return by nightfall.

Frank's contact in Florida, Carmelita Viscaya, impressed him.

Over the years, he met many women who, in his opinion, belonged in the kitchen or in the bedroom. She rarely disagreed with Frank's proposals and regularly provided him with funds. She also agreed to a large shipment of ammo and arms, in mid-September. Frank would accompany the filibuster and meet, once again, with Maceo. She provided Frank with additional funds and supported his efforts to eliminate Captain-General Weyler. The use of the *Olivette*, would no longer be necessary.

When evening fell, he entered the *Olivette's* storeroom as quietly as possible. The girl, perhaps sensing his watchful eyes, woke with a start.

"Good evening," he said.

The girl pointed to herself.

"Elena."

Then, she pointed to him. Frank understood. He pointed to his chest.

"Frank."

She rolled out of the hammock and fell to her knees in front of him.

"I make Mr. Frank happy. Yes?"

Frank jumped away, his back now against the bulkhead. He used both hands and pushed the air in front of him.

"No. No. No. My God. What have they done to you? Those bastards."

He suspected both the Spanish and the Cubans as the predators who abused the girl. But it didn't matter to Frank. He wanted to slit their throats. Every one of them. Elena set on the floor, legs crossed and her head cocked to one side. The girl's bright green eyes searched his face for an answer.

"Americano no like Elena?"

Frank stepped forward and dropped to one knee. He reached for her hands and pressed them against his chest. He swallowed hard and blinked the moisture from his eyes.

"No Elena. Mr. Frank likes you."

He brushed the long locks of dark hair from her face and cheeks.

She threw her arms around his neck. Frank, stiff like a board, haltingly hugged the girl. She whispered in his ear.

"Mr. Frank, my friend. Thank you."

"Yes," he said. "Your friend."

Frank held the girl's hand until she fell asleep, once again. He cursed his current situation in a desperate whisper.

"I'm a mercenary. Not a goddamn nursemaid."

Roberto thought of Isabella almost constantly.

But there was no returning to the girl and with Frank no longer at his side, he decided to strike out on his own. He would seek out the nearest rebel stronghold, preferably the campsite of General Maceo. Making inquiries, without exposing himself as a rebel, would be tricky. He thought of Marianao. Roberto would start there.

With no weapons, the boy felt exposed. Accordingly, he avoided the main road unless he could see hundreds of yards in advance. When he heard loud voices, he took cover in the thick underbrush. The soldiers wore ragged uniforms. Many of them marched without shoes. Only one man, their leader, rode a horse. Roberto saw everything he needed. These men served in the Rebel Army.

He stepped out from the brush with his hands, high in the air.

"Don't shoot, please."

Roberto counted at least a dozen rifles pointed in his direction. One of the rebels rushed forward.

"On your knees, now."

Roberto did as he was told. The soldier searched him. After a rough pat down, the man's large foot sent the boy face down into the dirt.

"He has no weapons, sir," said the rebel.

Roberto twisted his head. The mounted soldier, older in appearance, dismounted and walked to Roberto's side.

"Stand up."

Roberto scrambled to his feet. The rebel with the rough hands objected.

"But, Captain, he could be a spy for the government."

Roberto, his jaw clenched and his lips pursed, ripped at his shirt and pointed to the scar tissue.

"I wear the scars of a Spanish bullet. Do you?"

The younger soldier jumped forward. He pointed the butt of his rifle at Roberto's head.

"You will show some respect."

Roberto stepped to the side, grabbed the rifle, and yanked. The soldier tripped over Roberto's extended foot. He fell face forward on the dusty road. The soldier sprang to his feet, machete in hand. Roberto pointed the rifle at the man's chest. The attacker's machete rose in the air. Roberto pulled on the hammer. Beads of sweat formed on the soldier's forehead. Roberto stepped forward. The soldier blinked and lowered his weapon. Roberto released the hammer and threw the rifle at the man's feet. He turned and faced the captain.

"I look for General Maceo. Can you help me?"

"Why do you wish to see General Maceo?"

"I was with him at El Rubi. I wish to serve him once again."

"You were wounded in the battle?"

"No. Havana."

"I don't understand."

"Bring me to Maceo and I will explain."

The captain turned to the fallen soldier.

"You will provide him with a rifle and a machete."

"But captain, we have none to spare."

"Then give him yours. He is much more acquainted with their use than you are."

Roberto shook his head and waved the soldier off.

"Keep your weapons. Maceo will have what I need."

The captain motioned the humiliated soldier to the back of the marching unit.

"What is your name?

"Roberto Alvarez."

"Walk with me, Roberto."

Isabella, encouraged and inspired by her uncle's unexpected and generous support, pursued her work at the hospitals with renewed vigor.

Despite the long days and short nights, Roberto's memory regularly invaded her thoughts. The Spanish soldiers in her care, some of them lucid and talking, described the cruelty and horrors which both sides inflicted on their victims. Perhaps her uncle was not the innocent defender of the government he pretended to be. And the rebels, despite the charms of Roberto, committed atrocities of their own. Isabella worked in a constant cloud of confusion.

"Isabella. I wish to speak with you. Alone."

The voice belonged to the doctor in charge. He regularly visited the hospitals but rarely announced his intentions, in advance.

"Yes, Doctor. Right away."

He led the young woman to an exit in the rear of the building. They sat together on a fallen tree.

"You have given generously of your time and your money. I thank you and the soldiers thank you."

Isabella, suspecting bad news, brushed the hair from her face.

"There is no need to thank me. Why are you here?"

The doctor exhaled loudly and, for a moment, closed his eyes.

"Your name is not Lopez. You are Isabella Hermoza, niece to Captain-General Weyler.

Isabella jerked in his direction and jumped to her feet. Her eyes flashed. She shoved an index finger in the man's face.

"Which is more important? My work or my name?"

The doctor's head drooped. He spoke softly.

"You do not understand. There are those who blame your uncle for their sickness, their wounds, and the death of their friends."

"I have not heard these complaints. Not once. And I have cared for hundreds of men."

"They love you, Isabella. But they hate and fear your uncle."

"Yes, I know. My uncle the Butcher."

"I do not call him by that name. Your uncle is the reason we have these hospitals."

Isabella brushed the dust from her long dark skirt. She paced in front of the doctor. After several moments she stopped abruptly.

"Is there anything else you require, Doctor?"

The doctor hesitated. He studied his shoes and avoided her gaze.

"There is talk among the patients and the staff."

"Talk of what?"

"The soldier who was abandoned and in your care. He suffered from a gunshot wound. You nursed him back to health. Fed him. Clothed him. And released him."

"I care for many men who are wounded."

"Yes, but how many of them are rebel soldiers?"

Isabella stood motionless. The color drained from her face. The doctor rose to his feet, his voice stronger.

"It is believed that this man you call Roberto killed two of our soldiers on the Sunday just before his arrival at this hospital. He was on the roof of the seminary. With a rifle. You and your uncle attended mass on that very morning."

"We attend the mass every Sunday."

The doctor continued.

"It is believed that your uncle was his target."

"And how is it that you know all of this?"

"One soldier was killed instantly. The second soldier lived long enough to tell his story. A third soldier witnessed the rebel as he escaped. Your friend was wounded and bleeding."

Isabella's knees buckled. The doctor reached for the girl's arms and held her steady.

"Roberto." she whispered. "Roberto."

Walter, unable to sleep for most of the return trip to Virginia, blamed the hallucinations on insomnia.

*And they must be hallucinations*, he thought. Walter could not explain the rat bite that miraculously healed in a few hours. Nor could he explain the pressure gauges, or the sabotaged hammock. Luther Burns came to mind. Walter no longer blamed the bully. He blamed himself.

"You look like death."

Walter focused on Bill Horn through bloodshot eyes.

"Can't sleep."

"Why not?"

"Don't know."

"Well, something's bothering you. You never needed more than four or five hours of sleep, before."

"I'm not sure I should tell you."

"Tell me what?"

"There's something wrong with me."

"All right. Tell me. It stays here. I promise."

Walter wet his lips and took several deep breaths. He wrung his hands like an old, wet rag.

"Bill, I . . ."

His voice trailed off.

"Jesus Christ, Walter. What the hell is it?"

Walter jumped back a step.

"I'm sorry, Bill. I'm sorry. It's quite simple actually. I think I'm seeing things."

"Like the pressure gauge, the other day?"

"Yes. And other things too."

"Like what?"

"Christopher bought a friend to dinner two days ago. The damn thing bit me."

"Well, that's to be expected Walter. The animal doesn't know you."

"I swear. It broke the skin. I was bleeding. Three hours later, when I woke up, the bite mark was gone. And so was Christopher's friend."

Bill grimaced and bit his lip. Walter caught the frightened look in Bill's eyes.

"It was all so real, Bill. Honest."

Bill stepped to the exit.

"Walter, I think you need some rest. Why don't you report to sick bay. Maybe the doctor can give you something."

Walter did not respond. Bill closed his eyes.

"Walter? Promise me you will see the doc."

"Yes, Bill. I will."

Bill busied himself in the engine room, trying desperately to push thoughts of Walter out of his head.

He thought of his own family. Walter reminded him of Uncle Cyrus. Strange, antisocial, and not easily provoked. Uncle Cyrus heard voices. And he imagined things that no one else saw. And when he lost his temper, things got ugly. Fast. Cyrus once tried to strangle his younger brother. Claimed his sibling set fire to the barn. It wasn't true. Cyrus fumed for days. He got his revenge, though. Hung himself on a Sunday morning when the family attended services. He left a note. Said the voices wouldn't go away. Bill muttered to himself.

"Walter just needs some sleep."

"Sorry, Mr. Horn. I didn't hear you."

Luther Burns stood in the doorway.

"I was talking to myself, Luther. But as long as you're here, can I ask you a question?"

"Yes, sir. What can I do for you?"

"Have you been playing your tricks on Walter again?"

Burns exploded. He started breathing heavily. He blinked repeatedly and his face turned a hot pink.

"I haven't even seen that little weasel or his stupid rat. What did he accuse me of this time?"

"Calm down, Burns. I'm just asking."

"I haven't seen him in at least two weeks. He was going on and on about his hammock. I just kept walking."

Bill put a hand on Luther's shoulder.

"All right, all right. I believe you. Just keep doing what you've been doing."

"Is something wrong?"

Bill looked away, unsure if he should share his concerns with Burns.

"I know you two have had your problems. But I think Walter is having problems of his own. Claims he's seeing things. I'm very concerned."

Burns rolled his eyes.

"I'm not surprised. He always acted a bit strange."

"Yes, but on a battleship, seeing things that aren't there can be dangerous."

"Let me know if I can help," said Luther.

"What happened to Luther Burns, the bully?"

Luther exhaled loudly, blowing the hair from his eyes.

"Truth is, I wasn't always this big. When I was a kid, I got the shit kicked out of me just about every day, at school and at home, too. My ole man said I wasn't tough enough."

"So, what happened?"

"I got tougher. And somewhere along the way, I started picking on people, just to prove how tough I was."

"Why the sudden change?"

Luther smiled.

"Walter fought back. And he's got a helluva swing. I still get headaches."

"Thank you, Luther. I appreciate the help."

"Anything you need, Mr. Horn. So long as I don't piss off Walter."

"I've been waiting for your visit."

Captain-General Weyler did not greet Isabella with a smile. She sat on one of the overstuffed chairs and focused on her uncle's steely, black eyes.

"You know why I am here?"

"Yes," he said.

"Please believe me, Uncle. I did not know that Roberto planned to kill you."

"You know this rebel by his first name?"

"Yes, my Uncle."

Weyler's face grew red. He raised his voice.

"And after he murders two of my men, you nurse him back to health? You wish for him to kill again? To kill me?"

Isabella leaned forward her eyes filled with tears.

"No, my Uncle. No. That was not my intention."

The angry man sprung from his chair, circled the large desk, and stood in front of Isabella. He looked down on the girl. Isabella saw something in his black eyes that scared her. She began to tremble.

"You will bring this Roberto to me. Now."

Isabella threw her hands in the air.

"But Uncle, I do not know where he is."

Weyler's face burned red. With both hands, he slammed the arms of her chair. She flinched. He spoke in an angry whisper.

"You will deliver this man to me or you will no longer be my niece."

"How am I to do such a thing?"

"Lie to him. You are an accomplished liar. It should not be difficult."

Isabella sat on a bench in the plaza, wiping the tears from her eyes.

Her uncle, fully prepared to abandon the young woman, could no longer be trifled with. He admonished her to tell no one of the attempt on his life. He feared a panic among the Spanish people. Isabella saw genuine fear in her uncle's eyes. He clearly worried about more attempts on his life, by Roberto or by others.

She secretly mourned the loss of Roberto. In her mind, the young man acted more like a would-be rebel. His dream, minus the revenge he sought for the loss of his sister, resembled her own dreams. A dream of peace. A part of her wondered if the accusation against Roberto could be inaccurate. She wondered if they identified the wrong man. If not, this incident changed everything. Roberto became one of them. She could no longer daydream about a relationship with the handsome young man. He was the enemy.

Still, she hoped and prayed that Roberto's near-death experience would sour him on life as a rebel. Perhaps it would change him for the better.

A stubborn voice in the recesses of her mind said, "No."

After a night on the *Olivette*, Frank and his young charge went in search of the *Dauntless*.

The smugglers refused to allow the girl on their ship. The captain could not guarantee that his men would leave the girl alone. Frank assured him. She would be safe with the American at her side. His guarantee, plus a hefty fee, persuaded the captain to let the girl on board.

It would be a trip fraught with danger. The *Dauntless* carried more than 500,000 rounds of ammunition, 2000 pounds of dynamite, and a cannon with one hundred shells. The tug also carried three dozen experienced Cuban fighters. The filibuster would land at Puerto de la Guira, on the western part of the island. The team included General Juan Riuz, a good friend of Antonio Maceo.

When Maceo greeted Ruiz, the conversation quickly grew tense. Despite the throng of cheering men, Ruiz grieved. He handed Maceo a folded piece of paper.

"What is this?" asked Maceo.

"A war bulletin. It is a tribute to your brother, José, from General Gomez."

Maceo yanked the paper from his officer's hand. He swallowed hard and refused to look up when he finished reading. Maceo's brother, José, died in battle almost 3 months ago. Although General Gomez published a stirring eulogy, no one thought to inform the senior Maceo of his brother's death. The general's son, Pancho, tried unsuccessfully to comfort his father. Pancho watched helplessly as the rebel leader disappeared into a field of overgrown brush and palm trees.

Maceo's schedule did not allow for the luxury of mourning his deceased brother. His troops, laden with the massive shipment of ammo and arms, would move quickly to their hideaway in the mountains of Pinar del Rio. They would wait there until Captain-General Weyler's previously announced offensive reached the mountain range.

Maceo expected the bloodiest battle of the war, thus far.

Roberto learned from his new-found friend, the rebel captain, that the officer's small company of men travelled to Puerto de a Guira.

Maceo issued a call for more recruits. Word also spread that a large shipment of arms and ammo would soon arrive. This triggered the enlistment of rebels throughout the region. Weyler's decision, to shut down the sugar industry, also expanded the rebel army. When given the choice between starvation and the army, most of the locals chose the army.

"And you, my young friend, why do you wish to fight with the rebels?"

Roberto focused on the road ahead. He thought of his murdered parents, his slaughtered grandparents, and his missing sister.

"The Spanish soldiers killed my parents and my grandparents. My 14-year-old sister is missing. I will have my revenge. But in the end, my family will still be gone. Forever."

"You are very young to have suffered so much," said the captain.

"I feel very old," said Roberto.

"How often do these hallucinations occur?"

The ship's doctor grilled Walter, exhibiting little sympathy for his patient.

"Well, doc, often enough that I'm worried about it," said Walter.

The doctor wagged his index finger in Walter's face.

"Let me give you some advice, sailor. Stop playing with that stupid rat, stay in bed, and get some rest, even if you're not tired. And make sure you eat three good meals a day."

"But doc, I . . ."

Dr. Heneberger interrupted.

"And I am not going to give you a single day off. If you ask me, this is silly. Now, get back to work."

Walter scowled at the man. He hopped off the examining table and stormed out of the room.

Christopher's dish, empty of food, told Walter that his rodent friend would not reappear until the next day. Walter slipped into his hammock, hoping for a few hours of sleep before the night shift began. As he fell into a restless slumber, a knock on the door pulled him back to consciousness.

"What did the doctor say?"

Bill Horn stood at Walter's side.

"He says I need more sleep. Doesn't think it's a problem and has no medicine for such a thing, anyway."

"That's good news, Walter."

"He thinks I'm looking to get out of work."

"Well, is that what you're trying to do?"

Walter gave Bill the same angry scowl he gave to the doctor.

"No, sir. And I find that insulting."

Bill closed his eyes and bowed his head.

"I apologize. That was uncalled for. Please forgive me."

"That's all right. But I'm worried, Bill."

"About what?"

"What if it happens again?" asked Walter.

"Come and get me," said Bill. "Immediately."

# Chapter Eleven

## SEARCHING

After several hours of tears, angry thoughts, and prayers, Isabella decided on a course of action.

She would take temporary leave of the hospitals and visit the surrounding towns. She would search for Roberto. Isabella wanted to question him. She wanted to hear, for herself, his version of the events that made him a wanted fugitive.

She harbored another objective. She wanted to see, firsthand, the work of her uncle's soldiers and the work of the rebels. She would be an unbiased friend to both sides. She would assist the sick and injured, with equal fervor. In the end, she would know with certainty, which side in the rebellion inflicted needless suffering and death.

Isabella began her search in the town where Roberto grew up, Guatao.

When she arrived in the village, it appeared to be deserted. The driver of her two-wheeled, horse-drawn buggy turned in his seat.

"Miss Hermoza. What would you like to do?"

"Wait here."

A small garden, tended by an elderly woman, caught Isabella's attention. The old woman survived the massacre. She had visited her sister, several miles down the road, on that day. She described in detail what she saw upon her return: mutilated bodies of her friends and neighbors, homes burnt to the ground, and possessions, destroyed or stolen. She could not locate her only son and, for weeks, visited the local prisons.

"I hope and pray for his safe return."

The woman remembered a girl with green eyes. She reported what others told her. The girl with the green eyes, along with a dozen other young woman, were taken prisoner and led away by the soldiers.

"And Roberto Alvarez?" Isabella asked.

"I know of Roberto. But I did not see him on that day. I have not seen him since."

"Do you know of an Americano? Frank is his name."

The old woman's eyes lit up.

"Yes, I remember. In the village of Marianao, soldiers were killed and the prisoners released. They said it was a young boy but he was with an Americano."

"And you know this how?"

The old woman studied Isabella's face.

"We cannot grow food. We cannot eat and we cannot travel. But we can talk," she said.

"Where did they go?"

"This I do not know."

For another coin, Isabella's driver traveled to Mariano.

Many of the villagers recalled, with clarity, the release of inmates from the local jail, the Americano, and his handsome young friend. Several of the peasants described Roberto in detail. No one could tell Isabella where the heroes traveled next. Isabella chose to leave Mariano and return to Havana.

During her trip, several groups of men, some armed, some not, traveled on the same road. Isabella accosted one of the leaders and inquired as to their destination. She triggered a series of suspicious looks.

"You are not Cuban."

"I am a native of Cuba. I can prove it."

Isabella produced a few coins. The senior man scooped up the money and started talking.

They travelled to the western portion of the Cuban island, in response to a call for volunteers, by General Maceo. They hoped to gather at the general's camp in the Pinar del Rio mountains. Isabella considered the possibilities. Havana would be a dead end. Without calculating the danger, she requested permission to join the men. After all, women of almost any age assisted the rebel cause. Many of the rebel strongholds included women who cared for the troops, carried rifles, and fought alongside their male counterparts. In this instance, Isabella's request generated a series of smiles. Concerned only that her true identity remain a secret, she fell in behind the small group of men.

Roberto, the captain, and their small company of rebels arrived at Maceo's temporary camp, shortly after the arrival of the *Dauntless*.

Hundreds of soldiers celebrated by drinking rum and shooting their rifles into the air. Boxes of ammo and rifles, stacked in the middle of the camp, told Roberto that the men celebrated a recent shipment from the United States. He searched for a quiet place to rest.

"Are you lost, boy?"

Roberto's head swiveled. The smiling face of Frank Lamb made him scowl.

"You left me for dead, Frank."

"I'm no doctor, kid. Hell, I didn't think you'd make it."

"I had a great nurse."

Roberto thought it best to omit the woman's identity.

"I have a surprise for you," said Frank. "Follow me."

He led Roberto to a small tent at the edge of camp. Two men stood guard at its opening. He paid each of them with a single coin.

"Thank you, gentlemen," said Frank, reaching for the tent's flap, as they walked away.

"It must be worth a lot of money, if you needed guards," Roberto observed."

"Priceless, actually."

Elena appeared at the entrance. Roberto fell to his knees. The girl screamed and rushed forward, wrapping her arms around the boy's neck. Between sobs and giggles, Roberto wiped the tears from her cheeks. Frank approached the deliriously happy siblings and rested a hand on the boy's shoulder.

"Roberto. Your sister did not escape unharmed. She has a story to tell. I will leave the two of you alone," he said, motioning to the tent.

Roberto carried the girl into the shelter. Frank could hear the squeals of laughter, even as he walked away.

Frank congratulated himself for arranging the reunion of Roberto and his sister.

Not surprisingly, Frank's brush with benevolence did not change the man. He intended to use the rescue of Elena as a means by which to manipulate Roberto. As he paced the ground near his tent, Frank's mind filled with possibilities. Roberto played a central role in all of them.

"She's sleeping," said Roberto.

"Did you give her something to eat?" asked Frank.

"Yes. She was very hungry."

Frank grinned.

"From what I've seen of your sister, she is always hungry."

Roberto laughed. Frank motioned the boy to a nearby rock. They sat on the ground, their backs to the large stone. Frank offered the boy a cigar.

"Made in America with Cuban tobacco."

"No, thanks. I don't smoke."

Frank lit his cigar. Large clouds of smoke enveloped the mercenary and the young rebel. They sat in silence for several minutes.

"My sister told me what happened when the soldiers took her away," said Roberto.

"She was abused by the Spanish soldiers and abused some more by the Cubans," said Frank.

Roberto's lips quivered. He squeezed his eyes shut.

"And it is all my fault. I was at the edge of the village when the attack occurred. But I did nothing."

"A machete against all those rifles? What did you intend to do? You would have been cut down in a hail of bullets."

Roberto's head drooped. He covered his eyes and face with both hands. His shoulders heaved. Frank put an arm around the boy.

"Roberto. Listen to me. You are not responsible for the harm that has come to your sister. Weyler and his thugs are responsible."

Roberto looked up. His bloodshot eyes flashed.

"But I cannot undo what has been done."

Frank reached for Roberto's head with both hands, forcing the boy to look him in the eyes.

"But you can avenge her honor. You *must* avenge your sister's honor."

Roberto pulled on the grass and flung the weeds into the wind. He mumbled.

"I'm just one among many. What can I do?"

"The captain-general is more cautious than ever before. He goes nowhere without his security detail. But his daughter goes wherever she pleases," said Frank.

Roberto jumped to his feet. His eyes drilled into Frank's face.

"What exactly are you saying?"

"You know the girl. You can get close to her. Persuade her to live with the rebels for a while."

"You mean kidnap her. Hold her for ransom."

"She owes you, Roberto. You rescued her from certain harm on that train to Matanzas."

"No Frank. You are wrong. I am the one, indebted to her."

"I don't understand."

"It was she who nursed me back to life at the hospital."

Frank's jaw dropped. He scrambled to his feet and pulled the boy close. He spoke in a hostile whisper.

"Did she recognize you?"

"Yes. Of course."

"And the government soldiers in the hospital. Do they know who you are and what you did?"

"I don't know. Perhaps. I spoke to a handful of the other patients. I suppose so."

"On that day at the seminary, there were two soldiers, correct?"

"Yes."

"You killed them both?"

"One for certain. The other was still breathing when I ran. But not for long. I'm sure."

"Did he live long enough to talk?"

"I do not know. Oh. I saw a third soldier when I ran down the street."

"You must find Isabella Hermoza, as soon as possible."

"Why?"

"You are in danger, my friend. And she is your insurance policy."

Bill Horn hovered close to Walter for several months.

He noticed that without any obvious stress, Walter reverted to his normal behavior. The eccentric sailor kept to himself, spent hours with Christopher, and did his job as a coal passer. Both Bill and Walter kept busy, the USS Maine now making regular trips between Hampton Roads in Virginia and Tompkinsville in New York.

They eventually settled into a peaceful routine that would bring them well into the Christmas season.

Frank disclosed the latest intelligence from his friends in Key West.

"We have received several confirmed reports that Weyler's protection detail has tripled in size. In my opinion, the captain-general knows of the attempt on his life."

"I don't see how that puts me in danger," said Roberto.

"Do you believe that Isabella worked in the hospital for all of that time and no one knew of her true identity?"

Roberto's eyes twitched. He gnawed on a lip, deep in thought.

"The captain-general's niece works in an army hospital, surrounded by yellow fever, and does so without her uncle's knowledge? Without Weyler's protection? Think, Roberto. Think."

Roberto covered his ears and yelled.

"I understand what you're saying."

"And she treated you no better than the rest. Is that correct?"

Frank knew the answer.

"Isabella was especially kind to me. She came to my bedside, several times a day."

"And do you suppose that any of the Spanish soldiers received similar attention?"

Roberto looked crestfallen.

"She also brought me clothes and gave me money."

"Roberto. If Isabella did not reveal your identity to the doctors or other patients, you did. You did it by your very presence, by your wounds, by your appearance, and by your familiarity with this woman."

Roberto shook his head in despair.

"More than likely, the dying soldier provided a detailed description. And the third soldier was a corroborating witness. It was only a matter of time before Isabella and her uncle figured it out."

"What do I do?"

"You must be careful, my friend—very careful. And we must find the Butcher's niece, as soon as possible."

"The general has invited you to join him."

The voice belonged to one of Maceo's aides. Frank and Roberto went immediately to the general's command-sized tent, where a dozen officers spoke in hushed voices. When Maceo appeared, a wave of salutes swept through the room. A reverential silence enveloped the enclosure.

"Gentlemen, we leave base camp tomorrow. We will not wait for the Spanish soldiers to attack us. We will attack them."

The room exploded in cheers. Roberto screamed his approval. Frank silently studied the general. Maceo, holding his hands aloft, continued.

"We have been told that Captain-General Weyler launched a major offensive just days ago. He desires to attack us in the west. I thank the captain-general for this opportunity to utilize the arms, the ammunition, and the men, brought to us by General Ruis and *Señor* Frank."

Maceo waved an arm in Frank's direction. The men cheered once again. Frank acknowledged the general with a quick jerk of his head. Maceo's objective would be the recently completed western trocha. The barrier, designed to keep Maceo and his troops in the western portion of Cuba, took months for the Spanish government to complete. The large ditch, with dirt berms, searchlights, barbed wire, artillery, and new fortifications with interlocking fields of fire, would be difficult, if not impossible, to traverse.

"You don't look very pleased," said Roberto, studying Frank's sullen face.

As the two men left Maceo's headquarters, Frank appeared to be pouting. He reminded Roberto of Maceo's previous battles with the Spanish army.

"We must occupy more than a series of trenches. We must control the capital."

"We did not finish our conversation about Isabella," Roberto said.

"Yes, I know. When the bullets stop flying, we will search for your lady friend."

After a half day's march, the young rebel and his mercenary friend took up positions in the same trench.

The Spanish troops, marching in formation, appeared within the hour. They suffered dozens of unnecessary casualties, refusing to adapt to the rebels' preferred method of guerrilla warfare. Easily routed, the Spanish quickly withdrew and the rebels moved forward, finding cover behind trees and freshly-dug trenches.

In the space of a week, the rebels scored victories at Montezuelo and Tumbas de Estorino. Frank seemed pleased. When the rebels reached a place called Ceja del Negro, on October 4th, the circumstances of the conflict changed. Weyler's forces abandoned their previous tactic of marching in formation. They took up positions in trenches, behind trees, and in the thick brush. They also expanded their numbers. An additional 200 volunteers swelled their ranks. The attacking force now outnumbered Maceo's army by more than two to one. It quickly became the bloodiest battle of the insurrection, thus far.

When the rebel forces approached a significant number of casualties, Maceo ordered a retreat. The Spanish troops took possession of the rebels' hand-dug trenches. Frank began to complain.

"We're doing it again," he said.

"Doing what?" asked Roberto.

"I would estimate that we have already used 10% of our ammo. And we have accomplished nothing."

Surprisingly, the Spanish did not maintain their positions for long. They surrendered the trenches, returning to their supply dumps, at the rear of the battlefield. When darkness fell and the shooting stopped, Maceo addressed his small band of rebels, gathered behind the lines.

"We have inflicted great damage on the enemy. We will proceed tomorrow and we will reach the trocha. I promise you."

The men cheered loudly, lighting cigars, and exchanging congratulatory toasts of rum. Maceo, perhaps as an acknowledgement that his army did not achieve a truly significant victory, encouraged the troops with an additional announcement.

"Our friends in the United States will soon intervene. And when that happens, our ultimate victory will be assured."

He asked that his men spread the word. Frank could barely hide his disgust. He whispered to Roberto.

"The general believes McKinley will be our next president. McKinley is known to be sympathetic to our cause. But McKinley's help is months and months away, if it ever arrives," he groused.

As if to confirm Frank's suspicions, the Spanish took Carcarajicara later that week. The government troops also seized a significant number of rebel rifles and ammunition. In their haste to leave, the rebels left the precious cargo behind. Frank saw it as the last straw.

"Roberto, we are wasting our time. We're leaving."

The two men crawled to the rear.

# Chapter Twelve

## REUNION

The tiny company of would-be rebels escorted Isabella into the mountains of Pinar del Rio.

They marched to within earshot of the firefight.

"I will go with you," she said.

The company commander shook his head.

"No. You will not. You have no weapons. This is where you are needed."

The officer pointed to an opening in the forest. A temporary field hospital, accepting the dead and wounded, operated there. Several rows of men, bleeding and wounded, lay on the ground. One man and two women tended to their needs. Isabella's instincts kicked in. She did not resist the captain's orders. As Isabella approached the doctor, he barked an order.

"That one there needs a bandage. Can you do a tourniquet? You'll find both by the cart, over there."

Isabella slipped into her usual routine. She went from patient to patient and in less than an hour, treated more than a dozen men. She stood by the doctor as he stitched up a wounded soldier.

"You've done this before, haven't you, *Señorita?*"

"Yes."

"I'm sorry. I do not know your name."

"Isabella. Isabella Lopez."

The doctor pointed to a dark-haired girl at the other end of the field.

"The young girl over there knows nothing. Please help her."

"Yes, Doctor."

Isabella approached. The girl pivoted. Her green eyes reflected the afternoon sun. Isabella stopped in mid-step, motionless and dumbstruck.

"Why do you stare at me, *Señorita?*" asked the girl.

"You are Elena."

"Yes."

"My name is Isabella. I am a friend of Roberto."

The girl giggled.

"Yes. You more beautiful than he say."

Isabella hastened to correct her.

"No, no. We are not friends. I mean, we are friends, but not like that. Do you understand?"

The girl shook her head no. She giggled some more and rushed forward. Significantly shorter than Isabella, Elena wrapped her arms around the woman and squeezed. The doctor interrupted them.

"I could use some help over here."

Frank and Roberto ran and crawled their way to the rear.

Several enemy snipers made their retreat both slow and dangerous. More than a hundred rebels surrounded the duo, all of them with the same idea. One soldier, desperate to reach the safety of base camp, abandoned his cautious approach and sprinted to the rear. The man's tall frame and white hat made him an easy target. A shot rang out and the rebel fell face forward. His loud groan, and proximity to Roberto triggered the boy's intervention. "Frank." Roberto yelled.

"Frank. Over here."

Each of them grabbed a hand and dragged the wounded man to safety. A growing splotch of blood on the man's back indicated a serious wound. The injured man, unable to stand, screamed in pain. Frank pointed.

"The field hospital is over that ridge."

When the doctor came into view, Frank yelled.

"He's hurt bad, doc."

The doctor rushed forward, yelling over his shoulder.

"Isabella. Here. Now."

Isabella pushed Elena.

"Let's go."

When Isabella came into view, Frank stood perfectly still, mesmerized by the woman's presence. Elena noticed her brother when she reached the wounded man.

"Roberto. You come back."

The boy did not respond. He studied Isabella as she knelt by her patient's side. The doctor, kneeling on the opposite side, grunted his orders.

"Let's roll him on his side."

"The bullet exited just below his heart," she responded.

"He's bleeding out. Get me some bandages. Now."

Isabella didn't budge.

"It doesn't matter, Doctor. He's gone."

Elena made the sign of the cross. Roberto bowed his head. Frank focused on the captain-general's niece. Isabella looked up, her face, set in stone. The doctor moved on to another patient. Isabella focused on Roberto.

"Put him over there," she said, pointing to an area of the camp where a dozen bodies lay in formation.

Both men jumped and carried the body away.

Isabella hopped from one wounded rebel to another.

The act of ministering to wounded and dying men allowed the woman to place her emotions on hold. In between bandages and tourniquets, she seethed at the sight of Roberto and simultaneously cursed his American friend. She blamed Frank for Roberto's decision to join the rebels. Isabella conveniently forgot his slaughtered family and the boy's search for justice.

The sight of Roberto, alive and well, also brought joy to her heart. She recalled, with clarity, how he rescued her from the rogue soldier on the train to Matanzas. And, despite their argument at the palace, she was touched by his concern for Elena and pleased that the siblings eventually reunited.

"My uncle is aware of your attempt on his life."

Isabella, holding her torch aloft, stood in front of Elena's tent. Roberto jumped to his feet. Frank, on his knees, poking at the campfire, did not look up. Elena lay sleeping in her tent. Roberto spoke softly.

"Isabella. We must talk. Please sit down."

Isabella stepped forward and swung her torch in Roberto's direction. The whooshing sound of flame against the nighttime air forced Roberto to step back. She hissed her anger.

"I should kill you myself."

"Isabella, please."

She turned to Frank.

"And you too," she said, spitting in his direction.

Frank poked at the fire one more time, dropped his stick, and slowly rose to his feet. He spoke slowly, slurring his words.

"You will not leave this camp unless I permit it. And if anyone should discover that you are the Butcher's niece, you will be executed. But I suspect you will die a very slow and painful death. You know, the kind of death that has become your uncle's specialty."

Isabella blinked her shock. Her eyes grew wide. Frank knocked the torch from her hand. It rolled in the dirt, causing a shower of sparks.

"Now sit down," he barked.

Isabella, unprepared for Frank's deadly threat, did as she was told. The spoiled woman, accustomed to getting her way, just assumed she would remain unharmed. Even in a rebel camp. A wave of embarrassed stupidity made her face blush pink. The young woman scooted away from the fire. She sat on the cool ground with both knees tucked under her chin. With trembling hands, she pulled her limbs close. Roberto noticed.

"Frank. This woman saved my life. Do not threaten her."

Frank said nothing, lighting his cigar and blowing smoke into the starless night.

Isabella spoke to Roberto, in a barely audible tone.

"You found Elena. I am happy for you."

Frank spit a loose piece of tobacco on the ground.

"I'm the one who found her, you stupid woman."

Roberto reached for the stars with both hands.

"Frank. Please."

"Shut up, kid."

Roberto jumped to his feet and gripped the machete hanging at his side.

"Will I, too, be executed?"

Frank, still sitting, removed the firearm from its holster and pointed it in Isabella's direction.

"The first bullet belongs to her."

Roberto put his hands up in surrender.

"Everybody is tired. Let's get some sleep. We can talk in the morning."

Frank shot an angry glance in the woman's direction.

"What about her?"

"She will be here in the morning. You have my word," said Roberto.

Frank staggered off. Isabella pulled on the flap to the tent she shared with Elena.

"Goodnight, Roberto."

Roberto waited until the sound of Frank's snoring became loud and regular.

Their lean-to made his escape both simple and silent. He retraced his steps to Elena's tent. Roberto noticed that neither of the guards, thoughtfully posted by Frank several days ago, remained at their post. He slowly approached the entrance. When he lifted the flap, a single form lay under one blanket. He could not tell if Isabella or Elena lay under the covers. When he turned to leave, the sharp end of a stiletto, pointed at his throat, prevented even the slightest movement. He could see Isabella's manufactured smile, in the light of a nearby campfire.

"I was expecting you," she whispered.

"But you do not welcome me."

"Why would I welcome my uncle's assassin?"

"I will answer your question, with a question. You were with your uncle on the steps of the cathedral, that morning. Were you not?"

"Yes."

"And yet both of you were unharmed. Why is that?"

Isabella's triumphant smile disappeared. She lowered her blade and thought for a moment.

"Were you not on the roof of the seminary with your rifle?" she asked.

"Yes. I was there."

"Why didn't you shoot?"

"Why didn't you leave me to die?"

Roberto reached for the hand that held the blade. Isabella let the knife fall harmlessly to the ground. He leaned forward. She turned away. He gently pulled on Isabella's chin, with a single finger. She could feel his hot breath on her lips. She leaned in and her eyes closed. He did the same, pressing his lips against hers. *The gentle kiss did not last long enough,* thought Roberto. She brushed the hair from his face. He caressed her face with trembling hands and spoke in a desperate whisper.

"Isabella. You must leave, immediately. You are in danger."

She nodded her head in agreement.

"Yes. Of course. Your rebel friends are less than friendly."

He surprised her with another kiss.

"Not all of them," he said, grinning.

Roberto's arms pulled her tight to his heaving chest. She reached for his head, a hand on either side. She pulled on his hair. His hands rolled up her back. They shared a long, hard, passionate kiss. She pushed him away. Each of them struggled to catch their breath.

"Roberto. What do we do now?"

"I have a suggestion."

Frank Lamb's voice boomed in the night air.

The boy reached for his machete. Isabella smothered a scream. Frank waved his side arm like a child waving a tiny flag on the Fourth of July. When Roberto's weapon left its leather sheath, Frank pointed his pistol at Isabella's head. His toothy smile, still visible on a cloudy night, morphed into a sneer.

"You two think you're so goddamn smart."

Roberto's machete dropped to the ground.

"Let her go, Frank. It's me you want," said the boy.

Frank could barely disguise his joy at catching his prey in each other's arms.

"I beg to differ, Mr. Alvarez. It is your sweetheart that I want. *You* are free to go."

Roberto's gaze fell to the ground. He shook his head. His voice trembled.

"I don't understand you, Frank. First, you rescue Elena and now you would harm the woman I love."

Frank smirked.

"I was feeling benevolent. Sorry. It won't happen again."

Isabella stepped forward, calm and smiling.

"Frank. I can make you a very wealthy man. Think about what you are doing."

Frank straightened his arm and pulled the hammer back on his pistol.

"And I can make you a very dead woman. Stay where you are."

Isabella snarled. The mercenary turned to Roberto. He spoke with no emotion, the tone of his voice, matter of fact.

"You. Leave. Now. Surrender to Weyler. Tell him the rebels have his niece. He resigns as captain-general immediately or she dies. And it won't be a quick death. She is much too beautiful for that."

Isabella's knees buckled. She reached for Roberto to steady herself.

"Go, Roberto, but not to my uncle. I will be dead before you get to Havana. The Americano is a snake. Don't trust him."

Frank stepped forward. He pushed on Isabella's forehead with the barrel of his weapon. Isabella yelled.

"Go, Roberto! Go!"

With his free arm, Frank backhanded the woman. She fell to the ground. Blood trickled from her lip. Frank reached down, yanked her by the hair, and forced the gun barrel into her mouth. He growled at Roberto.

"I will be her first lover. The officers will be next. Afterwards, she will be given to the men. And after that, she will beg me to pull this trigger."

Roberto ran. Frank pulled the woman to her feet.

"Come with me, Miss Hermoza. You are now a prisoner of war."

Roberto liberated one of the two dozen horses in the rebel camp.

He picked his way through the underbrush and utilized the narrow roadway only when he had to. He would go directly to the palace. He worried about the possibility that Weyler's guards would kill him on sight. At daybreak, he surveyed the Havana skyline from the outskirts of the city. The cathedral, one of its spires visible from his vantage point, prompted him to recite the Hail Mary. The prayer, taught to him by his grandmother, asked the Virgin Mary to intercede with the Lord Almighty when death approached. Roberto thought it unlikely he would survive the day.

"Halt."

A Spanish soldier, one of four, stopped Roberto, several blocks from the palace. The young rebel wasted no time in explaining his mission.

"You will bring me to the captain-general at once. His niece has been captured by the rebels."

The soldiers, temporally dumbstruck by the boy's message, pointed their rifles. Roberto reached for his machete with his left hand. He offered the weapon to his captors. A soldier stepped forward and snatched the weapon. Another one yanked the reins from the boy's hands.

"You will dismount. Now."

Roberto, his hands now tied behind his back, offered no resistance to his four-man escort.

Isabella did not object, when her movements were restricted by a long chain, manacled to her wrist and tied to a tree.

A nearby lean-to offered her some relief from the tropical sun. An overweight soldier, unable to take his leering eyes off the woman, brought her some hardtack and a canteen of warm water. When Isabella thanked the guard, he reached out and stroked the woman's hair. She grabbed his arm and bit him. Hard. He screamed in pain. The man reached for the machete hanging beneath several rolls of fat. The loud click of a gun, now ready for firing, brought his movements to a halt. Isabella's head jerked in the direction of her savior. She stared into the face of Frank Lamb. The mercenary closed his eyes and shook his head.

"Perhaps, if you go without food and water for a few days, you will be more respectful of your guard."

"You guard wishes to do more than just feed me. Perhaps you can instruct him as to the difference."

Frank used a jerk of his head to send the obese guard on his way.

"I expect to hear from your lover in the next day or so," said Frank.

"He is not my lover."

"But you're in love with him, are you not?"

Isabella refused to answer the question. She nibbled at the dry bread and took a swig from the canteen.

"Your silence speaks volumes," he said.

Isabella rinsed her mouth with another gulp of water.

"And *your* silence would bring me a great deal of joy," she said.

Isabella turned her back on the man. She did not want him to see her tear-filled eyes.

# Chapter Thirteen

## ᴛʜᴇ ᴘʀɪꜱᴏɴᴇʀ

"You will be executed at noon tomorrow. It matters not what you have to say."

Roberto, tied to a chair in front of Captain-General Weyler's mahogany desk, studied his captor. The Spanish officer wore the look of death. His inky black eyes, cold and beyond indifferent, betrayed no emotion. Tiny hairs on the prisoner's arms and neck rose in fear. The teen-rebel took a deep breath. His voice did not falter.

"Your niece is held prisoner in the camp of General Maceo. You are to resign your position, effective immediately, or she will die. I am told her death will be a slow and horrific process."

Weyler twitched. He immediately turned his back. Roberto noticed.

"My niece will die whether I resign or not."

"I agree."

Weyler spun in place. His eyebrows shot up.

The boy smiled.

"Explain yourself," said Weyler.

"Once you have resigned, neither I nor your niece are of any use to the Americano."

"The Americano?"

"Frank Lamb. A mercenary from the United States. Lots of money and good connections. Wants the Spanish government out of Cuba."

"Why do you tell me these things?"

Roberto bit his lower lip. His watery eyes closed. He cleared his throat.

"Because . . ."

The teenaged rebel choked on his words. He tried again.

"Because . . . I am in love with your niece."

The captain-general smiled.

"And now you will surely die."

Roberto slowly shook his head in disagreement. He spoke softly.

"I will not die. At least not at your hands."

"I have ordered the execution of thousands of rebels. Why should you be any different?"

"Because, my dear general, she is in love with me."

"I do not believe you."

"Allow me to explain. It does not matter if the rebels kill your niece or if you kill me. You will never see your niece again. It is a fact of life, my friend. A broken heart can do as much damage as a bullet."

Weyler exploded. He rushed forward and slapped Roberto in the face. First, with the palm of his hand and then with the back of his hand. Weyler did not stop. He slapped the prisoner, again and again. Roberto's lips oozed blood. The boy's eyes rolled to the back of his wobbly head.

"Take him away. And see to it that he is unharmed. I should like to kill this rebel bastard myself."

Frank chose to keep General Maceo in the dark.

The woman worked as a spy. Isabella's guards, bribed and less than intelligent, did not question Frank's story. Still, he worried. If word should leak out about her famous uncle, he could not control Maceo's reaction much less the reaction of hundreds of rebel soldiers. Soldiers who feared and loathed the woman's uncle. Soldiers who would happily do to her what so many of Weyler's soldiers did to their wives, mothers, and daughters. The American mercenary came to a quick conclusion. If Roberto did not return, Frank would be forced to leave.

Isabella would be on her own.

The *USS Maine* would spend more than a week at Hampton Roads, Virginia.

The cooler weather which characterized early October, plus a smooth-running ship, prompted Captain Crowninshield to grant shore leave. Even Walter decided to explore the taverns and eateries that dotted the water's edge. The locals, more than willing to help a sailor part with his money, welcomed the men with open arms.

"What's your name?"

Walter looked over his shoulder. He assumed the young woman addressed someone else.

"Yes. You," she said.

Walter's eyes opened wide. His search for an eatery landed him, by mistake, in a tavern. A dozen sailors nursed beers and sucked hard on their cigarettes. Walter did neither. He felt out of place and panicked when the woman approached him.

"My name is Angel. What's yours?"

Walter, wide-eyed and on the verge of panic, blurted the answer.

"Walter McDermott, ma'am."

The woman brushed the long brown locks from her face and extended a hand. Walter greeted the woman like a fellow sailor. Two firm pumps and a quick nod. She giggled.

"You haven't been here before, have you?"

"No, ma'am."

"Well, how about I buy you a drink, sailor?"

Walter wiped the beads of sweat from his upper lip.

"Well. I suppose that would be nice . . ."

His voice disappeared in the noisy room, unable to compete with clinking glasses, loud conversations, and scraping chairs.

"What do you drink?"

"Well, I don't really know."

"How about a beer?"

"No. Beer makes me sick."

"Whiskey?"

"I'm not sure."

"Whiskey it is."

Angel ordered two.

"Cheers," she said, raising her shot-glass to eye level.

Walter scrambled to do the same.

"Yes ma'am. Cheers."

"Call me Angel, please."

Their conversation, stilted at first, became much more cordial after Walter downed his third drink.

"I'm sorry, Angel. I should be buying the drinks," said Walter.

He reached into his pocket and retrieved a large wad of bills. Angel's eyebrows arched. She quickly looked away. The woman asked a series of questions—about his job on the ship, his family, his friends, and his hobbies. When Walter described Christopher, and the girl did not express her disgust, he became ecstatic.

"Angel. You are the first person I've ever met that approved of Christopher."

She finished her drink and took a deep breath.

"Walter, I think it's wonderful that you care so much about God's tiniest creatures."

She reached for Walter's hand. Several hours later, the nearly empty tavern echoed the bartender's loud cry.

"Last call, ladies and gentlemen. Last call."

Angel rose from her chair. Walter scrambled to his feet. He swayed, reached for the table, and collapsed back onto the chair.

"Oh my," he muttered.

"Let me help," she said.

She flung an arm around the man's waist and pulled his left arm over her shoulder. The woman, a bit taller than her new-found friend, navigated the exit with ease.

"Angel, you are a very nice lady," said Walter.

"I will never resign."

Captain-General Weyler paced the floor behind his oversized desk as quickly as his short legs would allow. A half dozen members of his senior staff showed no emotion. To a man, they predicted that Isabella would not survive her captivity. It mattered not what the captain-general did or didn't do.

"Very well, then. Release the prisoner. Inform him that I will not deal with the American. I will deal with Maceo only."

Weyler's officers looked flummoxed, exchanging furtive glances with each other. They questioned Weyler with their eyes. Weyler grinned.

"I want the young rebel escorted to the trocha and released. Have him followed. He will bring us right to Maceo. Use a small company of men. But you will have, in reserve, at least 1000 men.

Roberto woke to the sound of a key in the iron-barred cell door.

Two soldiers, unsmiling and with rifles pointed at the prisoner, stood by as a third soldier entered the cell. The trio escorted the young rebel down a long hallway, up a flight of stairs, and into a cavernous room. A Spanish colonel greeted him.

"Captain-General Weyler has agreed to your demands. He will meet with General Maceo only. His niece will be exchanged for the captain-general's signed letter of resignation. You will be given safe passage to the trocha."

Roberto bit the inside of his lip to prevent a smile. He did not believe the colonel. The captain-general, although fearful of Isabella's death at the hand of the rebels, feared the wrath of his tempestuous niece even more. Weyler did not want to be accused of murdering Isabella's lover. Nor would the captain-general resign his position as leader of the Spanish Army.

Roberto's dramatic release and the colonel's instructions could be no more than a ruse. Or a trap.

Isabella yanked on the chain that manacled her to a large tree.

Her wrist, bloody and swollen, evidenced the woman's frustration. She forced herself to believe that Roberto lived. She also believed that her uncle would have the boy executed. She too, would succumb, but at the hands of angry rebels seeking revenge for her uncle's excesses. When the fat soldier arrived with food and water, she tried to charm him.

"I owe you an apology," she said.

The overweight soldier stood perfectly still, except for his rapidly blinking eyes.

"I do not understand."

"You have brought me food and water every day. I am grateful to you and I should have shown my appreciation, long ago."

She walked behind the lean-to, where the two of them would be out of sight.

"I don't even know your name."

The soldier's head pivoted in every direction. Beads of sweat broke out on his face and forehead. His hands trembled. She motioned to him.

"Sit with me. Please?"

He dropped to his hands and knees, rolling clumsily to a seated position. She laced her arm around his arm and caressed his pudgy fingers.

"You have the hands of a working man," she observed.

"José," he mumbled.

"I'm sorry?"

"My name is José."

She leaned her head against his broad shoulders.

"José. You are my only friend in this horrible place."

"I have no friends."

"Why can't *I* be your friend?" she purred.

José shook his head and scowled.

"I am not a stupid man. You want to escape. But I do not have the key to the lock on your chain."

Isabella blinked, trying to hide her disappointment.

"José. Where would I go? A woman in the wilderness, without food, or water. I would never do that."

The fat guard appeared to relax. They sat in silence.

"I have to go," he announced.

The guard required a few moments to rise. He focused on Isabella, still seated.

"I'm sorry, Miss Isabella."

She scrambled to her feet.

"Goodbye, José. And, thank you."

Isabella retreated to the solitary confinement of her lean-to.

General Maceo flashed a sly grin.

"What have you learned from your beautiful spy?"

Frank Lamb's eyebrows shot up. He returned the general's smile.

"These interrogations take time," he said.

Maceo chuckled.

"Yes, of course. I understand completely."

"I did learn that Weyler's forces are on the move. We should expect them any day," said Frank.

Maceo grew serious.

"Yes. My spies have confirmed this. Once again, we will not wait for the enemy to attack us. We will attack them."

"Where?"

"The trocha."

José returned to Isabella's shelter that evening.

She no longer viewed the large man as her ticket to freedom. She would be kind to him, despite her disappointment.

"Dried beef," said José, placing a small pouch on the ground where Isabella rested.

She pointed to the grassy patch, nearby.

"Thank you, José. You are very kind."

The odd couple sat together in silence. Isabella nibbled at the extra helping of food. José searched the horizon in every direction. He spoke in a loud whisper.

"We will not be here for long."

"And you know this, how?"

"I heard some of the officers. General Maceo wishes to cross the trocha."

"Why?" she asked.

"Maceo must go east. He is trapped here in the west. He needs men and supplies."

"You are a wise man, José."

"I listen. I say nothing. I learn."

Isabella nodded.

"You are a very beautiful woman, Miss Isabella."

"Thank you, José. You are very kind."

With some effort, the big man rolled to his side and rose to his feet. Isabella did the same. He leaned forward and spoke softly.

"You are of no use to the rebel army while you are chained to a tree. I will tell the American that you are desperately needed at the field hospital. I will offer to accompany you. You will be free during the day. In the evening, we must use the chain. Do you agree?"

"Yes. I agree. And I am grateful. Thank you, my friend."

"Good night, Miss Isabella."

The guard turned to leave.

"Wait," she said.

The woman stepped forward. She stood on her toes and gave the guard a quick peck on the cheek.

"A soldier and his prisoner will never be good friends. But I like you. And I respect you. I hope that is sufficient."

José removed his cap and bowed at the waist.

"Yes, ma'am. It is."

Roberto and his military escort reached the east side of the trocha, after a day's travel.

He made a mental note of the men and massive amount of equipment guarding the oversized trench.

"You are free to go," said his captors, removing Roberto from his horse and shoving him in the direction of the trench. Although Roberto did his best to remain hidden, he encountered a rebel patrol within minutes.

"I am unarmed," said the boy.

A group of five Cuban soldiers raised their rifles. The senior man recognized Roberto.

"You were with the Americano."

"You are correct. I have just returned from Havana. He awaits my report."

"You may join us."

As they walked, Roberto discovered that Maceo dispatched a half-dozen reconnaissance patrols. They searched for a lightly guarded location along the trocha. The rebel army would cross there.

"Have you selected a place?"

The soldier shook his head.

"A rat could not penetrate the trocha. We are trapped. And now, I must report this fact to the general."

When they arrived at camp, the senior man ducked into Maceo's large tent. The remainder of the patrol rested in the shade of nearby trees. Roberto's first thought, to visit Isabella, disappeared with the sound of Frank Lamb's voice.

"She's fine. Unharmed and safe."

The American paused for a few seconds.

"Today, anyway."

Roberto approached Frank, ready to give the blackmailer a full report. Frank put his hand in the air.

"Not here," he said.

Roberto followed Frank well into the thick underbrush. Frank waited until they were out of sight and well beyond earshot.

"I see that you received a warm welcome," said Frank, noting Roberto's bruised and swollen face.

"Yes. He is a very charming man."

"Tell me what Weyler said. Word for word."

Roberto related his encounter with Weyler, his incarceration, and his sudden release, with specific instructions by the Spanish colonel.

"Do you believe them?"

Roberto surprised himself with an honest answer.

"No."

"Why not?" asked Frank.

"Because Weyler has Maceo, and what is left of his army, pinned up in the Pinar del Rio region. Crossing the trocha and moving east will be impossible for the rebels. Weyler will not resign his office when he is this close to victory."

"Why did he let you live?"

"Because he knew I would lead him to Maceo. And because . . ."

Roberto's voice disappeared in the hot jungle breeze.

"And what?" Frank asked.

Roberto said nothing. Frank reached for his gun. He stopped short of removing the weapon from its holster.

"And, he would rather see his niece killed by the rebels than be blamed for killing the man she loves."

A slow smile crossed the American's face.

"Roberto Alvarez. You are the luckiest man I know," said Frank.

Roberto's eyes drilled into the American's head.

"I don't feel very lucky."

"You're still alive."

"But soon, you will kill us both."

"I am certainly prepared to kill your lover if you refuse to cooperate. And you will cooperate, Roberto, won't you?"

"Yes sir. May I see her now?"

Roberto turned toward the camp.

"She is no longer in the lean-to. She is under guard at the field hospital," said Frank.

As Roberto pushed his way through the underbrush, Frank muttered to himself.

"I'm not done with you yet, Captain-General Weyler."

# Chapter Fourteen

## ANGELS

Walter collapsed on Angel's bed.

She removed his shoes, verified he passed out, and retrieved the sailor's wad of cash. Her eyes bulged when she counted the money. She looked again at the sleeping man. He looked like an aging child. No hair, a baby's complexion, and curled up in a fetal position. She finished counting and flopped into a nearby chair. After a minute, she cursed him.

"You are either very stupid or very naïve," she mumbled.

Angel folded the cash into a roll and returned it to Walter's pocket. With some effort, she pushed the sailor to one side of the bed and climbed in. Both, fully clothed, slept for hours.

Walter woke up first.

"Where am I?"

Angel, facing in the opposite direction, rolled onto her back. It took a minute to get her bearings. She rubbed at the sleep in her eyes and yawned.

"My place. How are you feeling?"

"I have a headache."

"You drank too much."

"I never drink."

"You did last night."

Walter sat on the edge of the bed with his back to Angel. He used both hands to hold his throbbing head.

"I'll never do that again."

"Don't you have to get back to your ship?"

"Not till tonight."

Without turning, he jerked and reached for his pocket.

"Don't worry. It's all there," she said.

"I don't remember how I got here. But I remember you. Thank you for being so nice to me."

Angel smiled, rose from the bed, and straightened her clothes. She retrieved a pack of cigarettes from the nightstand.

"Smoke?" she asked.

"No. I don't smoke."

"Let me guess. You don't gamble either."

"I gambled, once. Won a lot of money, too."

"You shouldn't be carrying that much money in your pockets. Especially in these parts. The next girl you meet won't be so nice."

Walter looked at Angel, as if for the first time. She wore her brown hair, long. A frayed dress exposed too much of her bosom. A pug nose, framed by eyes that matched her hair, pointed to a set of puffy lips. Tiny laugh wrinkles appeared on either side of her eyes and lips. He guessed her age at 25 but could not be certain.

"How old are you?" he asked.

"Never ask a lady her age, Walter."

"Why didn't you take the money and run?"

Angel fidgeted. She brushed her hair with the fingers of both hands and smoothed the front of her wrinkled dress.

"I don't really know, Walter. Probably because all you wanted was a conversation. And you know what they say. Talk is cheap."

Angel laughed at her own joke. Walter didn't understand her play on words. He started to make the bed. Angel's jaw dropped.

"Are you kidding me?"

Walter stopped.

"Habit, I guess. From childhood," he murmured.

Angel sat on the side of the bed and slapped at the mattress.

"Have a seat, Walter."

She took a long draw on her cigarette, blowing a large white cloud into the air.

"You're different, Walter."

Walter's head drooped.

"Yeah. I know. Most people think I'm strange."

"You are. But I like you. You're not like all the other men."

They continued their conversation of the previous evening. Walter no longer required the agreeable effects of alcohol to loosen his inhibitions. When he came up for air, Angel suggested breakfast at a local eatery. He insisted on buying. She agreed. Afterwards, they walked for hours, stopping to rest on a waist-high stonewall. The shade of a large cypress tree and a view of the water triggered a flood of memories and confessions.

Angel, a Louisiana native, confessed to a violent childhood, an abusive father, and too many nights trying to sleep on an empty stomach. Walter, ecstatic with the similarity of their lives, shared similar memories of his tragic upbringing. They giggled, they cursed, they laughed, and they took turns dabbing at watery eyes. When the words no longer came, she reminded Walter that the sun would soon disappear.

"Isn't it time you headed back?"

Walter's lower lip protruded, like a child, pouting.

"I don't want to."

She leaned in and kissed him on the cheek. Walter's face turned pink. He reached for her hands. He didn't dare look her in the eyes. She pushed up on his chin, forcing him to look up at her. She kissed him again, this time on the lips. Walter's eyes remained open.

"You're the first woman that ever . . ."

The breeze that flew in from the ocean and rustled the trees, covered the man's voice. Angel smiled.

"I know," she said.

Isabella, surrounded by sick and wounded men, preferred the chaos of the field hospital to hours of boredom in the lean-to.

Although Frank agreed to her relocation, he assigned a second man to prevent the woman's escape.

"You know what to do, Isabella. Get to work," said the doctor.

She shaded her eyes and searched for clouds in the clear blue sky. None. It would be a long and simmering hot day.

"Isabella."

The girl's head lurched and she quickly turned.

"Roberto. Oh, thank God you're safe."

She rushed into his waiting arms. José and his partner pulled them apart. The big man spoke firmly to Roberto.

"Do not touch the prisoner."

"Did you talk to my friend?" asked Isabella.

Roberto understood the woman's question.

"Yes. He complied with my employer's request."

Isabella, with a quick glance at José, confirmed that neither of her guards understood what the couple discussed.

"But I do not believe him," he said.

"I agree," said Isabella.

"You must go now," said José, as he pushed Roberto in the opposite direction.

Roberto started to object when shots rang out. José's head exploded. Isabella, her face, and chest covered with blood and brain matter, did not move. Roberto pushed her to the ground. More shots rang out. The second guard spun in a circle and fell to the ground in a crumpled heap. A hail of bullets whizzed just above Roberto's head. The doctor, yards away, reached for his shoulder and staggered backwards. He stumbled and found cover behind a large outcropping of rock. Roberto yelled for his sister.

"Elena! Elena! Where are you?"

The boy's head bobbed up and down, desperate for a glimpse of his sister. The enemy's gunfire pinned him to the dirt.

"Stay down," he ordered, pushing Isabella's head into the ground. Roberto crawled on his stomach to José's lifeless body. He relieved the corpse of its machete and Mauser rifle.

"This way," he yelled, motioning to Isabella to follow him.

They crawled on their bellies toward the trees. He looked behind him and could see Spanish soldiers dotting the landscape. Dozens hid in the bushes on two sides of the field hospital. Isabella's head jerked up.

"Elena!"

The girl, standing at the far edge of the camp, screamed uncontrollably. Isabella shouted over the sound of gunfire.

"Get down, Elena! Get down!"

Roberto scrambled to his feet. He ran a zigzag pattern toward the girl. Still yards away from his sister, he tripped over a wounded patient and fell. Roberto looked up. Elena flew backwards. Her arms rose in the air. A cluster of red splotches appeared on her white dress. Elena's mouth opened, but no sound came out. Roberto groaned in agony.

"No, Elena. No."

The girl fell to the ground and disappeared from view. Love and rage coursed through the boy's veins. He ran to his sister's side. A bullet tore through his left arm. Roberto took no notice. Isabella arrived seconds later, the front of her dress covered in dirt and debris. They dragged the girl into the deep woods. Blood streamed from her mouth. The girl's eyes fluttered. The white dress, now a bright red, heaved with each breath she took. Isabella ripped the blood-soaked material. Elena's chest, riddled with bullets, oozed blood in every direction. Isabella closed her eyes and crossed herself.

"Oh God, no."

Elena's breath grew shallow. Her eyes opened wide. She seemed to be looking at her brother.

Roberto screamed.

"No! No! Please, God, no!"

Elena, shivering in the heat, uttered her last words in a breathless whisper.

"I'm so cold."

The wounded girl's eyes glazed over. Her last breath, long and labored, told Isabella what she did not want to know. The woman brushed the girl's eyes closed. Roberto pulled Elena's head to his chest. He rocked the lifeless form, back and forth.

"Elena. My precious Elena."

The shooting stopped. The loud sound of Roberto's sobs filled the air. Isabella did not cry.

Her eyes, clear and dry, flashed with anger.

Frank could hear gunfire.

It came from the rebels' unguarded base camp. Nothing there but sick and wounded men, he thought. And two extremely valuable prisoners of war. He questioned his decision to leave the camp and accompany Maceo to the trocha.

In fact, the general gave him no choice. Despite the reports of reconnaissance patrols, Maceo insisted on probing the trocha in several places. He discovered electric searchlights, ubiquitous artillery, new fortifications, and Spanish troops. Lots of them. By midday, Maceo changed his plans once again. He would go around the trocha, rather than pass through it. He gathered a few dozen of his most trusted men, plus Frank. The American received an invitation because he represented a source of money, arms, and ammo. Maceo's invitation sounded more like a command, thought Frank. He could not say no.

The tiny cabal hiked to the water's edge, at the Bay of Mariel, on the northwest shore of the Cuban island. A limited number of rowboats forced the men to make a series of trips. Now well east of the trocha, Maceo waited for the balance of his army and proceeded to San Pedro. Frank could see the nervous look in Maceo's eyes. Surrounded and outnumbered by Spanish soldiers, the rebel leader moved slowly and with great caution.

A sudden crack of rifle fire forced the rebels to dismount and seek shelter behind a stand of large trees. Several companies of Spanish infantry and local guerrillas surprised the rebel force. The two armies exchanged gunfire but to no appreciable effect.

With his troops low on ammunition, Maceo ordered a machete attack. Such a maneuver often struck terror in the hearts of Spanish soldiers. Not today. The Spanish troops, wiser than in the past, did not march in formation. Nor did they flee from the rebel onslaught. Maceo's troops suffered significant losses and fell back in a disorderly retreat.

Maceo yelled in pain and fell from his horse. Slightly wounded, an aide boosted Maceo back onto the saddle. Frank urged the Cuban leader to retreat.

"General, this way, please."

Maceo ignored the request. The firing continued.

Maceo fell again. Frank could see a bullet wound in the general's neck. The rebel leader lay still, his death instantaneous. Poncho Gomez, the son of General Maximo Gomez, also succumbed to enemy fire. Frank chose not to linger.

The American used the remaining daylight for his hike to safety.

"Roberto, we must leave," said Isabella, as she tied a piece of her undergarment around Roberto's wounded arm.

Roberto, still at Elena's side, refused to budge. The massive firestorm of Spanish bullets came to an end. The respite did nothing to assuage Isabella's growing panic.

"We have no choice, Roberto. We must run for it."

"I must give my sister a proper burial," said Roberto, through red and swollen eyes.

Isabella, surprised by her unfeeling reaction to the girl's death, voiced her strenuous objection.

"She's dead, Roberto. Covering her with dirt will not change that. We must leave. Now. Do you understand?"

Roberto pounded on the ground with the blade of his machete. He chopped up the soil and used his hands to scrape the dirt. After several minutes, he stopped to catch his breath. Elena's grave would barely cover a dog's carcass. Isabella reached for the machete.

"Roberto."

He yanked the weapon away. The sharp edge left a cut on the girl's forearm. Isabella used her skirt to dab at the wound. She softened her voice.

"Roberto. Listen to me. Please."

He continued to dig in the dirt.

"I must do this for Elena."

A loud rustling in the nearby bushes ended their conversation. Roberto stopped digging and crouched low. Isabella's eyes darted everywhere. The click of hammers, pulled back and now ready to fire, sounded in every direction. Roberto reached for his rifle.

"You are surrounded, my friend."

The voice belonged to a Spanish soldier. He stepped into the clearing, along with a half dozen of his comrades. All of them aimed their rifles at Roberto.

"I wish to bury my sister," he said.

The soldier yelled for his captain. When the officer appeared, Roberto recognized him. He escorted Roberto from the palace to the trocha.

"We meet again, *Señor* Roberto."

The officer turned to Isabella and smiled.

"Miss Isabella. Your uncle will be pleased to see that you are safe and unharmed."

Isabella, no longer bleeding, jumped to her feet and shoved the officer. The captain fell back but remained on his feet.

"If my friend is harmed in any way, you will die. Do you understand me, Captain?"

The officer's smile disappeared.

"All rebels are to be shot on sight. Orders of the captain-general."

Isabella stepped forward, poking the captain with an index finger. She spoke slowly, in an angry whisper.

"You will shoot the both of us or I will testify at your court-martial and be a witness at your execution."

The Spanish captain took a deep breath and exhaled in surrender. He motioned to his men. They lowered their rifles. Roberto scraped at the ground. Isabella scanned the men which surrounded her.

"Elena was my friend. You killed her. And now you will bury her."

When the soldiers looked to their captain, he nodded his approval. The men fell to work, digging into the ground. Elena's grave grew in size and depth. Isabella glared at the officer. He squirmed and pulled at the collar of his jacket.

"I will construct a marker for the little one's grave."

Frank rested the horse and sipped from his canteen.

The warm water did nothing to assuage his anger and frustration. In a single day, he lost all contact with Roberto, Isabella, and now, the general. He cared less about the general and more about Isabella. She was the leverage he needed to affect a significant difference in the outcome of the Cuban insurrection. Additional funds, from his backers in the states, also seemed unlikely. He would return to Key West and meet with Carmelita. As he made his way through the dense underbrush, his thoughts turned to Isabella. He lusted for the girl.

Amidst all the suffering, death, and destruction, he lusted for the girl.

# Chapter Fifteen

## The Firing Squad

The Spanish soldiers hiked back to Havana, Isabella and Roberto in tow.

They resembled a funeral cortege more than a victory parade. Few of the government troops took great pleasure in the massacre of rebels, already sick, wounded, or dying. They followed their orders, nevertheless. Roberto mourned the loss of his younger sister, wiping at the tears in his eyes and avoiding conversation with Isabella.

Isabella, by contrast, walked with purpose. She intended to confront her uncle. Her time with rebel troops and government soldiers convinced the girl that both sides regularly engaged in torture and needless bloodshed. She stormed into the palace, Roberto behind her and struggling to keep up. The once-beautiful woman, covered in dirt and blood, brushed past the captain-general's bodyguards. Weyler scrambled to his feet when the office doors flew open.

"Isabella. You are safe and sound. Thank God almighty," said Weyler.

He smiled broadly until he saw the anger on her face, and Roberto behind her.

"I have Roberto and the rebel army to thank for that. From my uncle, I have seen nothing but death and suffering."

Weyler ignored her words and glared at Roberto. The teen rebel, no longer intimidated by the captain-general, fell into one of the overstuffed chairs. Weyler glared at the boy.

"I spared your life and this is how you thank me? You recruit my niece to your hopeless cause?" said Weyler.

Roberto jumped to his feet, stepped to Weyler's desk, and pounded on the surface.

"Your men have murdered my father, my mother, my grandparents, and, just this morning, my 14-year-old sister. None of them was a threat to your government. They carried no weapons. They were defenseless and they were massacred," he cried.

The captain-general sat speechless.

"Must I thank you for that, also?" asked Roberto.

Isabella reached for Roberto's arms.

"The rebel army is no better than the government army."

Isabella's comment stunned both men. A loud knock on the open door broke the silence.

"Sir. An urgent message from the San Quinton battalion."

The guard placed the message in front of Weyler. He read the note, looked up, and read it again.

"You may go," he said to the guard. "And close the door."

Weyler turned to his niece and pointed to Roberto.

"Their insurrection will soon come to an end."

Weyler handed the message to Roberto. A victorious smile covered the man's face.

"General Maceo and the son of General Gomez have been killed in battle. You are without a leader, my friend."

Walter, accustomed to days and nights with minimal sleep, returned to his duties at boiler number one.

He whistled while he worked and smiled often.

"I've never seen you whistle while you're working," said Bill.

Walter grinned and scanned the room. He used an index finger and signaled Bill to come forward. Walter whispered his secret.

"I met a girl."

Bill's eyebrows shot up.

"Well, that's great, Walter. Congratulations."

"Her name is Angel."

"Where'd you meet her?"

"In a tavern. Not far from the docks. She was nice. I hope to see her again."

Bill winced. The dockside taverns employed mostly "working women," he recalled.

"She let me sleep at her place. And then I bought her breakfast."

Bill's mind raced. He struggled for a response. To hell with it, he thought. Might as well get right to the point.

"Did you have to pay her?"

"Why would I pay her?"

Bill could not stop blinking. He laughed. Walter cocked his head.

"Why are you laughing?"

"Well, Walter. Sometimes when a girl sleeps with a guy, she expects to be paid."

Walter jerked his head in agreement.

"Oh. Sure. You mean like a prostitute. Angel is not a prostitute. She's just a nice girl."

"Well, I thought you said you slept with her."

"I did. But we had our clothes on. Nothing happened."

Bill exhaled.

"Oh. I'm sorry, Walter. I misunderstood."

Walter scolded his friend.

"Bill. It's not a good idea to hang around with prostitutes."

Bill stared in amazement. Walter shoveled more coal.

"Have a good night, Walter."

"Sure thing, Bill."

Bill turned his back, rolled his eyes, and headed toward the bunk room.

Roberto rushed to Isabella's side.

He deliberately stood between her and Weyler. He whispered in her ear.

"I wonder if Frank . . ."

Captain-General Weyler interrupted.

"There is no mention of your American friend," said Weyler.

Roberto took a deep breath. Isabella snarled.

"Too bad. I would like to have shot him myself."

The captain-general stood and bowed in Isabella's direction.

"Perhaps there is hope for my niece after all," said Weyler.

Roberto reached for her hands, holding them to his chest.

"I have lost everything, Isabella. The revolution appears lost. There is no reason for me to remain in Cuba. Please come with me. To the states. To Spain, if need be. I want only to be with you and to leave this horrible bloodshed behind."

Isabella softly caressed the boy's cheek with one hand.

"My work will end when the war has ended."

She jerked in Weyler's direction, her face red with fury.

"And I will help *all* of the sick and dying, rebel and government soldiers alike."

"Do as you wish, Isabella, But I can no longer guarantee your safety or the safety of this man who seeks my death."

Roberto sprang to Weyler's side of the desk. He grabbed the officer by the uniform and shoved him into the chair.

"I could have killed you on that Sunday morning, but I chose not to. Your life was spared because of your niece. And if you cannot guarantee her safety, I will not guarantee yours."

Weyler sprang to his feet, smoothing his ruffled jacket, panting like a wolf and ready to attack. The noise of his voice filled the chamber.

"Guard."

Two soldiers rushed into the office. Weyler pointed.

"Arrest them both."

Despite several trips to New York and South Carolina, the *USS Maine* lay docked at Hampton Roads, Virginia, much of the time.

Walter visited Angel every chance he got. The relationship remained platonic but they grew closer. She and Walter munched on fried chicken as part of a Sunday picnic at the beach. The woman took great pains to ensure their repast would please her sailor friend. Walter often complained about the mediocre meals on board the ship. She caught Walter staring at her.

"Why are you staring at me?"

"How do you earn your money?"

The unexpected nature of his question startled the woman. She responded with a question of her own.

"Why do you ask?"

"Bill tells me that most women are needy and can be rather expensive. You don't seem to be that way."

"Who is Bill?"

Walter explained that Bill Horn, possibly his only friend on board the ship, cautioned him in his dealings with women in general and Angel in particular.

"He doesn't even know me," she complained.

"I've told him all about you."

Angel clenched her jaw and leaned forward.

"I'm a prostitute."

Walter chuckled.

"Don't make jokes like that, Angel. It is unbecoming."

"You don't believe me?" she asked.

Walter returned his drumstick to the plate. He dabbed at his lips with the napkin.

"I don't believe you."

"Well, how do you think I make my money? I work in a tavern. Do you really think I make any money serving drinks? To sailors?"

Walter blushed. He carefully folded the red checkered cloth napkin into a perfect rectangle.

"You don't have to work anymore. In the tavern or elsewhere," he announced.

Angel rolled her eyes.

"Oh, let me guess. My rich uncle just died and left me a fortune."

Walter reached into his pocket and retrieved his large role of currency. He split it roughly in half and tossed a handful of bills on Angel's lap. The ocean breeze forced the woman to react. She needed both hands to stop the money from blowing away.

"Don't be crazy," she said, grasping for the loose currency.

"I'm not crazy."

"I can't accept this."

"Why not?"

"All I've ever done was kiss you."

Walter reached for the canteen filled with water. He gulped several times. With great care, he replaced the cap. He gripped the container like a drowning man would a life raft. He took a deep breath. The words spilled from his mouth.

"I love you, Angel. I want to marry you."

She chuckled and reached for his hand.

"Walter. You don't want to marry me. I'm just a whore and you and I are just friends."

Walter slammed the canteen into the blanket. He scrambled to his feet and shook an accusing finger in her face. His voice trembled and he had to catch his breath before speaking.

"Do not use that word in my presence."

"Walter. What's got into you?"

"Do not use that word in my presence," he repeated.

"I understand, Walter. Now please. Sit down and finish your lunch."

He refused, turned his back to her, and focused on the ocean.

"I'm not hungry anymore," he mumbled.

She packed their things while he pouted. They walked back to her place in silence.

"Do you want to come in?" she asked.

"No."

She gave him a peck on the cheek. He turned to leave.

"Wait. I still have your money," she said.

Walter kept walking.

Isabella, under house arrest and once again in her former room at the palace, opened the door.

Careful to make no noise, and peering through a small crack, she confirmed her suspicions. Two armed soldiers stood opposite the entrance. She slammed the door and flung herself into the over-stuffed chair. Her thoughts raced. How could she escape? What did her uncle do with Roberto? With General Maceo, dead, would the insurrection soon be over? Would she be forced back to Spain? A loud knock at the door jerked Isabella to her feet.

Captain-General Weyler strode into the room. Four guards accompanied her uncle. He pointed to the chair.

"Sit."

Isabella fell into the chair, her arms folded. She deliberately avoided her uncle's gaze. A soldier stood on either side of the chair. The other two flanked their commanding officer. He approached the woman and reached for the white gloves tucked into the sash around his waist. With his left hand, he held the gloves in a closed fist and struck the woman in the face. The soft leather stung her cheeks. Isabella's face turned to stone. He did it a second time and a third. He swung the gloves in both directions. She refused to cry out. The sides of her face turned red. She held her head high and forward, her flashing eyes daring him to do it again. He did. Again, and again.

When his breathing became labored, he stopped. She sprang to her feet and lunged. Two soldiers grabbed her by the arms and slammed her back into the chair. Weyler, gloves in hand, stepped forward. The woman leaned in. Her chin pointed at the captain-general. Her angry green eyes dared the little man to strike her again. Weyler turned his back to her and growled at the wall.

"Your friend will be executed in the morning. You will witness his execution. And then you will return to Spain. That is all."

Frank hiked to Havana, wandering through its back streets on his way to the docks.

Despite a change of clothes and a large floppy hat pulled low over his face, passersby recognized him as an American. The residents of Havana, both Spaniards and the locals, could barely disguise their dislike for Americans. Each side in the insurrection blamed the United States for the worsening conditions in Cuba. Frank's normal paranoia, made worse by the plethora of government spies and Cuban informants, left him frazzled and exhausted when he finally reached his destination.

He searched for the *Olivette*. He could hear Captain Randall cursing and yelling, two hundred yards away. The boat owner constantly chased the Spanish soldiers away. They regularly walked the docks in search of rebels and contraband. Randall threatened them with a visit from the *Amphitrite,* a U.S. gunship, docked at Key West.

"Her guns will turn that death trap into a pile of rubble," he yelled, pointing across the bay to the large grey walls of Morro Castle.

The soldiers scrambled in the opposite direction, afraid of any confrontation with the Americans.

Frank approached the captain as he stood on the dock.

"Captain Randall. Good afternoon."

Randall recognized the American and waved.

"Mr. Lamb. No trip to Key West until the day after tomorrow. We leave at sunup."

"That's fine, Captain. Mind if I spend the night on board?"

"Not at all. There should be an empty hammock in the bunk room."

Frank made himself comfortable. He planned to purchase supplies after a quick nap but would wait until dark. The cold, dreary walls of Morro Castle, visible from the tiny window in the bunk room, reminded Frank that his mission in Cuba lay in ruins. His backers in Key West, enthusiastic supporters of the insurrection, would not be inclined to throw good money after bad. He would require a convincing and realistic plan if he wanted more money for the cause. The plan, to impede if not remove the captain-general altogether, needed to be foolproof. Frank wracked his brain for an idea but quickly grew frustrated.

He closed his eyes and fell asleep.

Roberto, blindfolded since he left the palace, listened intently.

A group of soldiers led him on horseback through the streets of Havana. He estimated at least eight armed guards, split evenly, in front of him, behind him, and on both sides. With hands tied behind his back and no reins to hold, Roberto saw no choice but to comply. When the putrid smell of Havana Bay reached his nostrils, Roberto assumed his destination was a prison. A series of them dotted the water's edge. The worst, Morro Castle, rarely surrendered its inmates. Death, by disease or execution, would be the only way out of Morro Castle.

Rusty hinges, and the clang of steel against steel welcomed Roberto to his new home. He could hear the groan of a large metal gate. There would be three more, each closed and locked before the next gate opened. Someone tugged at the blindfold. He required a moment for his eyes to adjust. The blinding sun confirmed the boy's horrible suspicions. He stood in the courtyard of Morro Castle.

The quadrangle, contained within a large, modern building, featured a long stairway to the second floor. Guards, leaving and entering the premises, suggested the second floor consisted of sleeping quarters, supply rooms, and a kitchen. The first floor had, as its entrance, two large, oversized doors. When he stood before one of the large iron barriers, Roberto's hands were freed. He rubbed the red marks which circled each wrist. He could see dozens of faces, peering from the dark abyss. The emaciated prisoners wore the look of hunger, sickness, and death.

An unexpected shove sent him sprawling onto the muddy floor and into a large puddle of water, urine, and feces. There were no beds, no blankets, not even a hammock. A portion of the mud floor, covered in cold, wet stones, could serve as a place to sleep. But only for those inmates strong enough to claim a spot. In a series of terse conversations, he discovered that most of the inmates, young and old, arrived at the prison less than a year ago. A former merchant told the boy few inmates survived for more than a year. To do so, required a wealthy relative on the outside. The relatives would bribe the guards and deliver to their loved ones food, clothing, and perhaps, some money. Money was required for additional bribes.

Roberto identified government clerks, professional men, farm laborers, and political prisoners. He met two Americans, one British subject, and a boy, just 14 years of age. To a man, each prisoner claimed no knowledge of why they were arrested and when, if at all, they would stand trial. Roberto squatted in the corner. He focused on the large gate. There would be no escape, he thought.

He would die in this place.

Frank, nursing a cup of coffee, basked in the morning sun, still rising in the eastern sky.

Feeling adventurous and knowing the steamer would not leave its dock until the next day, he opted for a long walk. The place looked deserted. Although Havana Bay could easily handle several thousand vessels, trade and commerce slowed to a crawl when the insurgency began. After Frank circumnavigated most of the bay, he stood within yards of Morro Castle. He slowed his pace, knowing the area to be surrounded by armed guards, spies, and a variety of unsavory characters. The goose bumps on his arms reminded him to be especially vigilant. As a precaution, he stepped into an alleyway.

The clamor of horses' hooves on stone forced his eyes to the north. A large entourage of soldiers, at least 100, escorted an ornate horse-drawn carriage through the streets. The main gate at the castle opened in advance of the procession's arrival. Frank scurried down the alleyway in search of a higher perch. The large security detail could mean only one thing.

Captain-General Weyler would soon grace Morro Castle with his presence.

Frank discovered a small church, its door unlocked. Catholic Cuba welcomed its devoted flock at all times of the day and night. He quickly located the narrow stairway which led to the belfry. From there, he could easily see into the castle's courtyard. Frank knew, from local gossip, that the courtyard regularly hosted scenes of grisly torture and summary executions. He instinctively reached for his sidearm, carefully hidden beneath the drab green jacket he purchased long ago from a street merchant in Matanzas. The thought of assassinating Weyler sent a chill up the mercenary's back. He dismissed the thought. It would be an impossible shot.

Frank made himself comfortable, seated on the floor of the belfry, his head just above the windowsill. Weyler disembarked and disappeared behind his much taller protection detail. When a soldier opened the carriage door closest to Frank's side of the courtyard, he leaned forward. Frank stopped breathing. A dainty shoe, followed by yards of frilly, black lace, emerged from the carriage. When the lady's face appeared in the sun, Frank jumped to his feet. He banged his head on the wooden frame and immediately dropped back onto his knees. Despite her entirely black wardrobe, including a sun bonnet, he instantly recognized Isabella Hermoza. She stood in the middle of the courtyard, surrounded by soldiers.

Roberto, groggy from just a few hours of sleep, heard someone shout his name.

He chose not to answer. The large gate at one end of the oversized cell swung open. A dozen guards, rifles in hand, entered the chamber. They ordered everyone to be seated, pushing to the ground those inmates that did not immediately comply. Although he studied the muddy floor and kept his face hidden, two sets of boots stopped just inches from where he sat.

"Roberto Alvarez. Come with us."

Roberto did not budge. Muscular arms pulled the boy to his feet. When he resisted, a third soldier shoved the butt of a rifle into Roberto's empty stomach. The blow took the boy's breath away. His knees buckled. The soldiers dragged him from the cell. They pushed the young rebel through the series of gates. He recognized the courtyard as they dragged him in the direction of a thick post. A rope tied his hands together. Another rope tied his body to the post. A soldier stood by with a blindfold. Roberto spotted the captain-general and spit in the man's direction. A motion on the other side of the carriage caught his attention. Isabella stepped forward. Her eyes, red and swollen from crying, framed a face still pink from the blows of her uncle. The prisoner pulled against the ropes, scraping the flesh from his wrists. He screamed, his voice hot with passion.

"Isabella! Isabella! I love you!"

She looked up. Her legs gave way. Guards on either side of the woman steadied the girl. She sobbed her response.

"Roberto. I love you. I will always love you!"

Roberto refused the blindfold. The soldiers produced a hood made of thick burlap. They forced it over his head. The boy's world went dark. He could hear the footsteps of the firing squad as they marched into formation. He started to pray. Perhaps the Lord Almighty would forgive him his sins, in this, the hour of his death. Roberto recalled the vengeance he sought as retribution for his murdered family. His heart filled with regret. "Vengeance is mine, sayeth the Lord." For this too, he asked forgiveness.

And finally, he asked the Lord to forgive his killers.

Frank, his face glued to the window, rubbed and blinked his eyes.

The deadly scene unfolding below, did not change. His courageous but headstrong student would soon fall to the enemy. Frank tried to ignore the large pang of guilt in his gut. The kid did not deserve to die like this. In Frank's mind, the captain-general represented the worst kind of evil, unlike Frank's noble cause. The mercenary's twisted logic prompted the man to reach for his sidearm. He smashed the window. One of the guards below twisted in the direction of the noise. Frank ducked. After a short interval, he reappeared. He sighted his weapon on the captain-general. The Captain of the Guard stepped forward, blocking Frank's view of Weyler. Frank cursed and waited for the man to move.

"Please, uncle. You must stop this. I will return to Spain. I will do whatever you say. I beg you. Please let him live."

Frank could hear the woman's desperate cries. Weyler did not respond to the woman's supplications. Roberto squeezed his eyes shut. The burlap caught his tears. Weyler signaled the Captain of the Guard to proceed. The captain stepped forward. Frank's view, no longer obstructed, forced him into a low crouch.

"*Listo!*" (ready)

Frank pulled the hammer back.

*"Apunter!"* (aim)

Frank's hand trembled. The sight on his gun would not stop moving. The soldiers sighted their target. Roberto stiffened.

*"Fuego!* (Fire)

The soldiers fired their rifles. Frank pulled the trigger. Roberto remained standing. The rifles pointed at the clouds. Frank put his head through the window, refusing to believe his eyes. He sliced his forehead on a piece of glass. Roberto's head swiveled in every direction. He pulled on the ropes to no avail. Frank looked for evidence of his errant shot. He noticed the carriage driver inspecting the footrest. Isabella fell on her knees and sobbed uncontrollably. Weyler walked to her side. He showed no emotion.

"Your friend will remain in prison for the duration of the war. You will return to Spain as soon as arrangements can be made. Is that understood?"

Isabella pressed her lips against the man's dusty boot.

"Yes. Yes, my uncle. I will do as you say."

# *Chapter Sixteen*

## GRAVEYARD DUTY

A soldier yanked the hood from Roberto's head.

His face contorted in anger when he saw Isabella kiss the man's boot. Weyler climbed into the carriage. Two soldiers escorted Isabella to her side of the horse-drawn vehicle. She glanced one last time at Roberto. Roberto shouted.

"I will find you, my love! I promise! I will find you!"

Frank sat on the belfry floor smiling at his pistol.

"My money is on the kid."

Walter lay awake most of the day.

Christopher's arrival and the rat's ravenous appetite did nothing to improve the sailor's disposition. He thought only of Angel. He liked her. A lot. He did not care about her previous life as a hooker. He especially liked her honesty and opinionated ways. Strong women appealed to Walter.

But a tiny voice in the back of his head urged caution. He wondered about her feelings toward him. He saw little evidence that she loved him. She seemed to enjoy his company but little else. She spent a great deal of time with rowdy sailors and so-called gentlemen. Her clientele, motivated more by lust than honorable intentions, could only jeopardize his relationship with Angel.

Walter surrendered to his insomnia and dressed for work. He searched for his hat. It no longer hung on the wall hook. The shoelaces on his boots needed to be tied. Again. He cursed, certain that he tied the laces just moments ago. Walter reported to the boiler room, out of uniform, disheveled, and irate.

"Your hat's on backwards," said Bill.

Bill Horn startled Walter.

"Oh. That's where I left it," said Walter, a dismayed look covering his face.

"How's Angel?"

Walter lied, choosing not to discuss his last encounter with the woman.

"She's fine."

"By the way," said Bill, "what happened to your shoelaces?"

Walter looked down. There were no shoelaces in his boots. A look of panic covered his face. The hallucinations had returned.

Despite his promise, he did not tell Bill.

Isabella, smiling through tears, packed her few belongings in moments.

Months in the service of sick, wounded, and dying men, depleted both her wardrobe and her resources. Although exiled by her uncle, she would not miss the trappings of wealth and influence. Her imminent departure from Havana brought sadness but not regret. Isabella's genuine concern for soldiers on both sides of the rebellion triggered anger and frustration. So many of them required assistance. Her heart ached for those men. Fulfilling their needs gave her purpose in life. The once spoiled little rich girl underwent a soul-wrenching transformation. In truth, she now needed them as much, if not more, than they needed her.

Sitting alone in her room, for the last time, Isabella's thoughts turned to Roberto. She clenched her jaw and refused to cry. His last words rang in her ears. "I will find you. I promise." She smiled bitterly. She would never see him again. When the door opened without a knock, she knew that her uncle arrived. She refused to stand and spoke to the floor.

"Is it your practice to bid your prisoners a fond farewell?"

"I am doing this for you, Isabella."

She would not look him in the eyes.

"I do have one request," she said.

"If I am able, I will happily grant your request."

Isabella's head jerked up. Her angry face fixed on his beady black eyes.

"I would like a pair of your white gloves to remember you by."

Weyler froze in place. His face turned to a beet red. For a long moment the couple exchanged furious glances. He blinked, marched to the door, and barked at the guards.

"See that she gets on the boat and stays there until it leaves the dock."

The guards saluted.

Isabella jumped to her feet and slammed the door behind him.

The door reopened immediately. Four soldiers would escort her to the docks.

Frank returned to the *Olivette*, shellshocked by the harrowing scene at Morro Castle.

His steamer would soon leave the dock for Key West. And still, he possessed no plan of action. No promising initiative which would trigger additional funds from his backers in the states.

The image of Roberto flashed in Frank's eyes. The boy, standing in front of a firing squad with his head held high, made a lasting impression. Frank's stone-cold heart, for reasons he could not fathom, sympathized with the kid. Yes, Roberto had become a thorn in Frank's side. And he refused to take advantage of Isabella, the way Frank wanted to. Instead, the innocent boy professed his love for the girl. Frank didn't believe in love. An honest man would call it lust.

Whatever his character flaws, Roberto did not deserve to rot in prison. Frank surprised himself with such thinking. But with Isabella out of the picture, the boy would be a valuable comrade in arms. A crazy idea made Frank's head spin. With a little time and a lot of money, he might be able to get the kid released. Roberto would be indebted to the mercenary. Extremely indebted. And willing to please.

"We leave in 15 minutes," said a deckhand.

Frank grabbed the few items of clothing not already in his haversack. He reappeared on the deck, out of breath.

"Where are you going?" shouted the captain.

"I changed my mind," said Frank.

"Again?"

Frank returned to his heavenly perch above the choir loft in the church belfry.

Along the way, he refilled his canteen and purchased some food stuffs from street vendors. He planned to be in his hideaway for a while. Frank could think of no obvious plan to free Roberto. His instincts told him he should observe the Morro Castle courtyard, nevertheless. No prison is impregnable, he thought. Observing the comings and goings at Morro Castle might give him a solution. For now, he would wait and watch.

An entire day in the hot and humid belfry produced nothing of value. Frank now knew the precise times at which guards began and ended their shifts. Nothing more. As darkness approached, he heard voices and movement, down below. Although barely visible, a sliver of a moon, plus torches held aloft by two soldiers, revealed the nature of their activity.

Two inmates left Morro Castle, never to return. Frank watched as the lifeless forms were tossed into an ox-drawn cart. Two soldiers rode in front of the makeshift hearse. A lone inmate, this one very much alive, rode in the back with the bodies of his fellow prisoners. The scene set Frank to thinking.

The transport of dead bodies occurred after dark for a reason. Prison officials wanted no witnesses. The soldiers would dispose of the body. No one, outside of the prison walls, would ever know. But why bring an inmate along? Frank thought for a moment and chuckled to himself. To dig the grave, of course. The lazy guards considered such work as beneath them.

He rushed from the belfry intent on following the secret funeral cortege. The oxcart did as he expected. An abandoned cane field, not fifteen minutes from the prison, would serve as the cemetery. Although unable to see beyond the torch lights, Frank suspected that the cane field served as a final resting place for dozens of former prisoners. After the burial, the ox cart and its passengers left the way they came. Frank stayed in place.

"My new home."

The American assumed that it would only be a matter of time before Roberto would be tapped for the burial detail. A strapping young man, in good health, would be an obvious candidate for the job. If Frank knew Roberto at all, the young man would jump at the chance to leave the prison and perhaps escape. The American took refuge behind a nearby boulder, large enough to hide his presence but close enough for an ambush. Roberto's assignment as a grave digger might not occur for days. Frank could not know for sure.

He settled in for a long wait.

Roberto, with nothing to keep him occupied, studied the movement of guards for hours at a time.

The unexpected arrival of two guards at dusk got his attention. The older of the two searched the interior. He tapped one of the inmates on the shoulder. Neither of them said a word. They appeared to know, in advance, what the other one wanted. Roberto wondered if the prisoner would soon be executed. When the man returned, hours after sunset, the teenager stepped forward.

"I thought you might not return."

The inmate, hot, sweaty, and covered with dirt, shook his head.

"They needed a gravedigger."

Roberto's eyebrows arched.

"Does that happen often?"

The prisoner rolled his eyes.

"Someone dies in this hellhole almost every day. It stinks in here as it is. We don't need the smell of rotting flesh."

Thoughts of escape raced through Roberto's brain.

"Would you like a break?"

"What do you mean?"

"I'd like to take your place."

"I know what you're thinking."

Roberto smiled.

"I'm bored."

"Two guards, both with rifles and machetes. You don't stand a chance."

"I'd like to try."

"You are a brave young man and you are a very stupid young man."

Roberto's grin turned into a glare.

"That's my problem. Not yours."

"If I refuse, I'll get shot."

Roberto stepped forward, poking the man's chest.

"You'll be just as dead if you refuse me."

"I'll see what I can do."

Two days went by before another prisoner succumbed to illness.

Roberto knew him. An older man, formerly a government clerk. His crime, objecting when a soldier stole his lunch, cost him his life. When the guards made their usual rounds in the midafternoon, Roberto pointed to the dead man's body.

"He's dead."

The guards turned their heads in the direction of the body and left without comment. At dusk, they returned, one of them searching for the previous evening's gravedigger. The remaining guard stood near the unlocked gate. Roberto walked briskly to the gate.

"Halt or I shoot."

Roberto slowed to a stop.

"I have some money. Do you have any cigarettes?"

The guard snarled.

"No. Now step back."

Roberto retreated but remained in full view, a short distance from the gate.

The second guard emerged from the darkness.

"The sonofabitch is hiding."

The guard by the gate pointed to Roberto.

"How about this one?"

Roberto looked up. He thought it wise to resist.

"I'm not going anywhere."

"You will do as you are told or you will be shot."

Roberto looked up and away. He did not want the guards to see his grin.

Frank, unwilling to admit defeat, secured more provisions.

He vowed to remain at his temporary camp for days, if necessary. A combination of dried meat and a shot of rum pushed Frank into an uneasy slumber as darkness fell on the abandoned cane field. Voices, and the noise of wheels on a hardscrabble road, and jostled him awake. The burial detail for Morro Castle inched its way onto the field. When the guards' torch illuminated their volunteer grave digger, Frank easily recognized the facial profile and lean, muscular body of his young rebel friend.

Roberto lifted each corpse from the wagon and gently placed them on the ground. A guard handed the boy a shovel. Roberto dug without objection. After ten minutes, he stopped and threw his shovel to the ground.

"I'm taking a break."

One of the guards stepped forward and shoved the butt of his rifle into Roberto's midriff. Roberto fell to his knees, gasping for air.

"Dig or you will die," said the soldier.

Frank moved toward the guards, certain that his blade would do the job. The guard that struck Roberto wore a cocky smile.

"Are you enjoying your break?"

Roberto caught his breath. The guard carelessly lowered the barrel of his rifle. Roberto slapped the rifle to one side, jumped to his feet, and pushed his attacker to the ground. Frank pulled his knife. Roberto jumped the guard and the two of them wrestled for control of the weapon. The second guard stepped forward. Frank's blade flew through the night air. Roberto overpowered his opponent and took possession of the Mauser. Frank's knife plunged deep into the second guard's back. The injured guard dropped to his knees and fell face forward into the pile of dirt. Roberto's attacker put his hands up in surrender. Frank yelled.

"Don't shoot him. You'll wake up half the city."

Roberto barked.

"On your knees."

Frank pulled the bloody weapon from his victim's back. Roberto smirked,

"Good evening, Frank. What a nice surprise."

"No one has ever called me nice."

"Tie him up," said Roberto, pointing to the terrified guard.

"Sure thing," said Frank.

Frank approached the kneeling officer from the rear. He did not have a rope.

"Hands behind your back."

The soldier complied. He pulled the guard's head back, exposing the man's neck. The mercenary's blade sliced his victim's throat from ear to ear. Roberto heard the man gurgle. The guard fell to one side and rolled into the shallow grave. Roberto could see the man's terrified face in the flickering light.

"What the hell are you doing, Frank?"

"We're taking the guards with us."

"Why?"

"I don't want half the Spanish army following us."

Roberto swallowed his nausea and loaded the bodies.

Isabella, escorted to the *Antonio Lopez* by four armed guards, did not resist.

As she waited to board, the weeks in Cuba flashed in her mind like a series of paintings. Her near-death experience with yellow fever, the arguments with her uncle, the tumultuous encounters with Roberto, and the constant stream of hungry, sick, and dying soldiers, all took their toll on the young woman. Her initial reasons for accompanying her uncle—adventure, endless shopping, and plenty of men to flirt with—faded into the background.

She would return to Spain a different woman. For reasons she did not fully understand, her endless toil amongst row after row of helpless patients triggered a level of achievement, gratification, and empowerment previously unknown to the girl. Her job as a nurse brought no compensation, great sacrifice, and utter exhaustion at the end of insufferably long days. And yet, her memories of those times made her long for those times. Although she would return to an opulent, carefree lifestyle in Spain, she did not relish the thought. Isabella brushed the guards aside.

"I can manage, thank you."

She reached for the tiny piece of luggage that contained her extra dress, some undergarments, and a few toiletries. With guards surrounding her, she boarded the steamer. Isabella remained on deck, seated at a bench, observing the animated discussion between the captain of the ship and the Captain of the Guard. The boat captain yelled at the uniform. Isabella could not discern the nature of their dispute. She rose to her feet when the senior guard approached. The three remaining guards pointed to the bench.

"Sit."

She apologized to the Captain of the Guard.

"My uncle taught me to stand when greeting a member of her Majesty's army."

The captain ignored her remark.

"I have been informed by the ship's captain that the *Antonio Lopez* will not leave the dock until tomorrow morning. There appears to be a mechanical malfunction with the boiler."

Isabella chuckled. Her eyes sparkled.

"My uncle will never be rid of me," she said.

The captain shouted to his men.

"The three of you will remain with the girl. You are not to let her out of your sight. Is that understood?"

A chorus of "yes, sirs" cut through the morning fog.

"If the captain-general's niece should escape, all three of you will be shot."

The men looked at Isabella. They moved closer and stood at attention. Isabella took a seat on the bench. One guard took up his post on her left side, one on her right, and the third, immediately in front of her. Isabella rolled her eyes.

"Stay alert, gentlemen. I may jump over the side."

The soldiers looked straight ahead.

# Chapter Seventeen

## THE CABIN BOY

When Isabella rose in search of an onboard latrine, all three of the guards blocked her path.

"At ease, gentlemen, I wish to answer the call of nature."

She brushed them aside and disappeared into the bowels of the ship. A cabin boy directed her to the far end of the hold. On her way back to the deck, she encountered the young man once again.

"Where is the captain?" she asked.

"The captain and the crew went ashore. I am the only one here."

Isabella flashed a smile.

"Then I shall call *you* the captain."

"Captains do not have to load the cargo or clean the latrine," said the boy.

Isabella extended her hand.

"My name is Isabella."

He examined his opened hand and rubbed it on one leg of his trousers.

"My name is Roberto."

Isabella's smile vanished. She studied the young boy's ruggedly handsome features. Like her Roberto, the kid wore a perfect smile and long black hair. His piercing blue eyes searched the woman's face.

"Have I offended you, Miss Isabella?"

The beautiful woman blinked tears from her eyes. Her vision of the missing Roberto vanished as quickly as it appeared. She used both hands to wipe the moisture from her eyes.

"No. Not at all, Roberto. Could you tell me where I will be sleeping?" she asked

The boy showed her to a tiny room without windows. A straw-filled mattress, horribly stained and smelling of stale rum, lay on the floor. A chamber pot in the corner of the room would serve as her lavatory. A hook on the wall became her armoire. Isabella faked a slight smile.

"I left my bag on deck. Would you be so kind as to retrieve it for me? Oh. And tell the soldiers I will be resting for a while."

"Yes, ma'am."

Isabella stepped forward and caressed the boy's cheek with her hand.

"You remind me of a good friend of mine. He was young and handsome and so polite. Just like you. And he too, was named Roberto."

The boy blushed.

"How old are you?" she asked.

"Sixteen. Well, I will be sixteen, next month."

"When will the captain and his crew return?"

"Not until dark, ma'am."

"I will rest for a while. Please wake me in about one hour's time."

"Yes, Miss Isabella."

"Thank you."

Isabella remained dressed and lay on the dirty mattress. She thought of Roberto, imprisoned at Morro Castle. She daydreamed about the man she loved and imagined herself in his arms.

Her eyes closed.

Walter and the crew of *the USS Maine* spent their Christmas in Hampton Roads, Virginia.

Despite several attempts, Walter could not find Angel. No one answered the door at her second-floor residence. He inquired at several places and no one knew of her whereabouts. Angry and hurt, he made excuses for the woman. Illness or the death of a loved one would force her to leave, he thought. But what if she took sick? She could be seriously ill or dying, for all he knew. His frustrations grew by the day and the frequency with which he 'saw things,' also increased.

"Walter, we have new orders. We're going to Charleston!" shouted Bill.

Walter stared at the floor and mumbled.

"I've never been to South Carolina."

"You better say goodbye to your sweetheart. We will be in Charleston for at least 10 days."

Walter caught Bill's gaze. He spoke louder than usual.

"I haven't seen Angel in weeks."

Bill rested a hand on the little man's shoulder.

"I'm sorry to hear that, Walter."

"She just disappeared."

"Women can be so unpredictable," said Bill. "It's not your fault."

Walter, preoccupied with the woman, almost forgot to check the gauges. Bill started to leave.

"I don't know what to do."

"There's nothing you can do, Walter. Just focus on your job. We'll soon be in the water off Cape Hatteras. Lots of rough seas up that way."

Walter checked the gauges, again.

The cabin boy called for his sleeping passenger several times.

She didn't budge. The boy bit his lip and tiptoed into her cabin. He dropped to his knees and touched her shoulder. Her eyes opened wide. He leaned back. Isabella smiled through sleepy eyes.

"Roberto. You remembered. Thank you."

He rose to his feet and turned to leave.

"Please. Stay with me a while. We can talk."

The boy sat cross-legged on the floor, his back to the far wall.

"Please. Sit next to me. I promise not to bite."

He inched toward the woman, beads of sweat on his brow, eyes darting everywhere.

"Are you afraid of me, Roberto?"

The boy sat up straight and cleared his throat.

"No, Miss Isabella."

"Very well then, Roberto. Please tell me about yourself."

The boy feigned a cough. Isabella assumed he needed time to compose an answer. She waited patiently, her eyes wide and unblinking.

"I was born in Matanzas."

"I know where that is," she said. "A beautiful city by the water."

Isabella, now seated cross-legged on her bed and facing the boy, listened with genuine attention. The boy slowly abandoned his initial inhibitions. He talked, nonstop, about his childhood, his years on the water, the captain, and the crew. An inquiry about his family revealed that his parents died in a fire. With no siblings to care for him, the teenager survived on the streets of Havana by begging and stealing. A year ago, the captain of the *Antonio Lopez* offered him a job.

When prompted, Isabella recounted her life as a nurse, omitting any reference to her uncle.

"Why does a nurse require the presence of three soldiers?" he asked.

A guard stuck his head in the doorway. He said nothing and slammed the door behind him. Isabella used the interruption to create an excuse for her military escort. A germ of truth made it more believable.

"I nursed a wounded man back to health. He turned out to be a rebel. I have been exiled to Spain."

The cabin boy frowned but did not challenge her story. She focused on the boy as if he were Roberto Alvarez. The kid's eyes, his smile, and his animated voice reminded Isabella that a similar conversation, with her Roberto, would never happen. Roberto Alvarez would die in prison. The young Roberto that sat cross-legged, just inches from her, served as a temporary distraction for the girl. Without knowing it, the boy postponed the painful reality of her return trip to Spain. At least for today, she could hide from the miserable life that lay ahead. In her eyes, the Roberto in her cabin became the Roberto in prison.

When the boy stopped talking, she reached forward and pulled him close. Her eyes filled with tears. He held her tight.

"Miss Isabella. Why do you cry?"

She pulled back and ran fingers through his long locks. He mimicked her with trembling hands. She could feel his hot breath, quicken. She leaned forward and kissed him on the lips. He gasped; his surprise obvious. He kissed her in return, his inexperienced lips soft and warm. They held each other. Her hands cradled his head. She found his lips yet again. He discovered her cheeks, her neck and her throat. He returned to her waiting lips. A wave of passion and lust washed over her body. She pulled him onto the mattress and ripped his shirt open. He pawed at her bosom. She peppered his hairless chest with a series of erotic kisses.

"Oh Roberto. My dear, sweet Roberto."

The cabin boy, bewildered but tipsy from his first encounter with a woman, fumbled with the buttons on her dress. She reached for his pants and groped at the hardness. The boy could not catch his breath. Her hand disappeared. He groaned. His body stiffened. He squeezed both eyes shut. The boy whimpered. She could feel the spasms. And then, dampness on her hand. His breathing slowed. He turned and faced the wall. She sat next to him, a hand covering the exposed portion of her undergarment.

"Roberto?"

"Yes?"

"I'm sorry."

"You are disappointed that I am not the Roberto you love."

She pulled him in her direction.

"No. No. Don't say that. Please."

"I have not been with a woman, until today."

"Then it is good that our time together has come to an end."

"Why is it good?"

"Because. The first time you make love, you should be in love."

The boy sat up.

"It was that way for you?"

Isabella fixed her gaze on the mattress.

"I have not shared my bed with any man."

Roberto reached for her cheek and stroked the soft skin with the back of his hand.

"And when this happens, he will be, I am sure, the happiest man on this earth."

She smiled, redid the buttons, and smoothed her hair. He rose and pulled Isabella to her feet. She kissed him on both cheeks.

"I miss my Roberto. So much. Do you understand?"

"Yes, of course. But you go to Spain."

Isabella's frustration turned to anger.

"I will not go to Spain."

"You have no choice."

"I will drown in the ocean before I go to Spain."

The boy looked over his shoulder at the closed door.

"Perhaps I can help you."

"How?"

"We have a lighter. It is tied to the rear of the boat."

"And the guards?"

"I will tell them you are sleeping and that I must greet the captain."

"They will check the room."

"And they will find you sleeping."

He winked and dashed out of the room. The boy returned with several sacks of food stuffs and supplies. Roberto quickly positioned the items on her mattress and covered the lumps with a blanket.

"And now we must cut your beautiful hair."

She retrieved the stiletto in her bag. He gathered a fist full of her flaming red locks, tied it tightly, and sliced it off. He arranged the hair so that her "head" faced the wall. The exposed hair could be seen from the door. When he finished, he looked at her with a triumphant smile. She thanked him with the highest possible compliment.

"You are, indeed, the Roberto of my dreams. Thank you."

"You will see him again. Of this I am certain."

Frank and Roberto decided it would be too dangerous to remain in the vicinity of the canefield-turned-cemetery.

"Sooner or later, the security detail from Morro Castle will be dispatched. They will search for the missing guards and their missing grave digger," said Frank.

The duo navigated their ox-driven cart in the opposite direction of the docks. At strategic intervals, they disposed of the bodies, insuring their easy discovery. Frank wanted the authorities to believe that the escapees had traveled inland. Several hours later, the rebel and his mercenary friend stood in full view of the docks.

"Are we going somewhere?" asked the boy.

"Key West. My backers are there."

Roberto walked into the darkness, away from Frank. He sat on his haunches and used his finger to draw circles in the dirt.

Frank searched the horizon. He saw no sign of the *Olivette*.

"Our ride to Key West may have come and gone. We will have to wait until she reappears."

Roberto did not acknowledge the mercenary. Frank got closer.

"What's wrong?"

Roberto jumped to his feet and spun around.

"We have some unfinished business to settle."

"You mean the girl?"

"Yes."

"She was never in any danger."

"You threatened her and you threatened me. You are a blood-thirsty madman and you will do anything to overthrow the Spanish government."

Frank tried to explain.

"When we get to Key West . . ."

The boy's rising voice interrupted the American. His red face forced Frank to step back.

"And that's another thing. Why am I taking orders from you? Your family wasn't slaughtered by the government soldiers, mine was. As far as I'm concerned there isn't much difference between you and the government soldiers. The rebels do as much harm to the Cuban people as the Spanish do."

Roberto paced the ground as he tried to catch his breath. Frank's eyes darted everywhere. He avoided eye contact with the boy.

"Look, kid, if it's money you want, I can't give you anything right now, but the folks in Key West have a lot of money. We can make a big request. I promise."

"Yeah. Sure. You get the money and I get my head shot off."

Frank changed the subject.

"It's gonna be light soon. We need a hiding spot."

Roberto didn't budge. Frank pleaded.

"Please."

Frank directed the young rebel to an old tobacco warehouse. It lay empty because Captain-General Weyler ended the export of tobacco. Roberto continued to fume. They untethered the oxen and shooed the animals away. The ox cart, now tipped on its side and lying against the rear wall of the warehouse, would make a suitable shelter.

The two fugitives from justice could not be seen by passersby but lay less than a half mile from the docks.

Tragedy struck the *USS Maine* long before it sailed into Charleston Bay.

In the ship's hold, Walter could feel the pitch and roll of the ship as it encountered one giant sea swell after another. He estimated that the battleship rolled at least 20 degrees on either side of its vertical. When his shift ended, the battleship, now in warmer waters, pitched and rolled even more. Sleeping through it would be impossible. Walter lingered in the boiler room, secretly concerned that he might be imagining things. When the day crew straggled in, many of them bouncing against the bulkheads, Walter knew otherwise.

As the ship steamed into Cape Hatteras, excited crew members recounted the fatalities and accidents which occurred there, over the years.

"We're rolling as much as 25 degrees," said one crew member.

Anything that was not secured to the walls fell to the floor.

"This is one of the worst storms I've ever seen," said another sailor.

A loud cry from up above interrupted the chatter.

"Man overboard!"

The message, passed from one man to the next, made Walter's stomach turn. Bill Horn, with his head peering just above the hold, described the pandemonium as heavy seas broke over the bow.

"Two men overboard. A third one jumped in after them. I think one of them is Kogel."

Kogel, an apprentice second class, enjoyed widespread popularity. Life buoys, thrown over the side, would have to suffice until a port side whaler could be lowered. The crew, fighting against severe rolling and pitching, required several attempts before clearing the ship with their small boat. Despite a superhuman rowing effort, the struggle cost the victims precious minutes.

When the captain maneuvered the *Maine* portside to retrieve the whaler, the battleship wallowed in a deep trough of sea water. The ship tipped to one side, a full 45 degrees. At least two more men, on deck at the time, disappeared. Captain Crowninshield screamed over the din of crashing waves.

"Clear the deck."

After several desperate attempts, their rescue efforts ended. A ship-wide muster announced the bad news. Of the five missing men, only two survived. Ironically, the first man to be washed overboard, Kogel, escaped his encounter with the monster seas. Walter looked like death.

"Walter, are you all right?"

Bill Horn followed his friend back to the bunk room. Walter could not stop trembling.

"I'm so co-co-cold," he mumbled.

Bill pushed and pulled his eccentric friend into the hammock. He piled extra blankets on top of him, uncertain as to why

Walter would be so cold and wet. He reached for the man's clothes and brushed against the man's skin. Bone dry and warm.

"Don't leave me, Bill. I don't want to drown."

Bill closed his eyes and shook his head in despair.

Isabella, curled up in a fetal position, lay perfectly still in the bottom of the lighter.

Roberto, the cabin boy, covered the woman with a stained piece of canvas. It smelled of rotten fish. Isabella did not complain. Roberto approached the guards.

"I must greet the captain. The woman is in her room," he said.

The two guards exchanged suspicious glances. The older guard poked the boy's chest.

"You must think we are stupid. But it is you, the Cuban people, who are stupid."

The Spanish soldier brushed past the cabin boy and yelled to his partner.

"You search the rowboat. I'll search her room."

The cabin boy slow walked between the two guards. The senior guard reached Isabella's room before the second guard reached the tiny boat. The first soldier yelled his findings.

"The boy is free to leave. The woman is sleeping."

Roberto stopped and turned.

"Thank you, officers."

Isabella, after hearing the man yell, could breathe again. Roberto untethered the lighter and used an oar to push away from the ship.

"You are safe now, Miss Isabella. They can no longer see us."

She lowered the canvas to her chin. Her eyes darted in every direction.

"Roberto. You have saved my life. I am forever in your debt."

"You help the Cuban people. I am the one who is grateful."

Isabella closed her eyes and bowed her head. She looked up, her eyes filled with tears.

"I am truly blessed to have known not one, but two, very brave men."

Roberto flashed a sly grin.

"If I were older and more experienced, Miss Isabella, we might never have left your room."

Isabella giggled like a little girl. Roberto slid the rowboat alongside a small dock.

"Go. Quickly. And may God be with you."

"But the guards. What will you tell them?" she asked, hopping onto the dock.

"My captain has been delayed, again."

Roberto pushed on the dock with his oar and floated across the water. She could see the young man's silhouette against the moonlight.

Isabella gripped her bag and ran into the darkness.

Frank and Roberto waited less than a full day for the *Olivette* to reappear.

They stayed hidden while several Spanish soldiers searched the boat for contraband. Although the guards found nothing, they lingered, forcing the mercenary and the young rebel to wait until dusk. When the guards left, in search of food and drink, the two fugitives scrambled on board.

"Mr. Frank has a friend," said Captain Randall, emerging from his cabin.

Frank twisted in every direction, worried they would be discovered.

"We need a secure location. Please."

The captain scratched at the white bristles that covered his chin and cheeks.

"The boiler room. Use the canvas if you have to. It's a bit warm down there but it will cool off in a few hours."

"When do we leave?" asked Frank.

"Tomorrow. Mid-morning."

"Not soon enough," said Frank, as he motioned to Roberto.

The duo scrambled below deck and quickly fell asleep.

"Once again, there's nothing wrong with you, Mr. McDermott."

Doctor Heneberger visited Walter in the bunk room. Walter, refusing to leave his hammock for several days now, would soon be charged with insubordination. Thus far, Bill dissuaded Walter's commanding officer from punitive measures. The Lieutenant would wait until the doctor rendered an opinion.

"As far as I'm concerned, you're fit for duty," said Heneberger.

He packed his medical bag and marched out of the bunk room. Bill turned to his friend.

"Walter, I've done everything I could."

"I'm not going back. We are all going to die."

Walter's objections drowned in the noise of a loud explosion. The ship trembled. Walter screamed.

"We're going to die on this boat, Bill, I'm telling you. I've had these feelings before and I'm never wrong. We are all gonna die."

Bill scrambled down the narrow passageway and through the hatch. The scene on deck stunned the experienced sailor. The distinctive smell of artillery fire filled his nostrils. One sailor lay sprawled on the deck, his arms and upper chest covered in blood. A second man, obviously injured, sat upright screaming in pain and clutching his leg.

Bill could see Dr. Heneberger rushing to the scene. The doctor barked orders and attended to both men. Bill learned from two sailors, sent below for a stretcher, that a cartridge from a one-pound artillery gun exploded. The sailors described the episode as an accident. Word of the incident spread quickly throughout the ship. Walter saw it as confirmation of his worst nightmare.

"I'm leaving, Bill. You can't stop me. I swear to God, I'm leaving."

Bill watched as the little man shoved his few belongings into a cloth duffel bag. He felt certain that if Walter went AWOL, the unstable sailor would end up in the brig. Bill played what he thought would be his strongest card.

"Walter, what about Christopher? You can't just leave Christopher."

"He's coming with me. As soon as he shows up for dinner," said Walter, glancing at the floor beneath his hammock.

Bill grimaced, unsure of what to do or say next.

"You're going to end up in the brig, Walter. You realize that, don't you?"

"I'll be miles from here before they even discover I'm missing."

Bill pursed his lips and shook his head.

"Unless you tell on me," said Walter.

Bill refused to respond. Walter raised his voice.

"You wouldn't tell on me, would you Bill?"

Bill marched down the hallway.

"Bill?"

Bill yelled over his shoulder.

"I don't know, Walter. I don't know."

Walter, sitting on the edge of his hammock, scanned the room and the passageway.

He fingered the handle on his duffel and wiped the sweat from his brow. He liked Bill Horn. The man came to Walter's rescue on several occasions. Bill never picked on Walter. He always showed courtesy and respect. But would he report Walter's absence to the officer in charge? Walter did not know.

"Mail call."

The announcement, shouted from one sailor to the next, triggered nothing more than a yawn from Walter. He never received mail. He rechecked the area around his hammock. No sign of Christopher.

"You got a letter, Walter."

Bill Horn delivered the note with a wink and a smile.

"It's from Angel."

Walter grabbed the note, his hands shaking. Bill excused himself. Walter stared at the envelope. The return address did not include her last name but listed a New Orleans address. He ripped the envelope open.

*Dear Walter: I am very sorry that I didn't write sooner. I received a letter from my father. He said he was very sick and wanted to see me before he died. I didn't make it in time. But I found real work in New Orleans. Hope you're doing well.*

*Angel*

Walter carefully placed the missive into its envelope and slid the letter into his pants pocket.

He smiled for the entire time it took him to unpack.

Isabella dashed from one dark alley to the next.

With only a few coins on her person and nowhere to stay, she questioned her decision to remain in Havana. The woman found a temporary resting spot under the overhang of a decrepit building. The monotony of a drizzling rain transported the girl back in time. A time when personal hardships, desperate poverty, and danger were the things that other people suffered. Since her arrival in Cuba, such experiences became an almost daily occurrence. In moments, her tears mixed with raindrops. She hung her head in despair.

Loud voices and the sound of a struggle emanating from the end of the alleyway caught her attention. She dared not move. In time, the noises stopped. She walked slowly in the direction of the disturbance.

Two Spanish soldiers lay in the gutter, both severely beaten and partially stripped of their uniforms. The instincts of a nurse overruled her fear. She kneeled at the side of the first man. He suffered a deep gash on his forehead plus cuts and bruises over most of his body. She suspected a serious concussion. He groaned in pain.

The second soldier lay perfectly still, a look of fear frozen on his face. Isabella searched for a pulse. His chest did not move. She arrived too late. She removed the remains of the dead man's undergarments. They would be useful as bandages. She held her handkerchief under the pouring rain which fell from a nearby roof. It allowed her to clean the survivor's wounds. Several trips turned the puddle of water a light pink.

She dragged his limp body to the nearest wall and propped him up to a sitting position. It would be light in just a few hours, Isabella thought. She sat with the man, unwilling to abandon him.

The officer, who could easily die from his wounds, would not die alone.

# Chapter Eighteen

## CARMELITA

The *Olivette* pulled alongside the docks at Key West.

Roberto, glued to the scene unfolding before him, twisted his head in every direction. The environs of Key West, its beautiful homes, buildings of two and three stories, plus dozens of colored drivers in their open hacks, reminded Roberto of his childhood. At that time, Havana bustled with activity and the Cuban people lived in peace. In Key West, cigar factories and government buildings dotted the landscape. Newspaper reporters, starved for news about the revolution, rubbed elbows with guests and competed for their next news flash. Roberto, lost in the luxury that surrounded him, temporarily forgot the miseries which delivered him to the state of Florida.

"Wait here, I'll be right back," said Frank.

Before Roberto could object, a scrum of reporters and guests surrounded the boy.

"Did you just come from Cuba?"

"Are you a Cuban rebel?"

"Is it true that the rebels are giving up?"

"How do you feel about President McKinley taking office?"

"Are you counting on his administration for additional assistance?"

Roberto's head pivoted in the direction of each voice. He did not respond to the scattered inquiries. A beautiful woman came to his rescue.

"Gentlemen, leave the boy alone. He is my guest."

The woman, in her early thirties, wore a fine dress and long locks of yellow hair. Her string of pearls matched the oversized earrings. When she grabbed Roberto by the elbow, he followed without objection.

The lobby of the Key West hotel, modest by U.S. standards, included overstuffed chairs, a large mahogany reception desk, several couches, and a dozen circular tables with chairs. She chose a table in the far corner of the cavernous room. As they sat down, she motioned to a colored servant, dressed entirely in white.

"Tea, on ice please. For both of us. Will that be acceptable, Roberto?"

"Yes, and thank you, ma'am. You are most gracious."

"Frank Lamb is a friend of mine. Do you work for him?"

Roberto grimaced and struggled to respond. The arrival of their servant plus a long sip of tea gave him the time he required.

"I work *with* Mr. Lamb. I do not work *for* him. But I suppose that is a distinction without a difference."

"You are an educated man."

Roberto recalled his first conversation with Isabella. He leaned in her direction and snarled.

"Why do woman of means automatically assume that young Cuban men are illiterate and ignorant?"

"I have hurt your feelings, Mr. Alvarez. Please accept my sincere apologies. I will start over. My name is Carmelita Viscaya."

Roberto sighed loudly. The anger drained from his face.

"Please, call me Roberto. And it is I who should apologize to you. One should not be short-tempered after so gracious a welcome."

"Tell me about yourself, Roberto."

Roberto spoke in a soft voice about the murder of his family, his meetings with Isabella, Elena's death, his fake execution, his time in prison, and his escape.

Carmelita, mesmerized by Roberto's tragic tale of woe, reached across the table and held the boy's hand.

"So much suffering and yet so young."

Roberto studied his empty glass of iced tea.

"I see you have met Carmelita."

Roberto and his host snapped to attention when Frank appeared at their table. Frank reached for a third chair and turned to the woman.

"Our friend has not yet checked in."

She shrugged.

"He does not wish to invest in a losing cause," she said.

Frank's ears turned red. He yelled at a nearby servant.

"Rum and a cigar. Now."

The servant bowed and scurried across the lobby.

"And my own funds are limited," she added.

Frank leaned forward, a sense of urgency in his voice.

"The rebels will be victorious. McKinley's election makes it a near certainty."

Carmelita looked at Roberto and turned to Frank. Her eyes flashed.

"Then we do not require your services, do we, Mr. Lamb?"

Roberto concluded that Carmelita represented the "backers" to which Frank continually referred. The colored man placed a small glass of amber colored liquid in front of Frank. The American grabbed the glass and, with two large gulps, consumed its contents. He retrieved the cigar and yelled again.

"I need a goddamn match."

The woman ignored Frank's rude behavior and turned to Roberto.

"And you, my friend. What are your plans?"

"I wish to go to Spain."

"Why?"

Roberto blushed. He took a deep breath but the words did not come. She reached for his hand again, leaned forward, and smiled.

"Did I mention that I have a soft spot in my heart for handsome young men from Cuba?"

Roberto grinned.

"Her name is Isabella. I am . . ."

Frank interrupted the boy.

"He's in love with the Butcher's niece. And now he wants to chase her all the way back to Spain. A stupid idea if you ask me," he grumbled.

Roberto slammed his empty glass of iced tea on the table. Carmelita hissed.

"Is there no one in this miserable world that you care about, Frank? Other than yourself?"

"The boy isn't thinking straight."

Roberto jumped to his feet. His chair skidded across the wooden floor. His lips flared and the boy's eyes drilled into Frank's head. Clenched fists, poised for action, hung on either side of his muscular frame. Carmelita stepped between them.

"Nobody asked you, Frank."

Frank pointed to his chin.

"Go ahead kid. Take your best shot."

A tense silence bathed the hotel lobby. Dozens of guests gawked at the threesome. Carmelita reached for each man's shoulder.

"Gentlemen. Please sit down."

She gently pushed them into the chairs. Roberto sat first. Frank followed. He challenged Roberto again.

"I should have let you rot in Morro Castle."

"You are the reason I was taken prisoner, in the first place. And I got *myself* out of Morro Castle. All you ever did was leave me for dead in a hospital full of dying soldiers."

Roberto turned to Carmelita.

"Isabella Hermoza, Weyler's niece, nursed me back to health. We fell in love."

"You left out the part where I warned you about that little witch," said Frank.

Carmelita slammed her drink on the table.

"That's enough, Frank. I think you should go for a walk. A long walk."

Frank jumped to his feet and stormed out of the lobby.

"Don't worry about him," said Carmelita. "He'll come around when he runs out of money."

"Can you help me get to Spain?"

"There's a steamer, the *Antonio Lopez*. It travels back-and-forth between Havana and Spain. It's usually loaded with

Spanish soldiers and supplies for the Spanish army. You'll have to bribe the captain. That is your only hope of getting to Spain, unless you go to New York City."

"I have no money."

"I can help with that."

"Thank you, Miss Carmelita."

"You're welcome. Now let's talk about Frank. My friends in New York City paid him a lot of money. He supposedly came very close to cutting off the head of the snake."

"The Butcher?" asked Roberto.

"Yes."

"That was me."

"Tell me all about it."

Walter could not believe his ears.

The *USS Maine* would accompany the *Texas* to the famous Mardi Gras carnival in New Orleans. There would be no time to notify Angel. Walter, like every sailor on board the *Maine*, eagerly anticipated their next assignment. They would leave on the morning of February 25, 1897. Despite lousy weather, the crew completed their assigned tasks in good spirits. Four days later, a local river pilot maneuvered the battleship up the Mississippi River and into New Orleans. By 4 o'clock that afternoon, the *Maine* lay docked, just yards from Canal Street in the heart of New Orleans.

Walter fumed when he learned that shore leave would be postponed for a few days. Captain Crowninshield ordered the sides of the ship repainted. The next day, the crew would march in the Mardis Gras parade. Only after King Rex, the leader of the carnival, made his grand appearance, would the crew receive three-day passes.

Walter made a beeline to Angel's address. He knocked repeatedly, but no one came to the door. He chose to wait at the bottom of the stairwell that led to her second story apartment. After an hour, he made inquiries of the neighbors. Most of them, still recovering from the celebration, knew nothing. Walter skipped lunch and still, the woman did not appear. At dinner time, he found a street vendor, purchased a sandwich, and hurried back to his perch on the staircase. At three in the morning, a woman's voice woke him from a restless slumber.

"Walter?"

The groggy sailor jumped to his feet. He rubbed the sleep from his eyes.

"Angel?"

"I didn't know you were coming," she murmured.

"The crew wasn't told until last week."

"Do you want to come in?"

"Yes."

"I'm sorry. I can't offer you much to eat or drink. I've been working day and night."

"Where do you work?"

"I cook at an eatery down by the water. Money's not bad but my social life is less than desirable."

"We leave day after tomorrow."

Angel plopped into a chair and exhaled loudly.

"Walter. Why are you here?"

Walter posed a question of his own.

"Why did you write that letter to me?"

Angel studied the floor. Her head jerked up and she raised her voice.

"How the hell do I know?"

"You stopped working as a prostitute."

"Yeah. What of it?"

"You did it for me."

"Don't flatter yourself."

Walter smiled.

"I want to get married."

"Oh Walter. Be sensible."

"I am the most sensible person you'll ever meet."

"You're serious, aren't you?"

"Yes."

"Walter, I have a long and checkered past."

"I don't care."

Angel groaned as she stood up.

"My feet are killing me."

"You are on your feet all day. It's to be expected."

Angel slipped out of her shoes and stood in front of Walter.

"You really don't care about my past, do you?"

"No, Angel. I don't."

"Yes."

"Yes what?"

"Yes. I'll marry you."

The first rays of sun warmed Isabella and her injured patient. She thanked God for another day.

"And please, Lord, help me help this man."

An occasional groan and the constant flutter of his eyelids told her that the Spanish officer might eventually recover from his injuries. When a detachment of officers appeared at the end of the alley, she yelled.

Four soldiers ran in her direction. She did not wait for their questions.

"The other officer is dead."

"Did you see the attack, ma'am?"

"No. I found them on the street. I've been with him all night. He needs water. And so do I," she said.

The men produced two canteens. The colonel's eyes opened. He focused on Isabella.

"Thank you."

"Get a cart. We will bring him directly to the palace," said one of the soldiers.

Isabella shook her head.

"No."

"Why not?"

The woman's mind raced.

"He may have several broken bones. Too much movement could make his injuries worse."

"You are not a doctor."

"I am an experienced nurse and you will do as I say."

The officer in her arms spoke to the men in a weak voice.

"She knows best."

They brought Isabella and her patient to a nearby government office. They cleared a large desk, using a cushion from a chair as a pillow. The colonel agreed to some bread and fruit. He instructed the soldiers to stand guard at the entrance. They were not to come inside. Isabella checked his wounds. The colonel's gaze, unrelenting, forced her to stop her ministrations.

"Is your pain getting worse?"

The colonel forced a smile.

"I am in great pain. It is temporary, I am sure. It is my great curiosity, however, that you must attend to."

Isabella removed a bloody bandage and folded the material into a perfect square. For a moment, she studied her handiwork. She frowned, crumpled the cloth into a bloody snowball, and flung it to the floor. Isabella blinked back her tears.

"Does everyone in this godforsaken place know my face?"

"A beautiful woman is hard to forget."

"I do not recall having met you."

"I am the commandant at Morro Castle."

Isabella closed her eyes.

"Yes. I remember now. You were at the so-called execution."

"That is correct."

"Is he? Is Roberto still . . . ?"

Isabella, unable to finish her inquiry, turned away.

"I do not know."

"How is that possible?"

"Your friend escaped several weeks ago."

Isabella's green eyes opened wide. A huge smile covered her face. She squeezed the colonel's hand. He groaned in pain.

"I'm sorry. I didn't mean to hurt you. Oh, but I am not sorry. My Roberto lives. You may now deliver me to the palace, or to the castle, or to Spain, or wherever you wish. Because you have made me the happiest person in all of Cuba."

The colonel did not share her joy.

"He was assigned to a burial detail. Two of our guards were killed. We do not believe he was alone. He had help. Who this other man was, we do not know. If your friend should reappear, he will be shot on sight."

Isabella scowled.

"And me? Am I to be shot on sight?"

"I am not an ungrateful man, Miss Hermoza."

"Thank you, Colonel."

"There is one more thing you should know."

"What is that?"

"Two men, one fitting the description of your friend, were seen boarding the *Olivette*. The steamer makes regular trips from Havana to Key West. In my opinion, your friend has traveled to Florida."

Isabella, her bag already packed, stood at his side. She gently pulled his hand to her lips.

"You have been most kind."

"As have you. I wish you well, my friend."

Carmelita invited Roberto to her room at the Key West Hotel.

She insisted on privacy and gave instructions she was not to be disturbed. By anyone.

"We have much to talk about," she said, pointing to a small table and two chairs.

Roberto, fascinated with the room's four poster bed, complete with mosquito netting and plenty of white lace, fell into a chair. His head pivoted in every direction as Carmelita disappeared behind a large dressing screen.

"Pardon me while I get into something more comfortable."

Roberto watched with great interest, as she draped her dress, and several undergarments, over the large wall of flowers.

She emerged in a floor-length silk robe, entirely pink, except for the white cuffs.

"I left instructions to have lunch brought to our room. I assume you are hungry."

"Yes, ma'am."

"Carmelita. Please call me Carmelita."

"Yes, Miss Carmelita."

The woman's eyes rolled to the back of her head.

"Fine. Miss Carmelita it is."

Her endless questions made Roberto squirm in his chair. She quizzed the young Cuban on every possible subject. Frank, Isabella, Captain-General Weyler, the palace, Morro Castle, the massacre at Guatao, the burial detail, and the trip to Matanzas. Roberto slowly realized that Carmelita, despite her appearance as a beautiful woman of privilege, played an important role in the revolution. When her interrogation paused for a moment, Roberto announced his conclusion.

"Your appearance, although beautiful, is deceiving, Miss Carmelita."

Carmelita understood his meaning.

"There are people in New York City who consider a free and independent Cuba of the utmost importance. I work on their behalf."

"I understand."

"Do you? Really?"

"The Spanish Army murdered my entire family. I seek justice for their crimes. But I must tell you, Miss Carmelita, the rebel army has also committed atrocities against my people.

"The situation in Cuba will soon change. President McKinley will see to it. But I need you in Cuba. As soon as possible."

"I must find Isabella. Only then, will I return to Cuba."

"I will help you to find the girl. Will you promise to help your people?"

"Yes."

"I need your word as a gentleman."

Roberto rose to his feet, hand extended. She refused his gesture, leaning forward instead. She kissed him lightly on both cheeks.

"I can think of other ways to seal this deal."

Roberto's face blushed pink. She chuckled.

"But your heart is elsewhere."

"Yes. I am afraid so."

After an awkward embrace, Angel invited Walter to sit on the edge of her bed.

She reached for his hand.

"Walter. Have you ever? I mean. Are you still? Well. You know."

Angel blushed. Even for a normally blunt woman, such inquiries proved difficult. Walter understood her meaning.

"You are my first girlfriend. I mean fiancée. Is that what you are asking?"

Angel flashed a sly smile and whispered.

"There is still time for a quick honeymoon before you report back to the ship."

Walter took a deep breath and held it. He exhaled loudly. He could feel the heat covering his face. She stood up and pulled him to his feet. She kissed him and undid the buttons on his shirt. Walter looked away. The buttons on her dress came next. He watched, mesmerized, as she removed the dress and her undergarments. Walter recalled his early days in the navy. Several of the men shared photographs of naked women. This was different. She slipped off his shirt, undid his trousers, and pulled his underwear to the floor. He used both hands to hide his excitement. She smiled.

"I've seen it all before, Walter."

Walter's eyes looked glassy. He appeared on the verge of panic.

"Angel. I'm not sure what I'm supposed to do."

"I'll teach you," she said

Walter basked in the afterglow of his first time with a woman. Angel lit a cigarette.

"You're going to miss your boat."

"I don't care if I miss my boat."

"I do. Write when you get back to Hampton Roads."

"I'm not sure if I can get shore leave or not."

"I'll find you. One way or the other."

"Write me, Angel."

"By the way, you owe me a ring."

A sly smile crossed the sailor's face.

"Sure. But I have a question."

"What?"

"Can we do it again?"

"Wait. Please."

Isabella, her hand on the door, could feel the dread rising in her stomach.

"Yes, Colonel."

The colonel removed a sock and recovered a single paper note.

"It's not much but it will get you to Key West," he said.

Isabella dropped the currency in her bag.

"Thank you, Colonel. You are most generous."

"You should know that I will not be so generous should we ever meet again."

"I understand, sir. Thank you, nevertheless."

"Please cover your head and face when you leave. My men do not know your identity. I prefer that we keep it that way."

Isabella grabbed her things and exited the building.

Frank raised his voice.

"What does that mean, that you are dealing directly with the boy?"

Carmelita leaned across the table and poked him in the chest.

"Must we have yet another scene in the lobby of this hotel? Have we not called enough attention to ourselves already?"

"I never trusted that kid."

"Have another drink, Frank, and know this. I trust him to do as he promised. Which is more than I can say for you. Besides, the girl will most likely turn him away. He'll be back."

Frank shook his head.

"You are assuming that he secures passage on the *Antonio Lopez*. It's a government vessel, for Christ sakes."

"He is an engaging and creative young man. And from what I have learned, he has no fear."

"I will not argue with you on that point. But this obsession with Weyler's niece is dangerously stupid."

"He is in love, Frank. You should try it sometime."

"I'd like to try her, some time."

"You're a pig, Frank."

Roberto could not remember carrying that much money on his person, at any time during his short life.

In less than two days, he secured passage on the *Olivette* and returned to Cuba. He remained hidden, although now dressed like a government clerk. The suit proved hot and itchy but Carmelita insisted on a disguise.

"You are much smarter than your enemy, Roberto. Use your brains more and your muscles less," she advised.

Roberto smiled to himself. He considered the meeting with Carmelita as nothing less than a miracle. He could now search for Isabella and plot his revenge against the Spanish army. The possibility of a reunion with Isabella took precedence over his search for justice. The lust for blood no longer burned in Roberto's belly. The suffering and dying that both he and Isabella witnessed curbed his appetite for more of the same. His honest thoughts triggered a pang of guilt. Although his thirst for revenge should be his top priority, it wasn't.

Isabella Hermoza changed all of that.

For most of the day and well into nightfall, Roberto studied the steam-powered transport.

Passage on the *Antonio Lopez*, almost always with Spanish soldiers on board, would be difficult to secure. Only the captain of the ship would have the ability to protect Roberto. Even then, bribes would be necessary. A jealous crew member or a low-ranking member of the military could ruin such an arrangement. Would they remain silent when they discovered a rebel on board their ship? Any one of them could trigger Roberto's execution.

When the captain and his crew left the ship, Roberto noticed that the Spanish soldiers also vacated the vessel. A lone cabin boy wandered the deck performing a series of manual duties. Roberto calculated that a poorly compensated cabin boy would require a small bribe and yet possess a great deal of useful information.

"I seek passage to Spain. Can you help me?"

"We do not leave for Spain for three days. You must speak to the captain."

Roberto grabbed the boy's hand, pressing a coin into the kid's palm.

"I would prefer to speak with you."

"I have nothing to tell. The soldiers are mean, sometimes cruel. The *Antonio Lopez* is a military transport. Our kind is not welcome here."

Roberto extended his hand and gave the boy another coin.

"Tell me, my friend. Do they transport prisoners?"

"Yes."

"Female prisoners?"

The cabin boy stepped back. His eyes grew wide with fear.

"You work for the government. That is why you question me."

The boy tossed the coins at Roberto's feet.

"I refuse to help you."

Roberto picked up the coins and placed them on a nearby trunk. He scanned his surroundings, confirming their privacy.

"Her name is Isabella. She was delivered to Spain against her will."

"I know nothing about this beautiful woman you call Isabella."

Roberto smiled.

"I never said she was beautiful."

The boy's face reddened. Roberto laughed out loud.

"She is the niece of Captain-General Weyler. And I am in love with her."

The cabin boy blanched. He fell back onto the trunk. His chest heaved.

"You are Roberto."

"I trust she made it safely to Spain."

The boy's terror-stricken face triggered Roberto's worst nightmare. He lunged at the boy, pulled him off the trunk and slammed him against the bulkhead.

"Tell me the truth, boy. Did she make it to Spain or not?"

The boy shook his head, slowly, from one side to the other. He silently mouthed the mouth word no. Roberto fell to his knees.

"My poor, beloved, Isabella."

The cabin boy spoke in an urgent whisper.

"No. No. You don't understand. She remains in Havana. She escaped the ship. I helped her."

Roberto's head jerked up. He jumped to his feet and wiped the moisture from his eyes. He made a clumsy effort to smooth the boy's shirt.

"She lives? Are you certain of this?"

"Yes. I am certain. And . . ."

The boys voice trailed off.

"And what?"

The cabin boy smiled.

"And I am also certain that she loves you very much."

Roberto offered the boy a fistfull of coins.

"No. I refuse your money. Miss Isabella is a kind and gracious woman. She cares for the Cuban people. It is an honor to help her."

Roberto extended a hand. The boy returned the handshake but did not immediately release his grip.

"Find her. Please. There are government soldiers everywhere. She is not safe."

Roberto ran into the darkness shouting for joy.

"I will find you, Isabella. I will find you find you no matter where you go."

# *Chapter Nineteen*

## ᛏHE ᛁNGLATERRA ᚼOTEL

Isabella rushed to the docks at Havana Bay.

Although unlikely to find Roberto with the *Olivette*, she arrived intent on talking with the captain or a crew member. Learning the precise day on which Roberto left for Key West, would be helpful. Her visit came with risks. The *Antonio Lopez* would be docked nearby. She would need to exercise great caution. Spanish soldiers would be everywhere.

Her hair, still short from the cabin boy's labors, would fool some people. She wanted more insurance against the possibility of being discovered. Isabella stopped in an alleyway and used mud and animal dung, she guessed it was from oxen, to spoil her appearance and ward off anyone who might get close. Her dress, looking shabby already, and looked more so after she ripped it.

When the docks came into view, she could see the *Antonio Lopez*, it being one of the larger ships in the bay. She avoided the steamer and searched for the *Olivette*. Isabella did not know the ship. She watched for passengers, instead. Men and women, wealthy enough to pay for passage to Key West. Her perch, behind a storage building not far from the water's edge, gave her the panoramic view she required. After several hours, her empty stomach growling in protest, she thought more about food and drink than she did Roberto. The money given to her by the grateful colonel, did not last long.

When she prepared to leave, hoping to secure some water, Isabella spied a man, dressed like an American. He walked rapidly, his head pivoting in every direction. When he got closer, Isabella's hand jerked to her mouth. She smothered an involuntary scream. Isabella dared not call his name. This man once threatened to kill her. He treated women like dirt. Her stomach growled in protest. Such logic did nothing to ameliorate her need for food and water. Although her instincts said otherwise, she yelled at him.

"Frank."

He didn't hear her.

"Frank. Over here."

He glanced in the woman's direction, hesitated, and resumed walking. She persisted.

"Frank Lamb."

The sound of his last name brought him to a standstill. She waved him over and ducked behind the building. Isabella waited for him to appear. He should be here by now, she thought. She inched toward the corner of the building. An unseen hand yanked her backward. The point of a knife pinched the skin on her neck.

"Who are you and what do you want?"

She remembered the voice that so often irritated her in the past.

"Frank. It's me, Isabella. Now get that knife off my neck."

"You smell awful."

Isabella faced him. Her eyes flashed.

"My preference is to kill you but I haven't eaten in several days."

Frank sat down, his back to the building, searching his haversack. He handed the starving woman some dried meat and a canteen of water.

"You were wise to disguise yourself. Does Weyler know you are still in Cuba?"

"Not sure," she said in between bites.

"I wouldn't want to be the armed guards who saw you off," Frank chuckled.

"Me neither," she said, wolfing the meat down and taking several large gulps of water.

"How did you know I'd be on the *Olivette*?"

"I didn't. I wanted to speak to the crew. Ask them about Roberto."

"He's here in Havana. Left two days before I did."

Isabella stopped chewing.

"I was told by a friend that he and another man were seen boarding the *Olivette* for Key West."

"That was us, about a week ago.

Isabella swallowed a burp.

"Why did he come back to Havana? He'll be shot on sight."

Frank groaned.

"Why did you stay in Havana?"

Isabella combed her hair with the fingers of one hand. She glanced at her dress and used a sleeve to wipe her muddy face.

"I'm in love with a rebel, Frank. Can you believe it?"

"He's been promoted. Can you believe that?"

"Promoted?"

"My backers gave him enough money to find you in Spain. After that, his orders are to disrupt and, if possible, overthrow the Spanish government in Cuba."

"Roberto? He's just one man."

"He thinks you're in Spain, by the way."

"Oh, God, No. Please no."

"Cheer up. There is no way he gets on the *Antonio Lopez*. It is a government transport ship. Troops and supplies. He would need to sneak past half the Spanish army."

"How do I find him?"

"I wish I knew. I'm guessing he reports back to Key West."

"What about you? What are your orders?"

"Oh, I'm just a nobody now. They gave me just enough money to eat. My orders are to find General Gomez and do what I can to help him."

"Gomez?"

"Yes. He's the rebel leader now. Maceo got himself killed."

"What do you have in mind?"

"I'm thinking we need something that will get the United States involved."

"I don't understand."

"An attack on American assets or American personnel."

"You're playing with fire, Frank."

"Maybe. But I've got nothing to lose at this point."

They sat in silence.

Isabella's eyes fluttered shut. Her head fell to one side and rested on Frank's shoulders. Despite her appearance and the foul odor, Frank could feel the desire stirring in his groin. He ran his fingers through her dirty hair. She slept soundly. He caressed her cheeks and held her hand in his.

She needed him. And he wanted her. An erotic fantasy took shape in Frank's mind.

"I must have fallen asleep."

Isabella stretched and yawned.

"You've been sleeping for two hours," said Frank.

"Well, I am rested now. Where are we going?"

"We?"

"Aren't you going to search for Roberto?"

"He's a big shot now. Doesn't need me. I am supposed to find Gomez and do what I can to help him."

"Where is Gomez?"

"Hiding in Western Cuba. I'm not even sure I can get through. The Spanish army is in control almost everywhere."

"I'd like to get cleaned up," she said.

Frank sensed an opportunity.

"There's an American hotel not too far from the U.S. Consul's place. It would be safe."

"Let's go."

The thought of sharing a hotel room with Isabella sent Frank into a sexual frenzy.

Walter reboarded the *Maine*, thinking his next stop would be Hampton Roads, Virginia.

Instead, Captain Crowninshield announced orders to Port Royal, South Carolina. The new destination would cost Walter more than two weeks. He posted a letter to Angel in South Carolina. Because he did not know it himself, Walter could not inform her as to when and where he would next arrive.

"I bought a ring too."

Bill Horn's eyes blinked repeatedly.

"Walter. I am stunned. You proposed marriage. She said yes. You bought a ring. And did I hear you say that you already went on the honeymoon?"

Walter grinned from ear to ear.

"Well, we only had a few hours before morning muster and we . . ."

Walter's voice disappeared as he drowned in a daydream of erotic desire. His eyes glazed over. He wet his dry lips. Bill poked the man's chest.

"Walter? Walter! Are you ill?"

Walter's fantasy came to an abrupt halt. He muttered his disappointment.

"Oh. Bill. I forgot. You're still here."

Bill glared.

"Yes, I'm still here. And you better get going. Your shift starts in five minutes."

Roberto, still at the docks, took great pains to remain hidden.

He searched for and found a suitable hiding place, behind a pile of rotting wood. Skeletons of abandoned boats. The pile of rubble served as a memorial for those days when Havana harbor bustled with activity. Despite a limited view of the entire area, he enjoyed easy access to the boats, especially after dark.

The whereabouts of Isabella dominated his thinking. He considered a mental checklist of her most likely hiding places.

Area hospitals, Morro Castle, if she thought Roberto was still a prisoner, and the palace. Seeing her uncle would be as risky as visiting the castle. And finally, the waterfront. But only if she believed Roberto would be traveling off the island. That last thought made his head spin. What if Isabella lay in waiting, at the docks, just like he did?

In the end, he decided to use the docks as his base of "operations" and check out the army hospitals that dotted the immediate area. Her compulsion to serve soldiers, on both sides of the Cuban struggle, would make the hospitals Isabella's most likely choice.

Roberto dusted off his disguise as a government clerk and began the search. Ox carts, carrying soldiers dead or alive, would show him the location of hospitals and burial grounds. When one of the carts came into view, he approached the driver. The odor emanating from the driver's cargo, told Roberto the cart was headed for a burial site.

"I have been sent to inspect the hospitals which serve the bay. I was told there is one, nearby. But I cannot seem to locate it."

"There are three on this road. Good luck," said the driver, pointing in the opposite direction.

Roberto appeared at the first hospital. He found nothing more than a large tent, crowded with sick and wounded. The stench of human waste, rotting flesh, and sweat, filled the air. He noted two women. Neither of them looked like Isabella. Roberto left as quickly as he arrived.

His next stop produced similar results. After the third hospital and still no sign of Isabella, he continued several miles in every direction. He limped back to the docks, feet aching and stomach empty.

A telegram to Carmelita, explaining his dilemma, would be necessary. She gave him strict instructions to solicit the U.S. Consul's office. They knew how to access the cable office and get a coded telegram to Key West. Roberto, not yet prepared to give up his search for Isabella, considered the alternatives. He could remain at the docks for several days longer or he could explore the other locations where Isabella might be found. He drifted off to sleep, uncertain as to what he would do next.

He dreamed of Isabella.

Isabella did her best to look presentable, as she and Frank walked under the cover of darkness to the Hotel Inglaterra.

First opened in 1865, and just yards from several government buildings, the Inglaterra catered to Americans. The U.S. Consul, Fitzhugh Lee, a descendent of the famous confederate general, did not hide his support for the Cuban rebels. Nor did he disguise his dislike for Captain-General Weyler.

Frank instructed Isabella to wait outside while he registered for a room. The long walk across the hotel lobby and one flight of stairs, made Isabella blush. Her downcast eyes followed Frank's feet until his key turned in the door. She rolled her eyes when she saw the single large bed in the room. Isabella, thinking only of a hot bath, reserved her complaints for later. A black servant girl helped the filthy woman with towels and toiletries. The servant also knew where to obtain a simple dress for a handful of pesos. Frank agreed. Isabella luxuriated in the hotel bath, for more than an hour. When she emerged, wrapped in towels because of her damp undergarments, Frank's voice choked with lust.

"You are the most attractive part of this dirty little war," he said.

Isabella sat on the bed, using the covers to conceal her exposed calves and feet. Frank rushed to the door.

"I'll be right back," he yelled over his shoulder.

Isabella enjoyed her newfound lodgings and relaxed. Frank returned just as her heavy eyelids closed.

"I've taken the liberty to have our dinner brought to the room."

He brandished a bottle of wine, holding it aloft so Isabella could see the ornate label. Isabella could feel the goosebumps on her neck.

"You *are* the Frank Lamb that wanted me tortured and killed, are you not?"

Frank's smile looked artificial.

"I never would have gone through with it, Isabella. I simply used you as leverage. I was doing my job. From now on, we are friends."

Frank's wide-open eyes focused on her exposed shoulders.

"Good friends."

"He filled two glasses with the red liquid and delivered them bedside.

"To the most beautiful woman I know," he said, clinking his glass against hers.

Isabella squirmed. She took a modest sip and slid off the bed.

"I think my undergarments are dry."

Isabella shut the bathroom door and frowned when she noticed the absence of a lock. She relaxed a bit when she heard the door open and a female voice. A knock on the bathroom door triggered a nervous response.

"Who is it?"

"Oh, for Christ sakes, who do you think it is?"

"Sorry."

"Your dress is here."

She opened the door a sliver and put her hand in the crack.

"Don't you want to see it first?" Frank asked.

"It's fine, Frank"

"Let me show it to you."

He pushed against the door.

"Frank, I'm not dressed."

She used both hands to cover her scantily clad bosom, forcing her to lean against the door. He overpowered her with ease. Frank held the dress in front of him. He peered over the top of the garment. She grabbed the dress with one hand and held it to her chest.

"Thank you, Frank. Now please excuse me while I finish dressing."

He leaned to one side, against the wall. His glassy eyes studied her perfect form.

"Frank. I said leave."

At first, he said nothing. And then he whispered, his voice drenched with lust.

"I would like to watch."

Isabella stabbed the air with her index finger.

"Leave, Frank, before you do something we both regret."

Frank stepped forward. He caressed her bare shoulder and continued to speak softly.

"After all, I fed you. I bought the dress for you. I paid for the room, the wine, and dinner. Wouldn't you like to show your gratitude, Isabella?"

He moved closer, tugging playfully on her towel.

"Isabella. You deserve much, much more than an inexperienced, teenaged rebel."

She raised her right hand. His lust blinded him to the threatening gesture. The loud crack of her open hand slamming into the side of his face filled the tiny room. He winced in pain and yelled.

"You spoiled little bitch!"

Frank backhanded the woman, sending Isabella falling to the floor. She screamed. The towel fell away. Her breasts lay exposed. He swallowed hard and licked his dry lips. She scrambled to her feet. A confident smile crossed his face. She kicked him in the groin. Her bare foot found its target. Frank groaned and fell to his knees. He clutched his private parts. She rushed past him, retrieved the dress, and ran from the bathroom. Isabella struggled with her undergarments and the dress, ignoring the buttons. She paused at the top of the stairs and stepped into her shoes. In seconds, she found refuge in a back alleyway. Her face contorted and she spit the awful taste in her mouth.

The dull gray surface of the walkway contrasted sharply with the deep red color of her blood.

After two weeks in South Carolina, the *USS Maine* departed for its home port of Hampton Roads, Virginia.

Walter, anticipating a visit with Angel, just assumed that Captain Crowninshield would grant a few days of shore leave. The request for shore leave came back denied. Crowninshield had been replaced.

Captain Charles Dwight Sigsbee resembled an aged professor more than he did a Navy veteran of 34 years. The bespectacled, white haired, 52-year-old man wore a handlebar mustache and rarely smiled. He demanded strict adherence to the Navy's rules, regulations, and protocols. Sigsbee took control of the *USS Maine* as the handpicked choice of Navy brass. The folks in Washington, DC, ever mindful of the deteriorating situation in Cuba, wanted a sure and steady hand at the helm of its finest battleship.

His mission, to rectify the battleship's checkered past, began on day one. Only after a lengthy series of inspections and follow-up tasks, did Walter receive his two-day pass. He waited for Angel at the tavern, their agreed-upon meeting place. He also knocked on the door at her old apartment. A strange man answered and chased Walter away. Walter blamed the post office for failing to deliver his letter to Angel. Mostly, he blamed the U.S. Navy. He muttered to himself on his way back to the ship.

"I should have walked off that ship when I had the chance."

Roberto arrived at the U.S. Consulate's office without incident.

His suit, although warm and itchy, gave him a nondescript appearance, as he walked among dozens of government employees. He announced his presence to the receptionist and informed her of his telegram for Carmelita Viscaya. The woman jumped to her feet and escorted Roberto to a tiny office. She left and reappeared moments later with a middle-aged man wearing a suit, not unlike Roberto's.

"May I see the telegram, sir?"

Roberto took a moment to reread the message he composed that morning.

*Nurse remains in Cuba, whereabouts unknown. Search will continue as feasible. Available as required. Please advise.*

The clerk required only seconds to review the message and left the room without comment. When he returned, he said little.

"The telegram has been sent. Good day, Mr. Alvarez."

"How did you know my name?"

The clerk smiled and left. In moments, the woman at the receptionist desk arrived.

"I will show you to the door, Mr. Alvarez."

Roberto walked slowly as he left the consul's office. A dozen questions swirled in his head. Who, exactly, does Carmelita work for? From where did they get their money? Is the United States officially assisting the rebel cause? And what are they expecting of me?

A disturbance, a hundred yards ahead of him, derailed his confused train of thought. Two soldiers, a civilian man, and a woman, appeared to be arguing. Roberto continued to walk in their direction. Their voices grew louder. The civilian man gesticulated, wildly. Roberto, still yards away, watched as the woman pushed the civilian away. Her victim wagged a finger at the soldiers and yelled.

"Bring her to the palace, at once."

The two uniforms turned their backs on the man. They talked quietly, punctuating their remarks with furtive glances at the woman. She wore her red hair short and looked dangerously thin in her drab grey dress. When she turned to leave the group, the civilian grabbed her by the arm. She spun in place and slapped him in the face. Hard. The blow sent the man sprawling. Roberto grinned and ran in their direction.

"Officers. I can explain. This is my sister, Juanita. She is delusional. Has been since we were children. She is in my care but I was delayed at the U.S. Consul's office. Please forgive me. I will take her home, immediately."

The civilian scrambled to his feet, rubbing the handprint on his cheek.

"I'm telling you. She is the niece of his Excellency, the captain-general."

The soldiers refused his entreaty and turned to the woman.

"You are free to go."

"Come with me, sister, and we will have lunch together."

Isabella, tears streaming down her cheeks, followed in silence.

Walter jumped from his hammock, screaming.

He rubbed his neck, certain that someone tried to strangle him while he slept. The bunk room appeared empty. Christopher the rat, also absent, most likely left when Walter yelled. *A nightmare* thought Walter. But maybe not. Several hours later, at his usual post, Bill Horn appeared in the doorway.

"Hi Walter. How are you doing today?"

Walter stepped closer.

"Do you see any finger marks or thumb prints on my neck?"

Bill tilted his head and peered at Walter's lily-white neck.

"No. Not really. Why? Did something happen?"

"I am certain that someone tried to strangle me while I was sleeping."

Bill groaned.

"Oh Jesus. Not that again, Walter. You are imagining things. Next, you're going to tell me that the queen of Spain is on the poop deck."

Walter stuck his lower lip out, turned away, and grumbled.

"You are my only friend on this miserable ship. Why can't you believe me?"

Bill threw his hands up, took a deep breath, and spoke calmly.

"Walter. Listen to me. Please. You are under a great deal of stress. I am sure this thing with Angel is getting to you."

Walter whirled around and thrust an accusing finger at his only friend.

"It's not a thing, Bill."

"I know. I know. I'm just saying that when you're stressed, you get a little confused. That's all."

"I am not confused. And another thing. This guy, Sigsbee, gives me a bad feeling."

"He seems fine to me. Not the friendly type but they say he runs a tight ship."

"I'm thinking of leaving, Bill. For good."

Bill shoved a finger in Walter's face.

"Walter, another word out of you about going AWOL and I will throw you overboard myself."

Frank required minutes before he could rise from the floor.

He dropped his pants and conducted an examination. No blood but lots of swelling. It made walking difficult. He hobbled to the front desk and complained about the condition of the room. His voice grew louder. He demanded a full refund.

"This place is a pigsty and unfit for occupancy," Frank lied. "I intend to warn all of my American friends."

Rather than risk a noisy scene, the manager complied. He breathed a sigh of relief when the "Americano" left the lobby. Frank discovered a lodging place more suitable to his limited budget. The boarding house, a dozen blocks away, lay in the middle of Havana's ghetto. Once in the room, Frank tended to his injury. A wet towel, not nearly cold enough, pressed against his genitals, provided some relief. The swelling remained and the throbbing pain continued. He cursed Isabella and vowed his revenge. A more pressing matter, however, consumed his thinking.

He contemplated the loss of funding for his mission. It made matters much more difficult. In the end, it didn't matter. With or without the support of his backers, Frank intended to strike at the heart of the Spanish government. He recalled the American guards, posted at the U.S. Consul's building. Frank wondered why Captain-General Weyler would tolerate the presence of Fitzhugh Lee. Lee made no secret of his support for the rebel cause. Clearly the Spanish government did not want to antagonize the Americans.

Frank bolted upright in bed, groaning from the pain. He allowed a slight smile to cross his face. U.S. intervention. That is precisely what this rebellion required. Frank could trigger American involvement in the revolution with an attack on the consul's office. If properly executed, the Spanish government would get the blame. There would be an immediate U.S. response. Frank's mind raced. How to make the attack appear Spanish in origin? Where to find a few sticks of dynamite? And how to accomplish the attack without being caught? His scheme would require a great deal of planning. But Frank convinced himself it could be done.

He soon forgot the pain in his groin.

Isabella and Roberto walked for two blocks and ducked down an alley way.

Isabella smiled through her tears. She threw her arms around his neck and pulled him forward. He held her face in his hands and hesitated. He kissed her, gently at first, but then, with great passion. She responded in kind. When he pulled back, they said the same thing at the same time.

"I love you."

"What happened back there?" he asked.

"The civilian recognized me. I remembered him from the palace. So, I said nothing. That's when he summoned the soldiers and demanded I be brought to the palace. I told him no. He insisted. I slapped him."

Roberto stared in her eyes.

"And that is the precise moment I recognized you, Isabella. I recall a similar incident."

"Bad habit. I'm sorry."

"We must get you off the streets, Isabella. I know just the place."

"Where?"

There is a hotel near the U.S. Consul's office, less than a block from here. They cater to Americans. It's called the Inglaterra.

She yanked her hand from his.

"No. I won't go there."

"Why not?"

"I ran into Frank at the docks. I was hungry, dirty, and tired. He fed me, took me to the hotel, and got me some clothes. I should have guessed his intentions when he ordered dinner and bought a bottle of wine."

"What happened?"

Isabella's eyes narrowed to slits.

"He insisted on dessert before the main course."

The large vein on Roberto's neck came to life. He clenched and unclenched his fists.

"I'll kill him. I'll kill him with my bare hands."

"I can handle myself, Roberto. When I left, he was clutching at his private parts and throwing up."

Roberto pulled her into his arms.

"Are you sure you are not injured?"

"I'm sure."

"You will be safe at the hotel. Besides, he's not there anymore. I am certain of that."

"How do you know?"

"He cannot afford to stay at a hotel like the Inglaterra. His backers cut him off. I'm surprised he brought you there in the first place."

"I think it was part of his plan."

"No doubt."

"How can *you* afford to stay there?"

"I now have more money than I need, Isabella. Now, let's get to the hotel before someone else recognizes you."

"You didn't say anything about my hair."

"I fell in love with your eyes, Isabella. And you are still the most beautiful woman in the world."

She stood on her toes and kissed him.

"And you, my handsome knight in shining armor, you are the most wonderful man in the world."

Roberto refused to leave Isabella's side.

Despite the hotel clerk's raised eyebrows, the young couple secured both a room and some food.

Isabella fell onto the bed and closed her eyes.

"You must be exhausted," he said.

"It has been a long and eventful day, Roberto. But my heart is full and I have never been happier."

She held her arms aloft, beckoning to Roberto. He sat on the edge of the bed and kissed both of her hands. He brushed the hair from her eyes. They kissed. She pulled him closer and smothered his head, face, and lips with passionate kisses. He drew a sharp breath and jumped to his feet.

"Roberto? What's wrong?"

He shook his head and stepped further away.

"I will not disrespect the woman I love."

Isabella rolled out of bed and smoothed her disheveled dress.

"In my lifetime, Roberto, I have shared my bed with no man. You will be the first. You will also be the last. With or without a band of gold."

Roberto fell into the nearby chair.

"I will sleep on the floor, Isabella. You will sleep on the bed. But soon, my love, we will sleep in the same bed. I promise."

# Chapter Twenty

## Poor Walter

The summer of 1897 would be a season of suffering for Walter.

It started with mail call. The seaman that delivered the letter noted its return address.

"Walter, is this Angel your girlfriend? You never told me about her. Does she look like an angel or is she ugly as the devil?"

"Get lost."

Walter ripped the letter open. He steadied his trembling hands against a nearby water pipe. He read her words several times. They did not change.

> *I am with child, Walter. And soon I will be without funds. I need your help.*

He sprang to his feet and paced the boiler room floor.

"How do I know the kid is mine? I gave her half of my money the last time we met. What am I supposed to do?"

"Do about what?" asked Bill Horn.

Walter jammed the letter into his pocket and grabbed the coal bucket.

"Nothing. I just can't seem to find my shovel."

Bill glared at the coal bucket.

"Walter. Your shovel is in the bucket."

Walter faked a giggle.

"Oh, silly me. I must be losing my mind."

"The thought has crossed my mind on more than one occasion."

Walter tried to brush past Bill. Bill stood in the man's way.

"You gonna tell me about that letter or not?"

Walter studied the floor. He shook his head, slowly, as if it pained him to do so.

"It's from Angel, isn't it?"

Walter's head jerked up.

"How did you know?"

"I didn't. Call it a lucky guess."

Walter pulled the crumpled note from his pocket and handed it to Bill. He didn't give his friend time to read the missive. He babbled, non-stop.

"Angel is with child. She wants money. How do I know it's mine? I don't have that much money left. What am I supposed to do? I think she did it on purpose. I haven't seen her in four months. We're not even married. What would you do, Bill? I think I'm just going to burn this letter. Will this Captain Sigsbee give me a week's leave when the baby comes? Jesus, Bill, what am I going to do?"

Walter came up for air. Bill, his open hands held aloft, urged calm.

"Take a deep breath, Walter."

Walter gulped a mouth full of air.

"Again."

After several minutes, his face still a ceramic white, Walter began to breathe normally.

"There is the possibility that her child is not yours."

"I must talk to her. Face-to-face. I want to see it in her eyes and hear it in her voice."

"The envelope says she's in Hampton Roads," said Bill.

"I didn't even notice."

"It's our home port, Walter. Why don't you write back and tell her that you intend to see her. You can write again as soon as you know the date of our next trip. It shouldn't be long."

"Yeah. That makes sense."

"There's no need to go crazy, Walter. This will all work out, I'm sure."

Walter's eyes watered up.

"You're my best friend, Bill."

Bill exhaled loudly.

"Just, take it easy, Walter. You know what happens when you get stressed."

Despite his shortage of funds, Frank felt certain he could secure a few sticks of dynamite.

His plan, to attack the U.S. Consul's office, did not require a great deal of explosives. Just enough to make it clear that Fitzhugh Lee could have been killed. There would be no real danger, of course. Frank would schedule the attack in the middle of the night when Lee and his staff were safely tucked in their beds.

It took days for Frank to discover even a handful of rebels, the Spanish army now exercising control over much of the Cuban island.

"You're an American."

"Tell me something I don't already know, Corporal. Do you have dynamite?"

"Why do you require dynamite?"

"I'm on assignment, corporal. And we do not share the details of our assignments with just anybody."

"We?"

"The American government, you fool."

"And your American friends, they do not have the money to purchase their own dynamite?"

"When's the last time you smuggled dynamite from Florida to Cuba?"

The rebel officer shrugged. Frank's logic and, perhaps his dismissive attitude, persuaded the man.

"Our base camp is 10 miles west of here. Is your horse capable of the journey?"

Frank kicked the old nag he confiscated from a stable, just that morning. He yelled to the rebel.

"The horse doesn't have a choice."

Isabella, although enjoying her room at the Hotel Inglaterra, grew bored and restless.

After replenishing her wardrobe, she neither left her room nor received visitors. Roberto said little about the frequent telegrams from Key West, now arriving at their room. He revealed even less about the nature of his many absences. Her frustration with their platonic relationship added to the woman's emotional turmoil. Roberto, a gentleman to the extreme and a Catholic since childhood, would yield neither to his temptation nor her solicitations. When Roberto announced that he would be gone for the day, once again, Isabella lost her temper. She threw a shoe at the door.

"Am I expected to live in solitary confinement for the rest of this miserable war?"

Roberto closed his eyes and allowed his head to droop. He joined her, bedside.

"Isabella, my love, you must be patient. There is important work to be done."

She reached for his hands and held them in her own.

"Am I no longer important to you?"

"You are the most important thing in my life. And soon, we will live happily ever after. I promise."

"Can we, at least, approach the priest at the cathedral?" she asked.

"Your uncle and his staff regularly attend mass at the Cathedral. You will be seen and recognized. Of this I am certain."

Isabella tugged at her hair, its length now well below her ears.

"I will disguise myself."

Roberto shook his head and started for the door.

"You will do no such thing."

"The rebel leader speaks as if he is my commanding officer."

Roberto glared at the girl.

"Isabella Hermoza. I will no longer tolerate your petulant and childlike behavior. It is time to grow up."

"How dare you address me in such a fashion?"

Isabella reached for her remaining shoe. Roberto turned the doorknob and slammed the door on his way out. The angry woman's footwear crashed harmlessly into the closed door.

Isabella buried her head in a pillow and cried,

When Frank rode into the rebels' base camp, he stared in disbelief.

The two dozen or so soldiers took no notice. Half of the men, assembled around a fire, appeared to be cooking something. A nearby carcass, a mule, he concluded, indicated that the men were starving. A dozen men, shivering in the hot sun and covered with open sores, lay in the dirt. Some of them begged for water. They stared at Frank through glassy eyes. Their pale, yellow skin hung on their bones like rags on a fence post. One of the men, motionless and with his mouth agape, showed no reaction to the bugs and mosquitoes that covered his flesh. Frank estimated the man died, days ago.

"I wish to speak with your commanding officer."

"That is not possible," said a soldier, tending to the fire.

"Why not?"

"He's dead."

Those that could approached Frank, eyeing his horse. One soldier held a rifle. The rest wielded machetes. They surrounded the American.

"We are requisitioning your horse," said the senior man.

Frank dismounted and approached the ringleader. He drew his weapon and pressed the muzzle against the man's forehead. The rebel blinked. His jaw fell.

"Your friends will be well-fed, tonight. But you, my friend, will be dead."

Frank allowed the rebel leader to step back. Beads of sweat appeared on the man's forehead. Frank pulled the hammer back on his gun. The Cuban's voice trembled.

"The Americano has big cajónes, yes?"

Frank flashed a toothy smile.

"Put your weapons down. All of you."

The machetes dropped to the ground. The rebel with the rifle caught Frank's gaze and laughed out loud.

"We ran out of bullets two weeks ago."

His comrades chuckled. Their leader smiled.

"Please *Señor*. We mean no harm."

Frank lowered his sidearm.

"We need food. Nothing more."

"I need dynamite. Do you have any?"

"Si, *Señor*. A whole box."

"I will give you American money."

"Come. I will show you the dynamite."

The crew of the *USS Maine* returned to Hampton Roads at the end of June.

Walter, desperate to visit Angel, immediately requested shore leave. When Captain Sigsbee granted him a two-day pass, he scrambled off the ship. He brought with him no change of clothes, a modest amount of money, and Angel's letter. He blamed the U.S. Navy for their separation of more than four months. The thought of going AWOL consumed him. Walter made a mental note to discuss his idea with Angel.

At ten thirty in the morning, the tavern where she used to work stood empty. Walter took a seat in the far corner of the large room. A middle-aged man, wiping down the bar, spotted him.

"No beer till noon time. But I got sarsaparilla."

"Sure," said Walter.

When his drink arrived, Walter paid the man and added a generous tip.

"Have you seen Angel today?"

"Haven't seen her in months," he said. "She used to work here you know."

"Yes, I know."

"I heard she got herself knocked up. Some sailor boy."

Walter blushed a hot red. The bartender's eyes opened wide.

"Say. That wouldn't be you, would it?"

"Leave him alone, Fred."

The bartender took one look at the woman in the doorway and scurried to a spot behind the bar. She stood with her back to the sun. Walter recognized the woman's silhouette. The bartender, pretending to clean the glassware, watched the couple with great interest.

"Get lost, Fred."

The man disappeared behind a door at the back of the saloon. Walter sprang to his feet but remained in place. Angel walked with purpose. He noticed her overly plump belly.

"Hello, Walter."

"Hello, Angel."

Walter's eyes darted everywhere. He tried not to stare. She stepped closer and planted a single kiss on his cheek. Walter motioned to a chair.

"Can I get you a drink?"

Angel studied his glass.

"Is that sarsaparilla?"

"Yes."

"I hate that stuff."

"A glass of wine?"

"Not good for the baby. At least that's what I'm told."

Walter sipped on his drink in silence. He cleared his throat. Angel responded.

"I didn't hear what you said."

"I didn't say anything."

"Oh."

Walter emptied his glass. He pretended to shoo a fly away.

"Jesus Christ, Walter. Talk to me."

Walter sat at attention.

"How are you feeling?"

"Fine."

"That's good."

More awkward silence.

"And you? How's it going on the ship?"

"Fine. Same old stuff."

"Is Christopher still your best friend?"

"Yeah, I guess so. Well, there's Bill Horn, too. He's really nice to me."

"Yeah. I remember you talking about him."

"We got a new captain. Sigsbee is his name."

"Is he nice?"

"Don't know. Haven't really met him yet. Looks like an old professor."

Angel studied the table.

"This place needs a good cleaning."

Walter leaned forward.

"Can I ask you a question?"

Angel bit her lower lip.

"You wanna know if it's yours," she snapped.

Walter's eyes dropped to his drink. He cupped the empty glass in one hand swirling an invisible drink.

"Yes."

"Three months before I met you, I was pretty sure I was knocked up. Turned out I was wrong. Scared the hell out of me. So, I started working here, waiting on tables. Damn near starved to death. And then you came along. You were the first man I slept with, in three months. That's the truth."

Angel sniffed. Walter looked up, fixing his gaze on Angel's glassy eyes. He reached into his pocket and pulled out a clump of bills.

"I'll bring more tomorrow."

She reached for the money.

"I'm sorry, Walter. Just till I get on my feet. After that, you'll be rid of me."

Walter's eyebrows shot up.

"What do you mean, 'rid of me?' We're getting married, aren't we?"

Angel used a sleeve on her blouse to wipe her eyes,

"I just thought you'd change your mind once you knew I was having a kid."

Walter frowned.

"Why would I do that? Like I said before. Nobody has been nicer to me than you."

"Thank you, Walter. And you have been especially good to me."

"I *do* have one request," he said.

"What's that?"

"If it's a boy, we ain't gonna name it Walter. I hate that name."
Angel giggled through her tears. She reached for his hand.
"I love you, Walter."

"I love you, too."

Isabella donned a black veil and a long, drab dress.

An hour of crying into her pillow triggered the woman's anger and frustration. Today, she would go to the cathedral. She didn't care if Roberto refused to go. She would do it without him. After Isabella climbed the steps which led to the oversized cathedral doors, she paused in the doorway. The long row of confessionals, which lined one side of the cavernous building, inspired an idea. She quickly blessed herself, dipping her right hand in the font of holy water, at the rear of the church. With her head down and face covered, she ducked into a confessional and closed the door.

The closet-sized chamber and the smell of burning candles temporarily transported the woman back to her youth. Her teen years, some of the happiest in her short lifetime, included frequent visits to the Catholic church in Mallorca. She received the sacrament of Confession on a weekly basis. Sometimes more. It did not matter if she had sins to confess or not. She happily visited with the priests anyway. In retrospect, she concluded that the innocent young woman brought joy to their otherwise beleaguered and boring lives. The small sliding door that separated confessor from penitent, opened. A deep purple, velvet curtain guaranteed her anonymity. She began her confession with the usual words.

"Bless me father, for I have sinned. It has been . . ."

Isabella hesitated, shocked when she could not remember the last time she received the penitential rights.

"Months since my last confession."

She went on to accuse herself of all seven capital sins. Unlike her childhood years, she easily recalled instances of anger, pride, greed, and spiritual sloth. She put people, the rebellion, and herself, before her relationship with God. She ended with lust, a daily occurrence, as of late. Her penance of five Our Fathers and ten Hail Marys would be accomplished on her knees, in a pew. The recitation of those prayers, memorized as a child and now mindlessly repeated, were necessary in order to receive the priest's absolution. The priest blessed and dismissed her.

"Go in peace, my child."

Isabella chose to remain.

"Father, may I speak with you for a moment?"

"Yes, of course."

"My fiancée and I wish to marry."

"Is the young man also a Catholic?"

"Yes, of course."

"You need only come to the rectory and all of the necessary arrangements will be made."

"But I wish a private ceremony. Simple and plain. Just the three of us."

When her query produced nothing but silence, she squirmed in place.

"Father?"

"And why do you wish to celebrate the joyous sacrament of marriage, in private."

Isabella stuttered.

"Well. Father. I am. I was."

Isabella froze. The priest waited in silence. The young woman's mind raced.

"My family is in Spain. Roberto has no family. It is just the two of us."

Her response came too late. His next question proved awkward.

"Are you with child, my dear?"

Isabella cringed.

"I am not with child, Father, and your question is hurtful."

"Forgive me. It is a question I must ask in these horrible days of suffering and chaos."

Isabella got up to leave.

"Where are you going, my child?"

"Clearly, you do not wish to help me."

"The Mother Church may dispense with the usual protocols in times of war. I will help you. What is your name?"

"Isabella."

"Bring Roberto with you. Identify yourself when the two of you come to confession. After both of you have made a good confession, I shall marry you."

Isabella beamed with joy. She pulled the velvet curtain to one side and kissed the priest on his forehead. The man's round and cherubic face flushed pink with embarrassment. He flashed a large and genuine smile.

"Thank you, Father. Thank you so very much."

He nodded and blessed the woman one more time.

# Chapter Twenty-One

## MARRIAGE

Isabella, in her room at the Hotel Inglaterra, paced from the bed to the door to the oversized chair and back to the door.

Every few minutes, she would peek into the hallway for any sign of Roberto. The prospect of a wedding, even without a beautiful white dress and a ring, left her anxious and excited. An angry reaction from Roberto would change all of that. She heard a key rattle in the door.

"Roberto? Is that you?"

Roberto stepped through the door, a cheery look on his face.

"You were expecting someone else?"

Isabella breathed a sigh of relief. She pulled him close. Their kiss, long and passionate, told her that he too, anxiously awaited their wedding and honeymoon.

"Roberto, I have something to tell you. But you must promise that you will not be angry."

Roberto ignored her plea, kissing the woman on her lips, cheeks, neck, and shoulders. He pushed her onto the bed and lay on top of her. She could feel his excitement.

"Roberto, listen to me."

"I can no longer resist your beauty, Isabella. Stop me or I shall have my way with you, here and now."

Isabella placed a hand over his mouth and forced him off the bed. He rolled onto the floor. Roberto, breathing hard, looked crestfallen.

"I had hoped you would ignore my request."

Isabella beckoned him.

"Come. Sit with me."

Roberto frowned and took his place at her side,

"I saw a priest. Today, at the cathedral."

Roberto's head jerked in her direction.

"Oh no, Isabella. Please tell me you didn't. You have placed us in danger."

Isabella recounted her meeting with the pudgy priest while in the confessional.

"No one will know, Roberto. It will be the three of us, no more."

Roberto took a long, deep, breath. His head fell forward.

"Roberto?"

"Please Isabella. Let me think."

The boy rubbed the sides of his head with the fingers of both hands. The would-be bride fidgeted in silence. Minutes later, Roberto looked up.

"Isabella, my love. You deserve so much more. A beautiful white dress, a church full of family and friends, and a ring of gold for your finger. We must wait. Just a bit longer."

Isabella surprised herself. She was overcome with sadness rather than anger.

"I don't want or need any of those things, Roberto. It is you that I want and need."

"Can we trust this priest to do as you requested?"

"He did not recognize me and he does not know you. We are safe. I am sure of it."

Isabella leaned forward and gently pressed her lips against his.

"You are very persuasive, Miss Hermoza."

Isabella smiled.

"Nevertheless, I will do whatever you ask of me."

Roberto sprang to his feet and rushed to the dresser. He reached for the inexpensive cigar, given to him by the hotel's management. He slipped the paper ring off the promotional item, rushed back to Isabella, and dropped to his knees.

"Isabella Hermoza. I have nothing to offer you except my promise to love you and cherish you with all my heart for the rest of my life. Will you marry me?"

"Yes," she cried. "A thousand times yes."

He slipped the paper ring onto the ring finger of her left hand. Isabella raised her hand. She recognized 'Por Larranaga', a tobacco company, established long ago and named for its owner. She smiled through her tears.

"It is the most beautiful ring I have ever seen."

Frank, anxious to leave the malaria-infected basecamp, paid the rebels for a single box of dynamite.

The physical condition of the men and their lack of military preparedness, stuck in his head. The only successful path to a

*Cuba Libre* would be as a direct result of U.S. intervention. During his slow journey to Havana proper, Frank contemplated the precise means by which his attack would be implemented.

A Spanish flag, readily available for a small amount of American money, would be the evidence used to condemn Spain. He considered, and then abandoned, the idea of utilizing a willing rebel to assist him. The delivery and detonation of dynamite could not be left to an amateur. He would do the job, himself.

A long fuse, attached to the remaining fuses, would accomplish the mission. He pulled up, well short of the city and retrieved six sticks of explosives from the wooden crate. Under the cover of dusk, he buried the remainder near a large rock, just north of the trail. It would be easy to recover, if additional explosives became necessary. He secreted a half dozen sticks on his horse and on his person. He waited in the shadows of the large rock. When the half-moon rose high in the sky, he trotted the horse into town. By now, he knew most of the back alleys, side streets, and poorly lit roads that led to the government buildings. Thirty minutes later, he could see the profile of the building he would soon reduce to rubble.

He used a length of vine from the large yellow flowers, golden chalice he thought, that dotted the landscape. It took a minute to tie the explosives into a neat and secure bundle. Frank calculated that the fuses would give him a full sixty seconds to leave the scene. He would require only a half-minute to run down the alleyway and take shelter behind an empty store front.

He tied the old nag to a wrought iron railing which decorated the stairs of an abandoned office building. Frank walked the half-block to the consul's building, approaching it from the rear. Before he stepped into full view, Frank searched for movement in all directions. The street, quiet except for two drunks sitting and singing in the nearby plaza, posed no hazards. When a cloud blocked the moon's dull glow, Frank made his move. He walked with purpose to the brick stairs which marked the front entrance. Lighting the fuse required only seconds, after which, he walked briskly to the corner of the building. Frank used the flag to muzzle the sound of his side-arm, as it broke the glass in a lower window. He draped the flag over the broken glass and ran as fast as he could to the location of his horse. He waited for the explosion. He caught his breath. The dynamite did not explode. He waited several minutes more. Nothing. He jumped on the horse and kicked hard, muttering as he did so.

"Those bastards sold me old dynamite."

The horse whinnied loud when he pulled her up at the nearest intersection. He could see the two drunks, staggering in the direction of the consulate. The first one climbed the stairs and tucked the dynamite, with its partially burned fuse, under his arm. They walked a little faster. When the second man spotted the Spanish flag, he slapped his friend on the back and tied it around his waist.

Frank's attempted destruction of the U.S. Consul's office failed miserably.

Walter gave Angel the balance of his savings and reboarded the *Maine*.

It would be two months before the ship returned to its home port. The *Maine* spent most of its time at the Navy Yard in New York. Walter wrote letters and always enclosed money. If Angel chose to respond, he never received the letters. He spent most of his time wondering and worrying about the state of her health. In mid-June, he received word that Hampton Roads would be their port of call for a full week. Walter's spirits soared. And fell. Precipitously.

"I don't understand it. I put in for shore leave a week ago and so far, nothing but silence."

Bill Horn refused to look his friend in the eye.

"Walter, I just got word myself. All requests for leave have been denied. Tensions are very high in Cuba. McKinley even sent $50,000 to the rebels. We may be headed south."

Walter stared in disbelief. He picked up his coal bucket and threw it down the passageway. He used a shovel as a hammer, and repeatedly pounded on the metal bulkhead, chipping the paint. He stopped when the wooden handle broke in two. The blade hit Bill in the face.

"Goddammit, Walter. You broke my nose."

Blood spurted on Bill's shirt and gushed to the floor. He used a sleeve to staunch the flow. The blood puddle forced Walter to look away. His face blanched. He swallowed rapidly and covered his mouth with one hand.

"The sight of blood makes me sick."

He doubled over and retched the contents of his stomach. Walter recognized the ham and corn he ate for dinner. Bloody footprints and vomit covered the floor.

"I'm not cleaning up this mess. This is your fault. You clean it," said Bill, as he stormed off.

Walter, spitting on the floor to remove the taste of vomit from his mouth, searched for a mop. When the floor looked respectable, he walked back to his hammock. Walter lay still for an hour, his queasy stomach making movement almost impossible. He fumed about his predicament and considered the alternatives. He needed to choose. Months on board the *USS Maine* or a blissful life with Angel. He yelled.

"To hell with you, Captain Sigsbee!"

The sound of his own words, echoing in the crew's quarters, surprised and emboldened the little man. He hopped off the hammock and stuffed his duffel with everything he owned. He leaned over the bed and searched the corner. Christopher's food dish lay empty. The rat made his rounds at this time of day. It could be hours before he returned. Walter paused. He thought of Angel, the first time he saw her naked. He remembered the ecstasy of their first and second lovemaking sessions. It was the most pleasurable experience of his young life.

"Sorry, Christopher."

He finished packing and hurried to the hatch. Walter climbed the ladder, shoving his duffle ahead of him. He squeezed through the hatch and headed for the gangway. No one took notice of a sailor crossing the deck with a duffel. When he descended the ramp and stepped onto the dock, a loud voice pierced the air.

"Walter."

He turned. Bill Horn, a large white bandage on his nose, yelled through cupped hands.

"Walter. Don't do it."

Walter shook his head. Bill yelled again.

"Walter. I'm warning you.'

Walter turned and ran.

The AWOL sailor made it halfway to the tavern when two Marines stopped him.

The men, two of twelve stationed on the *USS Maine*, were not to be trifled with. The muscle-bound sailors carried sidearms and stood two heads taller than Walter.

"Come with us, Mr. McDermott."

Walter appealed to their sympathies. And he lied.

"My fiancé is pregnant. She is sick and in the hospital. Please, I must see her."

"Take it up with the captain, sir."

They each grabbed an arm and turned Walter around. One of the men effortlessly slung Walter's heavy duffel over his shoulder. The other man pointed to the docks.

"This way, Mr. McDermott."

Walter's armed escort deposited him in the ship's brig.

The small but secure room in the forward part of the ship would be his new home. For how long, he did not know.

"I'm sorry, Walter."

Bill Horn spoke to the prisoner through a tiny, barred opening in the door. Walter, his face red and the vein on his forehead bulging, screamed at his visitor.

"You ratted me out, Bill. I thought you were my friend. But you ratted me out."

"I did it for your own good, Walter."

"You can go to hell, Fireman First Class, Bill Horn. And you are not my friend anymore."

Bill raised his voice.

"I am the only friend you have on the ship, Walter. And if you keep this up, you're going to spend the rest of your life behind bars."

Two marines walked into the room. The older marine looked to Bill.

"Excuse us, sir. The Lieutenant wants to see McDermott."

Bill seethed.

"I was just leaving."

Roberto and Isabella waited until the second week of August before they approached the priest.

They chose midweek, when the church contained few, if any, visitors. Roberto harbored great misgivings that they might be recognized and captured. He entered the confessional while Isabella waited.

"Bless me father for I have sinned."

The rebel did not confess his murder of Spanish soldiers. A just war and self-defense, at least in the eyes of Roberto, exempted him from the fifth commandment. Isabella entered the tiny chamber next. When she finished the recitation of her sins, the girl remained in the confessional.

"Father. My name is Isabella. We spoke several weeks ago. Roberto and I wish to be married."

"Yes, of course. Wait here please."

Isabella thought it odd that he would ask her to wait in the confessional. She could hear the priest as he left. The door to his portion of the booth remained open. The overweight priest walked as fast as he could, down the aisle. She opened the door to her portion of the confessional. The rotund man did not bother to genuflect when he flew past the altar. When Roberto saw the cleric rush out, he rose to his feet. Behind them, the large doors of the cathedral opened and slammed shut. Isabella saw four Spanish soldiers guarding the exit. She screamed.

"Roberto!"

Roberto rushed to Isabella's side and grabbed her by the hand.

"This way."

The two of them ran up the aisleway in the direction of the altar. Four more guards emerged from the vestibule, taking positions on either side of the altar. Roberto and Isabella, forced to stop at the railing where parishioners kneeled to receive Holy Communion, looked in every direction.

"We're trapped," she said.

Roberto reached instinctively for his sidearm and glared at Isabella. She insisted he leave the weapon under his pillow at the hotel. Isabella stifled another scream. Roberto looked up. Captain-General Weyler, hands clasped behind his back, walked slowly to the front of the altar. The rotund priest, still breathing heavily, followed several paces behind. Weyler looked first at Roberto, his eyes narrowed to slits. He then turned to Isabella.

"I have not given this marriage my consent."

Isabella reached for Roberto's hand.

"We are in love. With or without your consent."

Weyler looked in the direction of the priest, behind him.

"The good father is unable to marry the two of you."

Roberto stepped forward.

"Under the penalty of death, no doubt."

Weyler marched to the railing. He stopped just feet from Roberto.

"You, my rebel friend, are young and reckless."

Roberto snarled.

"So I am told."

Weyler held the boy's gaze.

"You are also without fear, a man of principle, and clearly in love with my niece."

Isabella's head jerked up. Roberto stood a bit taller. Weyler turned to the priest.

"The sacrament of marriage requires a witness, does it not?"

"Yes, your Excellency."

The captain-general turned to his niece.

"If your future husband approves, I should like to give your hand in marriage and serve as your witness."

Isabella burst into tears and rushed forward. A guard unlatched the gate which bisected the Communion railing. She fell to her knees at Weyler's feet. She hugged and kissed her uncle. He held her close and wiped the tears from her eyes, even as he blinked away his own tears. Roberto bowed his head.

"You are most generous, Captain-General Weyler."

Weyler pulled the girl to her feet. He descended the three steps to the aisleway and approached the boy.

"Mr. Alvarez. You have escaped my prison, murdered several of my guards and, I am told, have been given a leadership role in the rebellion. You should be, and may very well be, executed by the Spanish government."

Roberto cleared his throat, ready to defend his honor. Weyler held up a hand.

"Do not waste your words. Both of you will be pleased to know that I have been relieved of my command and ordered back to Spain. The next captain-general will deal with you."

Weyler turned again to Isabella and shrugged.

"Or perhaps not."

He extended a hand to Roberto.

"For me, the revolution has ended."

Roberto used his trousers to wipe his sweaty palms. He reached for his nemesis with both hands.

"Thank you, sir. Thank you, very much."

The marriage ceremony, with no mass, required less than a half hour. Roberto, numb from the captain-general's announcement and ecstatic with his new wife, could not erase the ridiculous grin which covered his face. Isabella, unable to contain her joy, hugged and kissed her husband, her uncle, and even the overweight priest. Weyler motioned the couple to the exit.

"I must go now. And so should you."

He reached into a pocket and removed a leather pouch. The small, overstuffed bag jingled when he pressed it into Isabella's hand.

"This is for you and your husband."

His eyes darted to Roberto.

"And not for the Cuban Liberation Army. Is that understood?"

Roberto signaled his agreement with a grin. Isabella made it official.

"I will see to it that my husband respects your wishes, my beloved Uncle."

Roberto stepped forward and reached for Weyler's hand, once again.

"It would appear, Captain-General Weyler, that a truce has been ordered by your niece."

"Yes. This is true. And it is the first of many orders by my niece, that you must now obey."

Isabella giggled.

Walter's meeting with the lieutenant did not go well

His commanding officer offered a choice. An immediate dishonorable discharge or a dishonorable discharge if he committed any serious infraction within the next 12 months. The ruling meant that Walter would be on his best behavior or get booted out of the Navy. He thought of Angel, his unborn child, and how he would support them absent a steady paycheck.

"Do you understand what I have told you, Mr. McDermott?"

"Yes, sir. I understand."

"Very well then. You are dismissed. And remember. One more problem and you are off this ship and out of the navy."

With a few hours before the night shift began, Walter returned to his hammock.

He brought with him pieces of bread and a handful of corn, left over from last night's dinner. As he filled Christopher's dish, the rodent appeared. When the food vanished, Walter coaxed the rodent into his hand and onto the hammock. The two cavorted on the sailor's chest. Walter smiled broadly when Christopher stood on his hind legs and begged for more food. When Walter surrendered his last kernel of corn, he noticed a dark blemish on Christopher's face. On closer examination, he could see and smell charred facial hair. The acrid smell suggested an electrical wire. The battleship's crude electrical system offered an endless number of opportunities for the rats. He recalled that a rodent's teeth do not have roots. They chew instinctively and constantly, to keep their teeth sharp and at a manageable size. Walter immediately delivered a stern lecture about the dangers of chewing on electrical wires.

Christopher, other than begging for more food, showed no reaction.

Frank, disgusted with the failed attempt to bomb the U.S. Consul's office, pouted in his room.

The cheap hotel reminded him of his uncooperative backers in Key West. Carmelita gave him just enough funds to sustain himself. An unemployed mercenary with no money made for an extremely ill-tempered man. Frank jumped out of his bed and walked the side streets and alleyways of Havana. At one point, he could smell the filthy waters of Havana Bay. He studied the scene for a few minutes. A slight smile crossed his face. When he turned back to the hotel, the smile grew into a joyful grin.

If an American merchant ship, and there were several in the bay, were to be destroyed or even damaged by a mysterious explosion, the news would trigger an immediate American reaction. It might even prompt the United States to declare war against Spain.

Frank's aimless walk took on a frenzied pace. From a distance, he studied the American steamer, *Olivette*, on which he rode so often in the past. Despite a passing pang of guilt, he speculated that the boat's destruction would create a massive uproar. Not unlike the consul's office, this mission would also be a challenge. Precisely how he would destroy the ship required meticulous planning. It must be done in such a way that the Spanish government got the blame.

He studied the steamer, as it prepared to pull away from its dock. Several men scurried across the deck. Frank could identify the captain, with his cap cocked to one side and a pipe in his mouth. He hoped that his friend, Captain Randall, would not succumb in the blast. Frank viewed such casualties as regrettable but considered them no more than collateral damage. The struggle for Cuba's freedom, like Frank's ego, always took precedence.

With a box full of useless dynamite, Frank considered other means by which to destroy or severely damage the ocean-going vessel. He knew boilers and he knew the *Olivette's* boiler room. As a passenger, he could easily distract the operator and quickly sabotage the boiler. Overfilling it with coal, or simply leaving its air valves wide-open would soon cause the water tank to explode. In the time it took for the water tank to overheat, he could escape.

The other possibility was a well-placed stick or two of dynamite. The *Olivette* housed a small stockpile of arms and ammo in a hidden compartment. But Frank could not be sure that the arsenal contained dynamite. Gaining access to the hidden compartment could also be problematic. He returned to the seedy hotel where he now lived, cursing the cabal in Key West.

"We'll see who gets the credit for winning this revolution."

Roberto and Isabella returned to the Hotel Inglaterra.

He stopped at the dining room for a bottle of wine.

"I'll be waiting for you, my beloved husband."

When Roberto returned, he found Isabella in bed, her bare shoulders exposed, and a sheet pulled discreetly over her bosom. His trembling hands removed the cork and filled two glasses. He sat on the edge of the bed and proposed a toast.

"To you Mrs. Alvarez. The most beautiful woman in the world."

When Isabella reached for the wine, she inadvertently exposed her breast. Roberto gawked, his eyes wide as saucers. She recovered, holding both her glass and the sheet, with one hand.

"Isabella, I must tell you something."

She finished her drink with a single large gulp and put a hand over Roberto's mouth.

"No Roberto. You will not let this revolution ruin our honeymoon. Say nothing about it. Nothing at all. Today, you will be my husband and my lover. Nothing more."

Roberto gulped the balance of his wine.

"Isabella, please. It is not the revolution I wish to discuss."

He cleared the imaginary frog in his throat and poured another glass of wine for himself and Isabella.

"Isabella. I will be your first lover, this I know. But you will be *my* first lover and I am inexperienced in such matters."

Roberto wiped the beads of sweat that formed on his forehead.

"I do not wish to disappoint you," he murmured.

Isabella leaned forward. She gently pressed her lips against his and she whispered.

"We shall learn the art of making love, together."

She placed her glass on the nightstand and leaned back. He tugged at his shirt. In moments, Roberto stood at her bedside, naked and obviously aroused. She pulled the sheet to one side.

"Come to bed, my love."

# Chapter Twenty-Two

## BOILER ROOMS

Frank quick-stepped across the *Olivette's* deck and greeted Captain Randall with a vigorous handshake.

"It's great to see you again, Captain."

"You too, Frank. How goes the rebellion?"

The smile on Frank's face disappeared.

"I prefer not to discuss it."

Randall lowered his booming voice.

"I am told that the Spanish army now controls all of the cities and much of the countryside."

"This is mostly true. But the revolution is far from over."

Mind if I bunk in the boiler room? That ocean breeze can be a bit chilly."

"Not at all. Make yourself comfortable. We leave in a few hours."

Frank surveyed the boiler room; its operator temporarily absent. He took a few minutes to examine the equipment. The boiler, a large horizontally positioned cylinder manufactured by Lancashire, appeared to be in good shape for its age. It required only one person to operate; its design that simple. He easily located the safety valve, the pressure gauge, and the fire door. Frank's plan, to overload the furnace and generate a dangerous level of pressure, would work. When he opened the fire door, he discovered a half load of unlit coal. When the time came to leave its dock, the *Olivette* would be fired up in a matter of minutes.

Frank also noted the manhole cover. The opening, located at the top of the cylinder, allowed a man to enter and clean the boiler. It needed to be sealed tight at the time of his sabotage. The American mercenary wanted the entire apparatus to explode. The "accident" would sink the ship.

"Who are you?"

The large man, completely bald and at least a head taller than Frank, blocked the opening to the boiler room.

"Frank. Frank Lamb. Captain Randall said I could bunk here for the trip to Key West."

Frank extended a hand.

The giant ignored the gesture and grunted his reaction.

"Just stay outa my way."

The giant removed his coal-stained shirt and glared at his unwanted guest. Frank, mesmerized by the man's massive biceps and chiseled abdomen, took a seat on the floor.

The big man smirked.

"Gonna get hot in here when I fire her up," he said, with a voice that sounded like a load of coal rolling down a steep hill.

Frank dismissed any thought of overpowering the brute. He reached into his rucksack for the rum. If he drinks enough, maybe the giant will fall asleep, he thought.

"How about a little swig before you go to work.?"

The boiler man growled, "I don't drink. Bad for your health."

Frank challenged him.

"Who the hell told you that?"

"My Momma."

The giant stepped forward.

"And don't be bad mouthing my Momma, you hear?"

"No sir. I would never question your Momma."

Frank exhaled loudly.

His second attempt on American assets in Cuba ended before it started.

The *Maine*, once again docked at Hampton Roads, would remain there for three weeks.

Despite his earlier troubles, Walter received permission for two days of shore leave. The lieutenant felt sorry for him. The expectant father walked to the eatery where Angel worked and lived. The cook recognized Walter in his navy uniform.

"She's not here."

"Where'd she go?"

"She's upstairs with a black lady. A midwife, I think. You're gonna have a baby, sailor man."

Walter let out a war whoop and ran out of the building. A long set of stairs, taken two at a time, delivered him to her one-room apartment. He burst into the room. The color drained from Walter's face. His wife lay on the bed, moaning in pain. Her hair, soaked with sweat, framed the dark circles under her glassy eyes. The midwife pressed cold compresses to Angel's forehead.

"What's wrong?" he asked.

The short black woman, bordering on obese, shook her head.

"She dun ben in labor for near on 12 hours. Weez in big trouble. There ain't no doctor man gonna come to these here parts."

Walter rushed to his wife's side.

"Angel. Can you hear me?"

The woman's eyes fluttered. Her dry lips moved but no words could be heard.

"You be the Walter she been askin for?" asked the black woman.

Walter spoke softly.

"Yes, ma'am. I'm her husband."

Angel's eyes opened wide. She screamed as her body doubled over. Her face contorted in pain. Walter yelled at the midwife.

"Do something. Anything. Please help her."

"Ain't nuthin I kin do," she said.

Angel screamed again. Walter noticed a growing stain of crimson red on the bedsheet. Angel's eyes closed as she slipped into unconsciousness. Her face, now ashen gray, frightened Walter.

"Is she . . . ?"

Walter could not finish his sentence. The black woman felt for a pulse. Angel's breathing quickened into a series of sharp gulps for air.

"The baby wanna cum out feet first. And it dun cum too early. The good lawd is gonna take em both. I'ze just knows it."

Walter backed away from the bed. The closed door ended his movement but he could still see her. He tried not to look at her. His eyes would not close. Angel's breathing slowed, stopped, and began again.

Finally, the noise of a long breath followed by a deep rattle in her lungs, filled the room. Angel's face became a frozen mask of gray. Her mouth, now ajar, matched her wide-open eyes. Walter thought they stared at him.

"I'ze truly sorry, Mr. Walter. She'z with her makeah now."

Walter's knees buckled. He slid to the floor and squeezed his eyes shut. Her image remained. He blinked several times and covered his eyes with both hands.

And still, he could see the death mask of his fallen Angel.

Roberto kissed Isabella goodbye.

He reluctantly left Isabella for a last-minute trip to Key West.

"Why must you leave?"

"The people in Key West have requested a meeting."

"When will you return?"

"In two days."

Roberto stopped and leaned against the door. He hung his head, frustrated, and discouraged.

"I'm sorry, Isabella. You deserve better than this. I am a fool. I seek justice for my family but it matters not what I do. My family will never return."

Isabella went to his side.

"And I am a bigger fool. I came to Cuba for fun and adventure and to be with my uncle. I found nothing but heartache, suffering, death, and destruction. And now, when I sleep, I dream of wounded and dying soldiers. Spanish soldiers and Cuban rebels, alike. And I am very tired. We are both tired."

"What are we going to do, Isabella?"

The newlyweds hugged each other in silence.

After accepting Carmelita's congratulations on his marriage, Roberto made his report.

"The Spanish army is in control of all the major cities. The rebels are dominant in portions of the countryside but only in western Cuba."

"I'm not surprised," she said.

"We are told that General Gomez is rarely on the offensive and seems unwilling or unable to challenge the Spanish Army. And Weyler has returned to Spain," she said."

"This is true and his replacement, General Blanco, has done much to silence the rebels."

"Like what?" she asked.

"He regularly pays his soldiers and feeds them. Weyler did neither when his regime approached its end. Blanco has abolished the reconcentration camps and thousands of Cubans have been freed," said Roberto.

He went on.

"Blanco no longer wages war on women and children and has gone so far as to donate funds for their well-being. Americans have been released from prison and Cubans on death row have been allowed to go free. The Cuban refugees, taken from their homes, have been told they can return."

"So, the revolution comes to an end," said Carmelita.

"Not quite. The Weylerites, supporters of the deposed captain-general, are angry and frustrated. They view Blanco as soft and weak. They threaten to riot," said Roberto. "And there are radicals who refuse Blanco's initiatives regardless of how much they help the Cuban people. They want complete independence from Spain. They will not end their resistance until total independence has been achieved. And so, the revolution continues," Roberto concluded.

Carmelita leaned forward in her chair.

"You have a new assignment."

"What is it?"

"The U.S. is very close to intervening in the rebellion. If that happens, the Cuban people will win their independence. We need and want the Weylerites to riot in the streets. Bribe them if you must, join them if necessary. Do whatever you have to do, to stir up trouble."

Carmelita approached the young rebel with a large envelope in her hand.

"American cash. Let me know if you need more," she said.

"Thank you, Carmelita. I think."

"You are most welcome. Now be careful. You have a wife to think of."

Walter sat in his bed, staring at the straight razor he used every third day.

He did not intend to shave. Walter removed the blade from the razor. He took a deep breath and rolled up the sleeve on his left arm. He studied the inside of his wrist. Several veins, clearly visible to his untrained eye, would make the job easy.

"I hate the sight of blood," he murmured.

"I know."

Walter's head jerked in the direction of the bunk room door. Bill Horn, no longer wearing the bandage on his nose, stood in the opening. His eyes flitted from the blade in Walter's right hand to the suicidal man's eyes. Walter gave him a dirty look.

"The lieutenant told me about Angel."

"Don't think about stopping me, Bill. I'm going to do it."

Bill turned to leave.

Walter frowned his surprise.

"Where are you going?"

Bill didn't stop until he reached the passageway and, even then, stood with his back to the man. He yelled over his shoulder.

"You don't need an audience, Walter. The men will figure it out. Besides, I don't wanna get stuck cleaning up the mess."

Walter's eyes turned glassy. He brought the blade to his wrist. His hand trembled.

Bill turned around.

"You should cut both wrists. That way, you can be certain of bleeding to death."

Bill leaned on the wall as if watching a poker game.

Walter put the blade down and rolled up the sleeve on his right arm. He flashed a triumphant look in Bill's direction. He reached for the blade. Too quickly. The sharp edge sliced into his thumb.

"Damn," said Walter, sucking on the finger.

Bill closed his eyes and smirked.

"Walter, you can kill yourself anytime you want. I'm not going to stop you. I just wanted to talk to you about Angel. That's all."

Walter checked his thumb. It continued to bleed. He sucked the wound some more, carefully placing the blade to one side. Bill re-entered the bunk room. He sat on the floor, opposite Walter's hammock and studied Walter's sad face for several long minutes.

"It must have been awful. Losing your wife and your child all at once. I'm not sure I would want to live, either."

"Do you have any kids?"

"Nope. I left right after we got married. Barely had time for the honeymoon."

"It's all my fault, Bill. I should have been there."

"Walter, if you were at her bedside holding her hand each and every day of her pregnancy, it would not have made a damn bit of difference."

They sat in silence for a while. Walter's empty stomach growled. Loud enough for Bill to hear it.

"How about we get something to eat?"

Walter did not immediately respond, choosing instead to reassemble the razor and return it to his duffel. When he slipped off the hammock he reached for Bill and pulled him to his feet.

"You're right. It is *not* my fault."

"That's the right attitude."

"I blame the United States Navy."

Isabella, bored with her surroundings, wandered downstairs in the lobby of the Hotel Inglaterra.

She took a seat in a chair made of white wicker. The fat cushions, covered with a colorful pattern of wildflowers, gave the cavernous room a festive air. As she sipped on a glass of lemonade surveying her view from the veranda, the woman allowed herself a slight smile. Isabella's thoughts drifted to her married friends, living in Spain. The newly minted bride now understood why lovemaking generated knowing smiles, plenty of giggles, and blushing faces. She and Roberto, although initially nervous and embarrassed, quickly discovered the pleasures of a marital bed.

"Mrs. Alvarez, I presume?"

The black servant at her side carried a silver tray with a telegram. She opened the envelope certain that Roberto, the only person who knew her whereabouts, sent her a message. When she read the telegram, Isabella's broad smile disappeared.

> *We will not rest until your uncle has returned. And you will soon be a widow.*
>
> ### *Friends of Captain-General Valeriano Weyler*

The thin paper fluttered in her trembling hands. She climbed the stairs to her room, locked the door, and checked it twice. Roberto's side arm, on his person, would not protect the girl. She paced the floor, visions of Roberto standing before a firing squad, flashing in her mind. A knock on the door, spun the woman around.

"Who is it?"

"Room service, Mrs. Alvarez."

She tipped-toed to the door.

"What is it you want?"

"I have a delivery for you, Mrs. Alvarez."

"What is it?"

"Flowers, ma'am."

Isabella opened the door. She could barely see the young boy who held an oversized bouquet of white mariposa, dotted with bright yellow blooms of golden chalice.

"Wait," she said, taking the flowers and rushing to the nightstand for a coin.

"Thank you, Mrs. Alvarez."

Isabella inhaled deeply and, for a moment, forgot about the threatening telegram. She opened the note that came with the flowers.

**Will be home by tomorrow evening.**

**Your loving husband, Roberto.**

She wanted to warn Roberto but did not know how to contact him. Isabella considered meeting him at the docks, but worried about the Spanish soldiers. Those still loyal to her uncle might recognize Roberto and take him prisoner. She too would be at risk of capture.

She chose to wait in the room.

Frank, no longer receiving regular dispatches from Key West, collected old newspapers.

He would find them on the benches in the plaza and in the lobbies of hotels nicer than his own. They became his sole source of information. On that day, they became a source of inspiration. A small article, originally published in the Port Royal times, found its way into a local newspaper. According to the article, the *USS Maine* received orders to proceed to Port Royal, South Carolina. It would remain there, on standby. The authorities in Washington thought it best to position the battleship closer to Havana where it might be needed. Widespread concern in the states, about Americans and American interests in Cuba, prompted the decision.

Frank fantasized about the *USS Maine* in Havana Bay. Such a high-profile target would strike fear in the hearts of the

Spanish army. It might also be a worthwhile target for Cuban rebels, looking to trigger a U.S. intervention. A growing number of Cubans, military and civilian alike, now believed that the rebels would not prevail without help from the United Sates. Frank agreed.

An attack on the U.S. battleship would be worth the risk of being captured or killed.

Walter's halfhearted suicide attempt faded into the background when Captain Sigsbee ordered the ship to the Southern Drilling Ground.

The ship's crew practiced sham battles, great-gun practice, shore landings, boat drills, and coaling exercises. All of which required a full head of steam. Walter regularly returned to his hammock, too exhausted to plan his revenge against the United States Navy. While at the Drilling Ground, 25 miles east of Cape Charles, Virginia, Walter learned of the ship's next destination.

"Why Port Royal, South Carolina?"

"Well, if you've been reading the papers at all, Walter, it is conspicuously close to Cuba," said Bill.

"Wouldn't Key West be even better?"

"That could very well be our next port of call. Things are going from bad to worse on that island and a lot of people in Washington want to intervene. So be careful what you wish for, my friend."

A week later, the *USS Maine's* executive officer accepted a transfer. Lieutenant Commander Richard Wainwright took his place.

The rumors surrounding his arrival suggested that Wainwright, handpicked by naval brass, came on board for the express purpose of preparing the battleship for a trip to Cuba. Wainwright pushed the crew hard, expecting them to be ever vigilant. The former Chief Intelligence Officer for the Navy received his 1864 appointment to the United States Naval Academy from none other than Abraham Lincoln.

He was also the Navy's foremost expert on the use and storage of coal.

When Roberto returned from Key West, four Spanish officers greeted him at the dock.

"General Blanco wishes to speak with you. Come with us, please."

Roberto reached for his pistol. The soldiers made no move to defend themselves.

"You are not under arrest, Mr. Alvarez. Please come with us."

As they left the dock area, Roberto noticed their soiled and ill-fitting uniforms. Their boots needed a thorough cleaning. The horses, only four of them, looked emaciated and each animal wore a different saddle. The youngest soldier surrendered his horse to Roberto and rode double with a comrade. Roberto said nothing until the docks disappeared. He turned in the saddle and grinned at the men behind him.

"The Cuban Liberation Army wears a different uniform these days."

The oldest soldier leaned forward in the saddle. He searched for unseen witnesses.

"There are dozens of us here in Havana."

"What do you want of me?"

"We do what we can to frustrate the government. Sabotage, mysterious explosions, accidental fires. But we are without a leader. We wish you to be our leader."

"Where is your General Gomez?"

"In the west. But he rarely confronts the Spanish Army and talks only of American intervention."

"I cannot be your leader."

"You mean you *won't* be our leader," said the soldier who donated his horse.

He slid off the back of his mount and approached Roberto.

"Have you forgotten Guatao?"

Roberto's eyes narrowed. His face turned hot red. The young soldier continued.

"Did you not lose your family on that day? Or did they rise from the dead? My parents, my brothers and sisters, they have not risen from the dead. Have yours?"

Roberto flew off his horse. He pulled the man closer and back handed the soldier across the face. The force of Roberto's blow sent the young man sprawling to the ground. He stood over the fallen soldier and growled through clenched teeth.

"I have not forgotten my family."

The young soldier rose to his feet, brushing the dirt and debris from his dirty uniform.

"You have married the Butcher's niece. He was present on your wedding day. You accepted the Butcher's blood money."

Roberto pulled his gun from its holster. He pressed the barrel against the boy's heart.

"You were not at the cathedral. You know nothing."

The young soldier stepped forward as if daring Roberto to pull the trigger.

"Priests do not lie."

Scenes of the massacre at Guatao flashed in Roberto's mind. His chest tightened. The mounted soldiers reached for their rifles. Roberto's head twisted from one soldier to the next. He took a deep breath. The young soldier pushed Roberto's revolver to one side. Roberto did nothing. The boy sneered. Their leader lowered his rifle and aimed a finger at Roberto.

"Today, we allow you to live. Tomorrow, you will die."

The rebels galloped away.

When Roberto reached his room at the Hotel Inglaterra, Isabella threw her arms around his neck. She refused to let go.

"Roberto. I was convinced that you would not return."

She kissed him, repeatedly, on the lips, his cheeks, and his neck. Roberto showed no emotion, pulled away, and fell into the nearby chair. He stared at the floor and said nothing.

"Roberto. What is wrong? Has something happened?"

He blinked back the tears, unable to speak.

"Roberto. Talk to me. Please."

He spoke slowly, relating the details of his encounter with the young rebels pretending to be Spanish regulars. He choked up when he got to the part about Guatao. He could say no more. The boy covered his face with both hands and sobbed. Isabella fell to her knees, at his feet.

"Roberto. I am so sorry. I have made your life a living hell. I am so sorry."

Roberto sniffed, his weeping coming to an end.

"No, Isabella. I am the one who is sorry. I am a coward and a traitor to my family and to my people."

Isabella sprang to her feet.

"How can you say such a thing?"

Roberto searched her face. Isabella went to the bed. She smoothed the covers and fluffed the pillows. Her eyes flashed. She glared at Roberto.

"You say these things because you have married the niece of the Butcher. I have brought shame to you and now you seek to please your rebel friends."

"No. That is not true. I seek justice. For my family and for my people. Nothing more."

"You seek the approval of your people and you will abandon your wife to get it."

Isabella stormed out of the room. Roberto waited for her to return. Several hours later, he left. Roberto walked to a tavern, widely known as a place where the most militant of Spanish soldiers often congregated. Weylerites, as they were called, pined for the return of the Butcher. They despised his replacement because Ramon Blanco catered to the Cubans and did not defend the Spanish Army when they were criticized and ridiculed in the local press.

"You don't look like a Spanish soldier," said a uniformed customer.

"No, sir. I am a native of Cuba, loyal to the government," said Roberto, grabbing a chair and motioning the servant for a drink.

"I wish to buy a drink for you and your friends."

The captain grinned. He and five of his friends, two without a uniform, scrambled to Roberto's table. When the drinks arrived, Roberto raised his glass.

"Gentlemen. I drink to Captain-General Valeriano Weyler, a true leader.

The men roared their approval and finished the rum in one gulp.

"You are a very generous host and a wise man," said the captain.

After an exchange of names, the men took their seats. Roberto purchased a second round. And then a third. Within the hour, the captain and his comrades in arms chattered non-stop and spoke in a pronounced slur. They complained and criticized Blanco for allowing the local papers to criticize their former leader and their ranks.

"You should organize," said Roberto.

"Organize? What do you mean, organize?"

"A demonstration. Ransack the newspaper offices, perhaps break a few windows and make lots of noise. Let the supporters of Captain-General Weyler know they are not alone," said Roberto.

The men nodded their approval. Roberto encouraged them a bit more.

"And afterwards, we will drink to the captain-general's return to Cuba."

Walter, in a long discussion with Christopher, asked the rodent for advice.

"What do you think, my friend? A so-called accident in the boiler room? It would do a lot of damage. Cost lots of money. Would that be enough payback for what they did to my Angel?"

Christopher, his belly full of chicken, lay in the bedding at Walter's side. The rat, his eyes closed, didn't budge. Walter raised his voice.

"Are you sleeping? Christopher, wake up. I'm talking to you."

The rat opened his eyes.

"If I open the air valve, the fire will grow, the water pressure will climb, and the whole thing will explode. I could leave ahead of time. I would tell them that the valve got stuck and that I went for help. It just might work."

Walter grinned his satisfaction. Christopher twitched his nose.

"You can't be hungry. I just fed you."

Christopher stood on his two hind legs.

"What's this?"

Walter examined the rodent's neck. He saw an irregular patch of black fur, roughly the size of a quarter. The grey fur, now charred black, emitted an odor of burnt rubber and singed fur.

"Again? That's the second time you've burned yourself. If you keep chewing on electrical wires, you're gonna get yourself killed."

Frank, desperate for funds, did not offer to pay Captain Randall for his passage to Kew West.

The skipper didn't seem to care. Frank intended to meet with Carmelita Viscaya.

"What are you doing here?"

Carmelita's greeting, less than friendly, told Frank he may leave Florida empty-handed.

"Please, Carmelita, just a few moments of your time."

She walked away from the open door. Frank let himself in and remained standing. Carmelita sat in an oversized chair, like a queen on her throne. She lit a cigarette and blew a white cloud in Frank's direction.

"You've got five minutes, Frank."

"The *USS Maine* is in Key West. It's only a matter of time before it's ordered to Havana."

"Tell me something I don't know."

"Well, if the *Maine* were to have, shall we say, a slight accident and that accident was made to look like sabotage by the Spanish Army . . ."

Frank allowed his voice to trail off. He searched Carmelita's face for a sign of approval. She took a long drag from her cigarette. The words, mixed with smoke, tumbled from her mouth.

"I won't support anything that will harm our sailors," she said, flicking her cigarette ash into a dainty pink ashtray.

"I promise. No Americans will get hurt."

"Sure, Frank. Just like you promised to eliminate Weyler. Just like you promised to get Maceo off his ass and score a victory. The only promise you managed to keep was recruiting some good help. Roberto has been a great help."

She glared at Frank and jammed her cigarette into the ashtray.

"You're all promises, Frank, and no action. Now please leave me."

Frank gripped the woman by her shoulders.

"Now listen to me, Carmelita. All I need is a couple hundred bucks. Cash. I can handle it from there. Please, I'm begging you."

"You're hurting my shoulders, Frank. Now get out."

Frank's lips curled into a snarl. His face burned red. He slapped the woman's face. She screamed. He snatched a lace doily from the nearby table, rolled it into a ball, and shoved it into the woman's mouth. Blood oozed from her lacerated lip. He yanked the electric cord from its lamp and tied her to the chair. Her muffled groans infuriated him. Using one hand, he grabbed her by the cheeks and squeezed.

"Listen to me, you arrogant bitch. Make one more noise and I'll finish the job."

Carmelita sobbed quietly. He searched her person, her belongings, and the drawers in her dresser. Nothing.

"Where is the goddamn money, Carmelita?"

She yelled something that sounded a lot like "go to hell" but Frank kept searching. He noticed her eyes dart in the direction of the bed. He threw the pillows onto the floor, stripped the bedding, and tossed the mattress upside down. Underneath, lay a large cloth sack. Frank's grin covered his face. He counted out $200, glanced in Carmelita's direction, and counted out $300 more.

"Have a nice day, Carmelita."

The Weylerites rioted on January 12, 1898.

Triggered in part by Roberto, but mostly by a newspaper. Its editorial vilified Weyler and the Weylerites as thieves and scoundrels. Several days of demonstrations produced no injuries but lots of property damage. They attacked the offices of four different newspapers. The protestors destroyed presses, scattered files, and broke windows. Shouts of "long live Weyler", "death to autonomy", and "death to Blanco", filled the streets. It required four days before Blanco could restore calm.

When word of the demonstrations reached Washington, the public outcry grew. Questionable stories of Spanish atrocities appeared in American newspapers. Calls for U.S. intervention increased. On January 23, President McKinley's administration ordered the *USS Maine* to Cuba.

It would arrive at Havana Bay on January 25, 1898.

Isabella returned to the Hotel Inglaterra, just hours after her argument with Roberto.

She considered all that he suffered. The loss of his family, a near fatal wound, and imprisonment. She could hardly blame him for seeking justice. Somehow, they would compromise. When she arrived at the room, penitent and anxious to reach an understanding with her new husband, no one greeted her.

She fell asleep, waiting for the young man's return.

# Chapter Twenty-Three

## SABOTAGE

Walter decided to go topside.

His shift finished just as the shores of Cuba appeared on the horizon. Overnight, the entire ship shifted into a state of military readiness. The *USS Maine's* big guns, thoroughly inspected, now included gunners hidden in the turrets. Piles of shot and ammo lay stacked in various spots across the deck. Armed sentries now stood on the main deck, forecastle, and poop deck.

As the battleship floated past the gargantuan guns of Morro Castle, every sailor on deck scanned the water in search of a potential threat. Even after the ship safely anchored at buoy number four in Havana Bay, additional guards took up their posts at both the portside and leeward gangways. There would be no liberty, save for a handful of officers. Even those officers would be ordered to wear civilian clothes. Captain Sigsbee, unwilling to risk a confrontation with the locals, thought it best to keep a low profile. Walter credited the captain for implementing a comprehensive plan designed to protect the battleship, at all costs. Walter's thoughts drifted to his own plan.

"I wonder if the good captain considered the possibility of an exploding boiler."

A loud knock woke Isabella from her uneasy sleep.

She rushed to the door hoping to see her husband on the other side. A messenger, telegram in hand, asked for Roberto.

"Mr. Alvarez is indisposed. I am his wife."

When the messenger hesitated, Isabella offered the boy a generous gratuity.

"Thank you, Mrs. Alvarez."

She ripped open the envelope and studied the message.

> *The bank has been robbed. A battleship is no place for a lamb. Your uncle's friends will be blamed. Stop. Stop. Stop. K.W.*

It took a few minutes for Isabella to understand the cryptic message.

Frank Lamb would attack the *Maine*. The Spanish government would be blamed. The 'KW', Key West, could only mean that the message came from Carmelita. Frank Lamb stole her funds.

Isabella ran from the room in search of a newspaper. She did not need one. The lobby, overflowing with guests, reporters, government employees, and businesspeople, buzzed with excitement.

The *USS Maine* lay anchored in Havana harbor.

"Is that a telegram for me?"

Isabella whirled in place.

"Roberto. Where have you been?"

"I will explain everything when we get to the room."

Roberto locked the door behind them.

"My mission was successful. The American Navy has arrived."

"Your mission, my dear husband, has just begun."

She relinquished the telegram. Roberto's eyes raced over the words. Several times.

"This can't be," he said, shaking his head, repeatedly.

"He must be stopped, Roberto. All those men. More killing. It would be a slaughter," she whispered.

"The American battleship is here to foster good relations with the government of Spain. That is the official explanation, anyway."

"I don't understand," she said.

"The public has been invited to tour the ship. There will be hundreds, if not thousands of visitors."

Roberto caught her gaze, his face a pale white.

"Frank Lamb will be one of them."

Walter, momentarily alone in the boiler room, stepped into the passageway and confirmed that no one was coming or going.

He opened the air valve. The flame grew in intensity. The pressure gauge started to rise. It would take minutes before the situation became dangerous. Walter waited in the passageway, just in case.

"Hi, Walter. Are you leaving early?"

Bill Horn's unexpected visit jerked Walter to attention.

"Uh . . . no. Not really. I was just taking a breather."

As Bill got closer, Walter deliberately blocked the man's view of the boiler room. He could not hide his nervousness and repeatedly wet his lips.

"Are you all right Walter? You look nervous."

"I'm fine, Bill."

Bill's eyebrows furrowed as he studied Walter's sweaty face. Walter lost track of how much time he spent in the hallway. Bill cocked an ear in the boiler's direction.

"Why is the boiler so loud? It sounds like you have a full head of steam. We're not traveling. You need enough steam for the dynamos and the turrets, and that's all."

Walter froze in place. Bill pushed him to one side and rushed to the boiler. He cut the air supply and peered at the pressure gauge. He didn't budge until the needle reversed its direction.

"Walter, you had her up to 130. What in God's name were you thinking?

"Oh, sorry, Bill. I guess I lost track of time."

Bill started yelling and waving his arms.

"Walter, you could have been killed."

"Sorry, Bill. It was an accident."

Bill looked away and took a deep breath. He grabbed Walter by the shoulders.

"Walter, you more than anyone, cannot afford to make any mistakes. Please, please, be careful."

"I understand, Bill. It won't happen again."

Bill disappeared in the passageway. Walter reopened the air vent, but just enough to keep the fire going.

"Now I know. I have about 15 minutes and then she blows."

Roberto reached for Isabella's hands.

"Isabella, I need your help."

"What can I do?"

"Frank will do his reconnaissance in daylight. He will attack after dark. We must monitor the ship whenever there is a public tour. We will take turns. The first group of visitors will be allowed on board, in two days."

"You must warn the captain of the ship."

"He is, or should be, as prepared as possible. We know what Frank looks like. The captain doesn't. We have the best chance of spoiling Frank's plans."

"How do I stop him?"

"Start a fight. Every man in the vicinity will come to your rescue. You are that beautiful."

Isabella blushed.

"I'll do the first day," she said.

She pulled him close.

"I'm frightened, Roberto. Frank Lamb is an evil man."

After returning to Cuba, Frank moved quickly.

He would be in the first group of visitors on board the *USS Maine*. Government officials, dignitaries, members of the Spanish military, and the locals, all looked forward to touring one of America's finest battleships. So did Frank. Today's visit would be a dry run for the real thing. He carried a pistol, concealed behind his jacket, plus a cloth bag, large enough to hold several sticks of dynamite. On this day, the bag contained no more than a small loaf of bread and some dried meat.

After climbing the gangway, Frank noticed the sailors and marines closely following each visitor. Certain areas of the ship remained off-limits. Most of the top deck, however, plus a half dozen opened doors, allowed the public to inspect large portions of the ship. The crew's bunk room, the captain's quarters, the officers' mess, an empty coal bunker, the large gun turrets, and dozens of other features, lay in full view.

Frank took great interest in several sailors wearing fabric booties over their shoes. They stood on either side of a locked door. He assumed they protected an ammo bunker. When his group returned topside, Frank got a closer look at the neatly piled shells and boxes of shot. The giant hills of explosives lay everywhere. He wandered away from the closely watched group, placed his bag on the deck, and pretended to blow his nose. When finished, he walked back to the scrum and deliberately left his bag on the deck. Less than a half dozen steps later, a marine guard accosted him.

"Excuse me, sir. You forgot your package."

"Oh, thank you sir," said Frank, reaching for his food.

The marine held onto it.

"Smells like lunch, sir."

Frank smiled.

"Yes. That's exactly what it is. Would you care to take a peek?"

The marine smiled.

"I already have."

Frank, startled by the marine's disclosure, did not know what to say. He flashed a fake smile. The unsmiling marine leaned forward.

"You're an American."

The man's inquiry sounded more like a statement of fact.

"Yes, sir. Kansas. And you?"

"Brooklyn. You better catch up with your group, sir."

Frank hurried to the clump of visitors, many of them disembarking as he walked.

He could feel the marine's eyes drilling into his back.

Frank's mind raced as he left the battleship.

The tight security impressed the mercenary. His attack would necessarily be scheduled after dark. It would require a distraction. If Frank could draw the attention of on-deck personnel to one side of the ship, the opposite side would be accessible. Gangways, on both sides of the battleship, would make his plan doable.

Doing the greatest amount of damage in the least amount of time would also be a challenge. He focused on the shells and shot, stored on deck in large quantities. They would be easy to access and would accomplish a great deal of damage when exploded.

As the small boat approached the docks, Frank spied a lone woman. She sat on a bench, her back to the water. She ignored the growing line of visitors waiting to board the ship. When Frank's group began the disembarkation process, she scurried behind a nearby storage building. The woman peeked around the corner of the building, inspecting the visitors as they left the dock. When the woman brushed bright red hair from the front of her face, he recognized her.

He turned to the side, stepped onto the dock, and walked briskly in the opposite direction.

Isabella scanned the small crowd as it left the boat.

From her vantage point behind the storage building, she saw Frank get on the ship. She did not see him leave. Isabella doubted he remained onboard and chalked it up to the large crowds. No matter. She would inform Roberto that Frank toured the battleship that morning.

"Looking for me?"

Frank's hand pressed against her mouth, before she could scream. He dragged her deeper into the alleyway. She dropped her bag and used both hands to loosen his grip. Without success. Breathing became difficult with the large man's hand over her nose and mouth. She tried to bite him. His fingers did not budge. Her eyes fluttered. She went limp. He lowered her to the ground and muttered to himself.

"Sorry, Mrs. Alvarez. You don't get to kick me in the nuts, this time."

After sending an update to Key West, Roberto returned to the Inglaterra.

When Isabella did not greet him at the door, he grew anxious. Horrible thoughts filled his head. After 30 minutes of nervous pacing, he left the room. Roberto searched the lobby, the dining room, and the block of streets which surrounded the hotel. Now close to a panic, he struck out for the docks.

A line of visitors, boarding and disembarking the transports to and from the *Maine,* gave Roberto a glimmer of hope. She may have taken the tour herself. Perhaps Frank arrived at the docks much later than Roberto anticipated. The mercenary could still be on board. Isabella could be hiding. Roberto decided to walk around the block. When he circled the abandoned warehouse, he spied a small bag in a puddle of water. It belonged to Isabella. Roberto took several deep breaths to calm his beating heart.

It did not work.

Christopher, always in search of food, did his best work in the dark of night.

Despite a rat's notoriously bad eyesight, rodents function well in the darkness. Rats enjoy excellent hearing, a great sense of smell, and long, sensitive whiskers. On this evening, Christopher left the area of Walter's hammock and explored the crew's quarters. He discovered an open duffel that contained a partially eaten chocolate bar. The paper wrapping posed no challenge. When his stomach grew full, Christopher scurried down the quiet passageway, past the sick bay, and down the hatch to the boiler rooms. When an on-duty fireman decided he needed more coal, Christopher followed the man to a coal bunker. The open hatch bathed the three-story-high mountain of bituminous fuel in a soft light. Christopher could smell the man's sweat, as the sailor shoveled the fuel into a bucket. He could also smell the damp coal. But not the natural gas it produced. Methane.

The gas, although nontoxic when ingested, rose to the top of the coal bins and could explode if allowed to accumulate. The ship's crew, constantly worried about spontaneous combustion, did not consider the dangers of coal gas. On the *USS Maine*, coal bins included electric-powered fire alarms which sounded when the temperature rose to dangerous levels. But the alarms sounded, almost daily. Each time, members of the crew would check the relevant bunker. The temperature would be normal and no evidence of fire could be found. The fire alarms were obviously defective. Crew members were instructed to respond, in any event. The alarms did nothing to warn against the accumulation of methane.

A loud bang and sudden darkness froze Christopher in place. He could no longer smell the sailor's sweat. Silence enveloped the large room. He decided to explore his new surroundings. The rodent discovered some electrical wires, leading to a box on the wall. His instincts took over.

Christopher gnawed on the wires.

"Good morning, beautiful."

Frank's voice made Isabella's fluttering eyes open wide. The tiny room, with no windows and spiders crawling in the dust, made her stomach turn. The sight of Frank Lamb gave her goosebumps.

"Where am I?" she asked, straining against the leather bindings which tied her hands together.

"When I noticed you were following me, I thought the least I could do is bring you home with me."

"I think I'm going to be sick."

Frank scanned the room.

"I didn't think my humble surroundings would please you. But money has been tight since your sweetheart took my job."

"Roberto is my husband. And I understand you just came into a great deal of money."

Frank winced. His eyebrows dipped.

"News travels fast in these parts."

"You're a dead man, Frank. If you want to live, keep the money and disappear."

"Oh, I intend to leave this miserable place. But first you and I have a job to do."

"You would kill American sailors for no reason other than your desperate need to feel important?"

Frank, momentarily startled by the woman's knowledge of his plans, quickly recovered.

"Why are you so harsh, Isabella?"

He stepped closer to the woman, using his fingers to caress her face.

"Don't touch me."

"You were much more appealing as a virgin."

Isabella snarled.

"Go to blazes, Frank."

"Roberto was your first, was he not?"

Isabella turned away.

"Isabella, my love. What does a boy know about lovemaking. We could have been a great couple, you and me."

Isabella pulled on the leather. Frank continued.

"As it is, we have more important things to accomplish. You're going to help me to destroy an American battleship."

"You'll have to kill me first."

"How prescient of you. That is precisely what I intend to do."

Roberto assumed that Frank held Isabella against her will.

He suspected Frank of wanting to use Isabella in his attack on the *Maine*. The question burning in Roberto's mind, how and when the attack would occur, could not be answered. The young rebel could only guess.

An attack during the daylight hours would be foolish. Accordingly, the boy chose to remain dockside at night. He would sleep during the day. He made himself comfortable in the dark shadow of the nearby warehouse. Except for an occasional lighter, crossing the waters of Havana Harbor, Roberto saw nothing that looked suspicious. On the night of February 15, the wind changed its direction. The *USS Maine*, still tethered to buoy number four, shifted its position and turned a full 180 degrees. If Frank installed an underground mine, its detonation would do no damage.

The mercenary would be forced to board the ship.

Walter, angry and frustrated that Christopher did not appear for his usual meal, worried that his best friend may have been injured or killed.

He wanted the rodent close by when his pre-planned accident occurred. Walter would wait until the firemen took their meal break. The junior coal-passer could be dispatched to the far end of the ship on a meaningless errand. Destroying boiler number one would cost the navy a pretty penny. There would be lots of downtime for repairs. The ship would survive and no one would get hurt. It was the perfect plan on the perfect day.

On February 15, 1898, Walter would commemorate the five-month anniversary of Angel's untimely death.

Frank's plan, to use Isabella as a distraction, would utilize the overcast skies in Havana for cover.

Her hands would be tied but not her feet. She would be gagged. He would dump her in the water near the portside gangway. Her flailing and splashing would attract a great deal of attention. As quickly as he could, Frank would row to the opposite side of the ship. While the *Maine*'s crew rescued the damsel in distress, he would scramble up the second gangway and fire into the nearest pile of shot and shells. The neatly stacked ammunition would explode with a fury. A well-aimed shot, from a distance, would allow Frank to escape safely. He hoped.

And the Butcher's niece would guarantee that Spain would get the blame for Frank's attack.

Roberto heard noises at the furthest end of the dock.

He thought he heard a woman's groan but could not be certain. He scanned the water's surface and stepped quietly in the direction of the disturbance. The splash of oars against water told him that someone launched a boat. He heard the high-pitched moan, once again. A man's voice, barely audible, followed by the sound of flesh hitting flesh, sent Roberto into a full-on run. The sound of his boots, pounding the dock, triggered the mystery man's anger.

"You loud-mouth bitch."

Roberto could not be sure but the voice sounded a lot like Frank Lamb. Roberto could make out the rough profile of two people in a small rowboat. He searched the dock for a nearby lighter. None. Roberto ripped off his shirt and removed his boots. He tossed his gun on the pile. Before he could jump in, a loud splash echoed across the water. The boat, now occupied by one person, grew smaller. Roberto dove into the dirty water. He glided effortlessly to the spot where he last saw the tiny boat. He could see the man's shadow against the lights of Havana. A weak splash caught his attention. He spun to his right. A single hand reached for the overcast sky. He leapt forward. The hand disappeared. He dove under the surface.

The filthy, inky dark water made his eyes worthless. With outstretched arms he grabbed at the water in every direction. Empty darkness everywhere.

He came up for air and dove deep once again. When he kicked, something brushed against his leg. With one strong swing of his muscular arm, Roberto turned. He extended his hand as far as it could reach. Hair. Short hair. He tightened his grip on a handful and pulled. A limp body floated into his arms. He kicked hard for the surface. His lungs screamed for air. The dim harbor lights exposed a woman's ashen face. And red hair. He pulled on the rag that gagged her. She did not react. He reached the docks. Roberto struggled to get the dead weight out of the water.

He rolled Isabella onto her back. He pulled her arms into the air, above her head, and then back again. Again, and again. He used two hands, positioned at the small of her back, to lift her motionless body. Her midriff rose and fell each time. He wanted to expel the water that filled Isabella's lungs. After several attempts, water flowed from the woman's mouth. He did it again. The woman gagged. He pulled her to a sitting position. She coughed. The color slowly returned to her face. Her eyelids fluttered. Her head wobbled. He pulled her close.

"Isabella."

Christopher wandered aimlessly through the coal bunker.

He returned once again to the wall-mounted thermostat. He gnawed for minutes, just as he did the day before. The chewy rubber fell away in pieces. He hit something hard and warm. His razor-sharp incisors sliced through the metal wire.

It sparked.

# Chapter Twenty-Four

## R.I.P.

Walter jammed the air vent wide-open.

He could hear the fire roar and watched as the pressure gauge inched its way past 100. He waited until it reached 115 and ran from the room.

"Walter. Who's watching the boiler?"

"Bill, I thought you had the night off!"

Bill pushed Walter to one side and ran into the boiler room. After seeing the pressure gauge, he closed the air vent and waited until the pressure subsided. Walter's appearance in the doorway sent Bill into a rage. He rushed forward and slammed the mentally unstable sailor into the bulkhead. Bill, using both hands, grabbed Walter by the neck and squeezed. Walter struggled to breathe.

The floor trembled beneath them. Bill released his grip and walked to the door. A wall of flame rushed down the passageway. The deafening roar forced the men to the opposite side of the boiler room. They searched for a place to hide. Another explosion filled the room with flying debris and flames. Bill covered Walter with his body. A third explosion knocked the boiler off its pedestal. Scalding hot water covered the floor and hissed in the flames. Walter screamed in agony. Bill groaned. A wall of seawater washed over their bodies.

Their suffering came to an end.

Luther Burns retired early on the evening of February 15, 1898.

His swinging hammock lulled him to sleep in minutes. A distant rumble and a sudden trembling of the ship forced his eyes wide open. He considered the possibilities. He was positioned just a few decks above large magazines filled with gun powder and ammunition. The explosion would kill him, instantly. It would be Luther's last thought. Seconds later, a flash he did not see, an explosion he did not hear, vaporized his mortal remains. On the metal ceiling above his hammock, etched in black dust, the outline of a person could be seen.

Luther Burns' body would never be found.

Roberto heard a low rumble.

He could see the lights on the *Maine* rise slightly and then fall. Seconds later, the sky lit up. A second and much larger explosion rained metal, wood, and body parts into the dirty waters of Havana Bay. Some of the shrapnel hit the docks. The ship, now a raging wall of fire, continued to explode. A handful of men on the poop deck, their silhouettes visible in the flames, stood just above the water. Several boats circled the red-hot metal carcass. They searched for the men whose groans and screams filled the air. Roberto closed his eyes and squeezed back tears.

Isabella, unable to witness the horror, pressed her face against the boy's bare chest.

Frank sprinted across the street and into an alley way. He stopped when he heard the explosion.

He could see the glow of a large fire in the otherwise dark night. The lights of Havana flickered. He turned and ran back to the harbor. Hundreds of people lined the docks and watched in horror. The crowd speculated as to the cause of the explosion and the culprits. Some accused the Spanish Army. Others accused the rebels. Everyone became a suspect.

Frank, forced to dump Isabella into the water long before he reached the battleship, wanted to be a suspect in the spectacular explosion. But he failed his mission, once again. His dream of rescuing Cuba with a dramatic and heroic gesture, ended with the explosion. Someone else, or something else would get the credit. Not Frank.

The Americans would declare war. Spain would be defeated. Cuba would be free. Frank did not rejoice. He wallowed in self-pity and anger.

He stood in the cold, drizzling rain for hours, watching the fireworks when munitions exploded. Eventually, he pulled away from the crowd of onlookers. When he arrived at his room, Frank stripped off his clothing. He lay in bed, naked, except for the pistol in his hand. For a moment, he studied the weapon. Smooth, shiny, and cold.

He wrapped his lips around the barrel, closed his eyes, and pulled the trigger.

Within days of the explosion, a Naval Court of Inquiry convened in Havana.

Its conclusions, announced just five weeks later, surprised no one. The report, much of it leaked in advance, concluded that an underwater mine caused the destruction of the *Maine*. The report did not allude to a culprit. Insufficient evidence. The American press and their readers reached a different conclusion. They blamed the government of Spain. A declaration of war would soon be made.

"I don't believe it," said Roberto.

"Why not?" asked Carmelita.

With Isabella at his side, Roberto explained.

"Frank never made it to the ship. The Spanish government would be foolish to start a war with the Americans. And the rebel army possessed neither the knowledge nor the money to install an underwater mine. Besides, the Maine moved almost daily, because of the winds and currents. A properly positioned mine would be impossible to install."

Carmelita wanted more.

"Well then, what happened?"

"It could have been sabotaged by someone on board, but I doubt it."

"What's left?" asked Isabella.

"An accident. An accident that will trigger a war and kill thousands more."

Carmelita lit a cigarette. A cloud of smoke hovered over the threesome.

"You are a very bright fellow, Roberto."

She glanced at Isabella.

"And you, my dear, have married wisely."

Roberto reached for his wife's hand.

"We wish to remain in America. Can you help us?"

Carmelita jumped to her feet.

"I can do better than that."

"As of now, you are employed by the American State Department. When the war ends, and it will end soon, we will want an Embassy in Cuba. Isabella, I am sure that we can find something for you."

Isabella focused on Roberto as she spoke to Carmelita.

"That won't be necessary."

Carmelita frowned.

"Why not?"

"My job is at home with our child."